INDIGO
TOWER

To all the Taffys, Petras, and Zaritas
of this and future worlds

Gray is the ocean
Blue is the sky...
We place our palms upon the dead
We embrace the art of 'shall not cry'...

From the poem:
"The Cost of Primitive Arrogance"
Preface to "The Book of Neil"

Experienced Cliff-Hunter, Ramon Baptiste Chang-Lee
Marcus O'Reilly[1], looked eastward over the gray ocean
before him. He noted how this endless expanse of water,
known as The Atlantic, slowly darkened as it neared the
horizon. "Almost charcoal, LULU," he said to an empty
lighthouse room of windows. Then, with a practiced calm,
he re-focused his gaze beyond the common sights and
sounds of the Florida shoreline stretching out below him.
Seagulls screeched as they soared through salty air.
Tourists splashed in breaking waves. And both ignored
the distant flashes of jagged lightning dancing in the
distance.

"Enjoy your lives," he murmured. "Enjoy your short,
ridiculous lives." Then biting his lip, he drew in a large
gulp of oxygen and placed his standard issue Ziter-1000
back on the tired wooden table to his right. "This is the
part," he said. "This is the part that stabs the heart..."

Glancing at the glowing display on his left thumbnail, he
noted the time...11:15 DST. Precisely three hours and fifty-
three minutes until his assignment would be
completed...that disturbing moment to which he had
never become accustomed. In less than four hours Cliff-
Hunter Class3 O'Reilly would disappear without a trace.
He would be transported instantly and miraculously to

---

[1] *It was once the custom of Tibetland III citizens to name their children after
those who had died in the 'build-out' of the island's infrastructure. The
custom was ended by decree approximately 200 years earlier.*

1

the *Historic Reconnaissance Branch* of Land III's *Research Agency.* He would arrive safe and well within a small, isolated launch/receiver room, fully aware that he had once again escaped the sudden death and destruction of a million helpless souls. As on countless other research missions, he would have vanished just seconds before others perished...the sounds of their suffering still ringing in his ears.

Even in his academy days, he had been beset by serious doubts. How, he wondered, would he ever achieve a rank beyond that of an entry level CH1? And what chance would he ever have of rising to the distinguished level of a CH5, that elite status to which his cohorts all so vigorously strove? True...as a young graduate, he had made a sincere effort to emulate the high standards of that consummate upper level. He had told himself that he too could become an aloof Cliff-Hunter, an explorer of history with perfect detachment, one of the special few who could calmly look on as oceans roiled and cities disappeared before them. But with every new assignment and its devastating human toll, O'Reilly had become less and less interested in achieving a successful climb up the CH ladder. And in the troubled years that followed, as his lackluster career unfolded before him, he had reluctantly come to accept what was so plainly obvious to his superiors. CH3 Ramon O'Reilly was quite simply not CH5 material. And so, with stoic determination he had come to accept the hurtful truth...he would forever be a mid -level agent, an insignificant pixel within the greater agency picture.

With nearly two centuries of faithful service behind him, he no longer chased after rank or reputation.
Instead, he sought something far more valuable, more elusive...a single night of solid sleep...a deep delicious slumber free of horrific nightmares and a deep persistent sorrow.

With the crooked smile of a condemned man, O'Reilly recalled his recent visit to the Council Review Board just two days prior to the current mission. Without advanced notice, he had been summoned to the notification chamber of Beatrix-AI47 and informed that a third cautionary entry would be recorded in his official file. It would read "Initiative Lacking/ Commitment Minimal/ Recommendation to Follow". Holding no illusions now about his future with *The Agency,* there remained little doubt. This *Florida Cliff Event* would be his last trek into the field.

It did not require much imagination to predict what carefully selected words *The Council* would choose before sending him down to the trades, or worse, to a population calming unit in *The Northside.* Even his impressive time in service would not save him. They would simply say...

"CH3 O'Reilly, you were privileged to be designated a Cliff-Hunter. You were granted gifts of daily living that others do not enjoy. Yet, on more than one occasion, you have disgraced your title and ignored the six-point-code to which you once swore allegiance.

> 1. *We walk through time*
> 2. *We seek out truth*
> 3. *We keep our distance*
> 4. *We monitor until we understand*
> 5. *We change nothing until we can be sure*
> 6. *We work in the knowledge that the* **Day of Days** *will come, and all will be made right once again*

You are therefore, as of this moment, relieved of your status as a Cliff-Hunter, all benefits commensurate with that position to be henceforth forfeited."

"And that, sweet LULU," said O'Reilly out loud, "will be that. Just a great big slice of karma cake and nothing to wash it down."

"Condolences, Commander O'Reilly," whispered LULU softly.

Max Takes the Helm

The USS Louisiana is one of fourteen Ohio Class ballistic missile submarines in the US Naval arsenal. Armed with a compliment of 24 multi targeting nuclear weapons, it is one of the three legs of America's triad deterrent strategy. It is also the newest such vessel in service, having been commissioned September 6, 1997. Though its home port is the Naval Base Kitsap in the state of Washington, the boat was now carefully making its way into the turn basin at Port Canaveral, Florida. Technically, US Naval ships were not required to take on a harbor pilot to navigate the waterway; but it had been a long-standing practice to do so. And so, one mile southeast of lighted whistle buoy #3, at the pilot boarding ground, the crew welcomed aboard the local harbor master, Maxwell (Max) Sturg.

Max had worked for the Port Canaveral authority for fifteen years; had passed his initial security review, as well as all periodic follow-ups, with flying colors. He did not drink alcohol; take drugs; gamble; or associate with the opposite sex. Determined to live his life more purely than the unrepentant Philistines around him, Max had long ago eschewed all temptation. Fellow employees considered him to be quiet, steady, and dependable. Though he lived alone, seldom socializing with workplace companions, he was well regarded professionally by his peers. So, it would have come as quite a surprise to all who thought they knew him to learn the three most powerful beliefs Max Sturg held.

1...Aliens walk among us

2...Four submarines (of four separate nations) that mysteriously sank in 1968 had been attacked and destroyed by alien spacecraft

3...The end times are near

Additionally, and above all else, Max had come to believe that whatever The Creator's final plan for planet Earth might be, it most certainly included him as an active participant. And so, with the unbounded determination of all true fanatics, Max had begun two decades earlier to consider how a social recluse, with two years of community college, could initiate the spark that would send the world up in a spectacular series of cataclysmic events. It had taken him twenty years to lay down the ground work that he prayed would push the world over the edge. Now, after many challenging years of careful preparation, that momentous day had finally arrived...the day that Max Sturg, acting in accordance with God's greater plan, would start the world down the path of total destruction.

"Welcome aboard, Max," said forty-two-year-old Commander Dwight Patterson. "You the man today? You gonna take sweet 'Louise' in for us today?"

"Absolutely," replied Max.

As per protocol, Max was carefully scanned for any weapons or threatening devices that might be on his person; his ancient worn tool bag receiving careful examination. The screening completed, twenty-year-old Seaman Baxter Dowd lowered a hand-held metal detector wand before turning to face his captain.

"All clear, Sir."

An almost imperceptible smile came and went as Max carefully slipped a temporary boarding badge and lanyard over his head.

"Well, be gentle, Max," said Patterson playfully. "Don't forget our Louise here is a mature 'ol gal and she needs lots of TLC."

"Will do, commander," said Max with a respectful nod.

Two minutes later, Max and his small leather boarding kit arrived in the control room. Carefully placing the kit down on the deck beside him, Max took up a position directly behind helmsman number one. Like an onlooker kibitzing a poker player, Max calmly looked on, now and then suggesting alternate minor changes in speed and direction.

"We had a foreign registry yacht sink here in the main channel just last week," said Max. "It should be resting well below us, but I suggest we steer 10 degrees starboard for approximately 100 yards, then return to our original heading."

"Sir?" asked the helmsman.

"Command confirmed," replied Patterson. "For the next twenty minutes, Max calls the shots; unless, of course, he yells 'Fire full complement!'" A shallow ripple of laughter tracked through the nearby crew.

"Understood, Sir," Baxter replied with a smile.

Though Max presented as something of an enigma to Patterson, the perceptive commander felt confident he had accurately assessed the man. Max, he surmised, was one of those brain-bound loner types, dedicated to his job and nothing more. In the several brief conversations they had shared, Max had come across as an inward-looking personality, preoccupied with the details of his job, uninterested in women or sports, apolitical in his views on the world. And on those truly rare occasions when Max grudgingly expressed himself in more than two or three words, it was to repeat one of several well-worn catch phrases. "The more things change, the more they stay the same ... Easy come, easy go ... When it rains, it pours."

Had Patterson been completely honest with himself he would have admitted to feeling a slight uneasiness when in the man's presence. He experienced the odd sensation that Max, though physically standing in front of him, was somehow looking on from a distant and detached location. Nevertheless, if asked to describe Max in a few adjectives, he would probably have summed up the man as "predictable, harmless and boring."

It was clear that Max wanted to keep his life to himself, and so Patterson made a strong effort to respect that. He never inquired into the man's past. He never asked Max how he had earned a living prior to becoming a licensed harbor master. Most certainly, he would have been nonplussed to learn that brain-bound Max had once served as a top welding specialist at the Navy's Trident refit facility at Kings Bay, Georgia. He would also have been surprised to learn that many years earlier, Max had been flown to Naval Base Kitsap in Bangor, Washington to help assess, supervise and repair damages suffered to the USS Louisiana following its collision with the offshore support vessel USNS *Eagleview* (T-AGSE-3) in the Strait of Juan De Fuca.

And even then, even if Patterson had learned of Max's previous work on the Louisiana, he still could not have conceived the threat he now faced. But then, how could anyone ever have imagined that multiple explosive devices had been carefully inserted within the bulkheads of the Louisiana long ago? How could any commander have guessed that multiple twenty-first century Trojan horses now passively rested somewhere below deck? And like children patiently awaiting the return of a wayward father, the explosive charges had silently awaited the return of their creator, Max Sturg. With the loving touch of a dedicated parent, that fanatic father would now install the required power sources to activate the timer and blasting caps attached to six blocks of extremely powerful composition C-4.

Max had no illusions about the outcome of his plan. He doubted that the nuclear tipped ballistic missiles on board would launch as a result of his actions. He knew that they would, instead, be brought off line either by their default fail-safe system or a manual electronic override from the subs' land based primary command and control center. What he was hoping for was a rupture to occur within the cooling system that maintained the reactor's fissionable material within safe temperature parameters. He assumed that, were this to happen, and temperatures were to rise exponentially, the superheated fissionable material would proceed to defeat all efforts to contain it...first melting through its substantial housing, then penetrating the boat's multilayered hull. From there it was anyone's guess. He was reasonably sure that massive amounts of radiation would be distributed throughout the boat through its highly efficient ventilation system.

All these events would certainly mean that Max would have succeeded in making an undeniable statement to the world at large. He would have caused the gruesome death of 140 enlisted men and 15 officers. He would have single handedly destroyed a 500 million-ton vessel of the United States Navy. And who knows, perhaps the United States would assume that they had been attacked by a foreign power and would respond "in kind". With any luck at all, Max surmised, such a response could then quickly escalate into a full-fledged nuclear exchange. Still, in his soberer moments of clarity, Max knew that such an outcome was highly unlikely, a splendid dream too grand to be hoped for. Nevertheless, whatever the aftermath of his vengeful plan, his carefully worded press release would arrive at all the major news services around the world. At last, he would have their undivided attention. This time, they would listen to him as he explained.

"A great conspiracy of nations has been taking place right before our eyes...a concerted worldwide effort to hide the truth from all of Earth's inhabitants.
Alien beings are here on earth. And it was alien spacecraft that destroyed the submarines of four nations back in 1968."

By the time the synchronized explosions had gone off, Max would be clear of the boat. Comfortably out of harm's way, he would return to his small apartment, turn on his TV, and enjoy the chaos and incriminations that would surely follow. His greatest hope being that one of the conspiring nations involved would finally come clean, would reveal what was so painfully obvious to anyone who cared to consider the facts. The truth of extraterrestrial interference on Earth would finally be told. Max would, at last, be vindicated in his beliefs, and the world would forever be changed, awakened to that which was undeniable.

An F-Bomb Queen Named Petra
Knocking at the Door

O'Reilly's uncomfortable reverie was suddenly interrupted by a thunderous pounding on the metal door at the base of the lighthouse. The sound seemed to expand and grow as it bounced its way up the interior iron and brick walls of the conical tower.

"LULU, full display of disturbance at lighthouse door," said O'Reilly.

Materializing before him, a three-dimensional image now provided him with a detailed view of the buildings entrance and the grounds within ten meters of it. In the fierce glow of a noon day Florida sun, an athletic barefoot female could be seen as she frantically pounded and screamed on the door before her. A stickler for detailed observation, O'Reilly examined her overall appearance. The left third of her head had been shaved clean, the remaining two thirds a choppy mix of unwashed blue strands. A pair of lime green sunglasses dangled from a purple cord around her neck, as a polished metal nose ring flashed in the bright sunlight. Her clothing consisted of torn and faded cut-offs, a red halter top, and a ragged cross-body surplus satchel (identifiable as a U.S. military issue - circa 1970). Her right arm was covered in a colorful tattoo sleeve of an uncertain topic; her upper left leg tattooed in similar fashion.

"Oh, sweet Jesus and all who dined with him," observed O'Reilly. LULU, are you seeing this?"

"Yes. Seeing this," whispered a soft female voice into his left ear canal.

"It's her again! Damn it all to hell. I hate this part. Why does she always have to show up?"

"Are you asking a direct question of me?" asked LULU. *"Or are you simply verbally venting your disappointment regarding a current circumstance?"*

"Verbally venting, LULU, ...just venting."

"Venting confirmed" whispered LULU.

"Please!" the girl shouted. There was genuine desperation in her plea. "Let me in. Let me in now! There's no time! They're coming! They'll kill me! Please...let me in!" Then looking up at a closed-circuit camera, one that had not functioned for 13 years, she pointed back in the direction from which she had come. "They're almost here. I need help! I need help now!"

O'Reilly shook his head slowly side to side then moved his gaze to the gray ocean stretching out before him. "Sorry, young miss," he said softly. "Just as in the past, I am not here on a rescue mission and this is not a safe house. This, dear child, is a *Class-3 beam-back reconnaissance-trek,* and you have not been gamed in." Then touching his left wrist once, the troubled young woman disappeared into the ether. "Damn it," he said to the ocean. "Just go away. One way or another, young miss, your time is up today."

As the young woman continued to pound and scream for help, two lean, darkly tanned males could be seen making their way toward her. Stopping sporadically to survey the surrounding grounds for potential witnesses, they were pleased to discover nothing but sand, sea grass, and a few tired Sago Palms looking on. Confident of anonymity, their hurried walk became a trot. When they were less than ten feet away, the frightened woman spun around to face them. As the first attacker reached out for her, she attempted to deliver a hurried groin kick. Anticipating the move, he pivoted his body a quarter turn to the right, the barefoot strike landing with a dull thud against his left hip. Striking- out with two muscular tattooed arms, he slammed her backwards against the metal door. Her second attacker then grabbed both her arms and dragged her away from the building. Pushing her down into the sand he shoved a knee into her chest.

"No use …you fucking sog!" he hissed in her ear. "No use at all. What did you think would happen? Huh? What did you think?"

Then roughly grabbing her neck with both hands, he began to squeeze. Contracting the muscles of hands and forearms he looked on with a joyful primal interest in the inevitable outcome. And that is when his brutal plan flew off the rails. At first, a questioning look of confusion crossed his face. This was quickly followed by one of total disbelief. To his astonishment, no matter the amount of force he attempted to exert; no matter how tightly he tried to squeeze, nothing happened. No amount of muscular effort could cause his hands to contract. It was as though he were trying to squeeze a pillar of steel instead of a vulnerable human neck. This surprising outcome was immediately followed by a weakness in both legs, fatigue, and an overwhelming desire to sleep. Without uttering a word, attacker number two slowly collapsed backward onto the scorching sand. As he did, a second muffled thump could be heard as attacker number one joined him in slumber. The amazed young woman drew in three deep breaths in quick succession before struggling to her feet.

"Holy shit!" she shouted. "Holy shit! What just happened?" Then, approaching the limp bodies with caution, she nudged the second attacker with her right foot. When there was no response, she brought her bare heel down with full force on to his rib cage. There was the muted snap of bone and cartilage. "What did you think would happen, 'honey'?" she mimicked. "What did you think?"

Her sublime moment of revenge was abruptly interrupted by a metallic rattle behind her. Spinning back in the direction of the lighthouse, she watched with a curious calm as its riveted iron door swung slowly open. Straining to focus, she could just make out the figure of a man standing there beyond the threshold. Half in light and half in darkness, he stared back coldly. He was a tall, pale man of perhaps 40 years. Dressed in green cargo pants, a pink and purple Hawaiian shirt and a vintage pair of brown wing-tips, he wore an expression of mild irritation just above a carefully knotted red bow-tie. Despite her terrifying brush with death just moments earlier, she now found herself smiling with wonder at the bazaar aberration before her.

"And what the fuck are you supposed to be?" she asked with genuine curiosity.

O'Reilly's expression changed to one of disdain. "I'm *supposed to be* doing something other than standing here talking to you."

"Well, fuck you too!" she replied. "But, do you think you could find the time to call the cops? These two ass-holes just tried to kill me."

"No" he said, "that's not something I can do."

"And why the fuck not, strange lighthouse-man?"

"Well, primarily because I have no phone."

"What the fu... So, you live out here in this giant brick penis, in the fucking land of hurricanes, and you *have no phone*?"

14

"Correct," he said. "No phone. Do not need it."

The woman stopped talking long enough to re-examine this odd life form a second time. She was just about to ask him about his strange wardrobe, when he spoke first.

"I dress like this to blend in. End of story."

"To blend in?" she blurted. But, before she could follow-up with a cutting observation, he interrupted a second time.

"I suggest you move on, get away from here."

"What?"

"I suggest you move on, get away from here. Get very far away from here."

"And so, what about these two jerks?"

"Well, angry young woman...that's the thing. These two perpetrators are going to be unconscious for no more than three and one-half minutes."

"Three and one-half minutes?"

"Approximately...yes. That's just an estimate based on their individual body masses, but I've seen heat related fatigue like this before. And, I'm guessing they'll be out that long...approximately."

"Listen up...whoever you are...right now I need a place that's safe."

O' Reilly shrugged with disinterest just as attacker number one began to stir.

"Hmmm," he said thoughtfully. "That was only two minutes and fifty-one seconds. Must have been the thick metal door... flow interference."

"'Flow?'...What the hell are you talking about?"

"Look," he said raising his voice slightly, "you've got to leave. You've got to leave right now."

Looking down at the male who was stirring back to life, the young woman shook her head.

"No," she said, "I don't think so. Asshole number one here is coming around and his pal's gonna be right behind. So, I am not going anywhere. And I am damn sure not going to take off running down the beach only to look back and see both these morons closing in. No thanks, lighthouse-man. No ...thank you very much!"

"And you have a better plan?" he asked.

"Yes," she replied with a wicked smile. "I do. It's simple. I'll stay here in this giant Florida phallus until these two losers are gone."

"That's your plan?"

"Bingo, Bosco!"

"Well, I'm sorry to have to alter your 'plan', but...*no*. You *cannot* stay here. I'm in the middle of a very demanding project, and I have no time for random chatter and distraction."

"Oh, gee. Sorry. I thought you might be interested in saving my life. But, gosh, sounds like you're really busy. So, guess I'll just stay out here and die so you can finish your 'very demanding project'. Jesus Christ, lighthouse-man...What's wrong with you?"

And before O'Reilly could share any additional concerns, the woman had darted passed him and begun the long climb up the 202 steps of the spiral staircase inside.

"Write if you get normal," she shouted over her shoulder. "I'm going up and look at the ocean. Close the door behind you, please."

O'Reilly drew in a long breath of thick, salty air. He looked down at the alpha attacker who had now managed to pull himself up onto his knees. Angry and confused, the man was struggling mightily to say something.

"Well, Jesus Christ and all who've dined *with* him," said O'Reilly to the midday sky.

Then touching his left wrist with the thumb and forefinger of his right hand, he watched as the dazed attacker fell backwards and unconscious for a second time. Turning back toward the building, he walked mindfully through its open door, stepping once again into the pleasant coolness of its dark interior. Carefully closing the door behind him, he reached up and pulled the large iron security bar into place. Installed a century earlier for the purpose of keeping the worst of Florida's storms at bay, the ancient crossbar was still effective in resisting any effort to dislodge the rust trimmed door. Grasping an iron railing, worn smooth by ten thousand hands, he paused to shake his head in disbelief. Then repeating a familiar reference to Jesus and his dinner guests, he began the long twisting climb upward.

"Holy damn!" echoed a voice from far above. "This place is fucking **awesome!**"

"Yeah," said O'Reilly, as he continued his snail-pace climb up the tower stairs, "fucking awesome."

The Sorrows of Zachary Pittkiss

"It has been said that good and loving parenting is the fertile soil from which mature, compassionate, and loving adults emerge. So, is it not reasonable then to surmise that bad parenting is the soil from which immature, heartless, and hateful adults arise?"
Excerpt from **"Kids to Killers"** *by Dr. Miles Perkins*
(TBIII copyright 2137)

Zachary Pittkiss had a horrible childhood. Both parents were alcoholic and easily riled to anger. Neither parent worked for a living. Both had spent time in jail for a string of misdemeanors ranging from DUI to petty theft. The family's primary source of income came from his father's disability checks, his injuries being the result of a drunken fall from a neighbor's rooftop. Had either parent been sober long enough to notice, they would have been surprised to discover that their son was not simply precocious in his ability to solve difficult problems, but was in matter-of-fact, a full-fledged genius in visualizing and comprehending algorithms, esoteric math concepts, and quantum equations. They would have recognized that they had miraculously given birth to that one in X-billion children, that single, gifted human anomaly capable of changing the world forever.

But Zach's parents did not stop drinking. In fact, their consumption increased as they developed tolerance to its effects. And as their drinking increased, so did their inability to relate to the needs of their son, or to be concerned with the consequences of their behaviors. The mild disagreements they had always had throughout their marriage, evolved into fierce shouting matches.

Predictably, Zach retreated more and more to the privacy and safety of his room. Once there, he poured over the many books he regularly carried home from the library.

He read and puzzled over all the major scientific formulas of the past century. He taught himself how to code software and to speak French and German. He reviewed scientific articles in their original language, making corrections in the margins as he read. He sketched models of turbines that he believed could efficiently run on 30% less fuel. He calculated the odds of nuclear war over the next ten years, fifty years, and one hundred years. He pondered his place in the world, and the world's place in the universe. Zach demonstrated in a thousand and one ways that he was, in fact, a genius who might very well surpass every intellectual master who had come before him. At age 10, he received, from his engineer uncle, a used high-end computer that he pretended to no longer need. The truth was that Zach's uncle Toby was the first person to recognize Zach's inherent gifts and potential.

From the very first day that Zach plugged in that generous electronic gift, he never looked back. His days, and most of his nights, were spent testing out his ability to reach out and touch the rest of the world. He challenged himself to crack the most formidable of data safeguards. And as the months and years slipped by, Zach's fascination with all other areas of science fell away. Like a laser beam, his focus was pure and singular. He became determined to hack the most sophisticated data security platforms in the world.

And one by one, they fell...Amazon, Disney, the Social Security Administration, NASA, the United Nations, and finally NATO. The exhilaration of each hack served only to feed his appetite for the next. At the tender age of 13, Zach had become the undisputed King of Open Doors. Around the world, computer experts, charged with protecting the privacy and secrets of their employers, could only scratch their heads and wait for the next shoe to fall. Such was his genius that, no trails could ever be found that would lead authorities back to him. Perhaps in time, as Zach matured, he might have found his way to a productive and legal career within the bright constellation of high-tech companies. Instead, a series of tragic events sent his life tumbling down a rabbit hole out of which he would never climb.

The most significant event occurred on a Christmas day. Zach awoke to the sound of his parents arguing wildly in the kitchen beneath his room. Apparently, to celebrate the birth of Jesus, both had stayed up throughout the night to drink to excess and to smoke cigarettes until the first floor was filled with a misty blue haze. Now, as the smell of fresh coffee filled the house, shouting and cursing suddenly erupted. This was followed by the clatter of metal pots being thrown and dishes smashing against walls. Zach had heard such sound before, but this time there was also the sound of his mother's piercing scream and then abrupt silence. Initially uncertain what to do, Zach finally determined to make his way downstairs. Once on the first floor, he moved with measured steps through the dining room to the swinging door leading to the kitchen. Pushing it gently open, Zach's gaze came to rest upon his mother's contorted, lifeless body. Standing over her, a bloody carving knife still in hand, his father turned in Zach's direction. "Mother's gone," he mumbled. "Mother's gone, Zach." A moment later, dressed only in his underwear, Zach walked calmly from his home.

Three houses down, Elliot Herman was about to get into his Toyota Corolla. His plans were interrupted by the arrival of a confused looking, partially dressed young man. Recognizing him at once as that strange Pittkiss boy, the one with the terrible parents, he asked.

"Are you alright? Where's your clothes, son?"

But Zach did not reply. Instead, he carefully removed his tee shirt. Then walking slowly beneath the Herman's sweeping yard sprinkler, he sat down gently on the soggy grass.

"Son, where's your clothes?" his neighbor repeated.

Zach turned his head slightly in the direction of the question. "Mother's gone," he said, repeating his father's words. "Mother's gone. My father killed her in the kitchen."

Six minutes later a patrol car pulled up. Twelve minutes later, a S.W.A.T. team arrived in full tactical gear. Fourteen minutes later, Zach's father emerged from his house, still grasping the knife he had used to kill his wife.

"Stop where you are! Stop where you are and drop the knife!" the S.W.A.T. captain shouted. But, before he could shout the command a third time, Zach's father pushed the knife out in front of his body and began to trot in the direction of the nearest S.W.A.T. team member. He made it as far as the team's 30 foot "safe perimeter", before twelve shots from three different weapons tore through his body. Zach's father fell instantly dead between a red Don Juan rose bush and a Hello Kitty skate board.

 A short while later, Zach was driven ...first to the police station for questioning, and then to the Department of Children and Families to await disposition. He would be there two months before finally being released to the full-time care of his uncle, the engineer.

On that very first night there in his uncle's home, as Zach sat quietly on the edge of his bed, he cried for the first and last time in his life. Then lying back on his pillow, he created a short poem...his one and only literary effort. It was called **"Zachary's Earth"**, and he fell asleep reciting its several lines ...

I shall melt all souls together
In a cauldron of despair
Kiss mountains into crystal sand
And awaken ancient air
And all who stand before me
All who've let the truth ignore me
Shall have my name carved in their bones
As their helpless God now weeps and moans
For I am death...And when I'm done...
The moon above...A lonely ONE

The Hand Grenade Heart

O'Reilly sat down on the top most metal step of the double helix staircase and tried to catch his breath.

"Wow! You're in fucking bad shape," said a voice from across the brightly lit room.

Shading his eyes, O'Reilly could just make out the silhouette of his impetuous guest. She was sitting cross-legged atop his work table, the noon day light flooding in around her.

"Well," he said between breaths "exercise is not a big part of what I do."

"Shows!" she said.

Pulling himself slowly to his feet, O'Reilly began to move in her direction, a look of irritation on his face.

"Whoa there, Bowtie!" said his guest. "Just what do you think you're gonna do?" Then picking up the Ziter-1000 beside her and gripping it like a weapon, she rolled forward into a defensive standing position.

O'Reilly stopped midway across the floor. Tilting his head to one side, he studied her now with the same curious interest a gardener might examine a hungry caterpillar. She was small, lean and angular...her green eyes filled with a fierce resolve. Having assumed a classic defensive posture, her feet were now shoulder width apart, one slightly behind the other.

"So, you've taken martial arts?" he observed gently.

"Believe it, Bowtie."

O'Reilly smiled despite his irritation with the young woman.

"Well the good news, strange miss, is that you won't have to use your deadly skills here today, at least not on me. So, if you would just please try to relax a bit and put down my Ziter, then I'll lower the shade on the window there behind you."

Glancing over her shoulder briefly, the young woman shrugged and stepped to one side.

"There," said O'Reilly tying down a dark rattan shade. "Sun's just brutal this time of day."

Feeling less threatened, the girl replaced her make-shift weapon back on its work table.

"So, you got anything to drink in this place?" she demanded.

"I do have something to drink in this place, but not before you tell me a few things...two things actually. No, make that three things."

"Which would be what?"

"Well...Number one...who are you? Two...why are those two men downstairs trying to kill you?"

"And three?" she asked.

"Well, three is just...why did one of them call you a 'sog'? What exactly is a 'sog'?"

"So, I'm three questions away from a cool drink?"

"No," said O'Reilly, "you're three *answers* away from a cool drink."

"Well fuck! Fine then...I am 'Petra' and those two angry idiot assholes are just a couple of total losers who had too much to drink...didn't like it when I said 'no' to their kinky party plans. And that's it. So, there you go...now where's my drink?"

"And number three...the definition of 'sog'?"

Petra rolled her eyes and crossed her arms.

"Well," she said with a forced calm, "that just depends on who you ask. Some locals say that it's short for '**Slutty Ocean Girl**', or their kinder version... '**Sad Ocean Girl**'. But *my* favorite is what the police call us... that would be '**Some-more Ocean Garbage**'."

O'Reilly stared at Petra dumbly for several seconds before breaking into unplanned laughter.

"You find that funny? Do you? Well how 'bout I put a funny fist in your funny face?"

O'Reilly shook his head and raised one hand.

"No," he said, "I don't find it funny at all. I find it troubling, cruel, and perplexing."

"And so...you are laughing because...why?"

"Because, young miss, where I come from, 'SOG' has a whole different meaning. In fact, it is a title of honor placed on very few."

"A title of honor?"

"That is a fact. 'SOG' in my profession refers to someone who displays a true *Spark **of** Greatness*."

"A spark of greatness?"

"To be sure. And I can tell you, there are not many citizens of my world who have ever qualified for that title."

It was Petra's turn to shake her head.

"You're a real piece of work, Bowtie. So, where's my cool drink?"

O'Reilly pointed to a small rust stained refrigerator across the room. "Help yourself!"

Placing her bag on the table beside her, Petra crossed the room with the air of a young princess. Then opening the tiny appliance, she rifled through it with growing irritation.

"So," she shouted over her shoulder, "you're telling me that in the middle of a fucking Florida summer you don't have one single cold beer in here?"

"That would seem to be the case," replied O'Reilly.

Petra pulled out a cold sugar free drink and wrinkled her face in disgust. First rubbing it gently across her forehead, she then twisted off its cap and proceeded to chug down most of its contents non-stop.

As she did so, O'Reilly stealthily placed two fingers of his right hand gently against the cross-body bag she had discarded. Then cupping his left hand over his left ear, he listened as LULU provided a detailed read out of the bag's contents.

"Interesting," he said softly.

Petra finished off the drink and grabbed a second one before kicking the fridge door shut and re-crossing the room.

"So, what exactly do you do here?" she demanded. "You some sorta hermit? Maybe a mad-ass scientist? And, oh yeah, why are you dressed like you broke into a friggin' Goodwill box? Seriously, Bowtie, here's *my* two questions. One ...who are **you?** And two ...just what is it you do here all day?"

O'Reilly placed both of his hands into the top pockets of his cargo pants.

"Well," he said thoughtfully, "I do research."

"Research? What? You mean like for the government or somethin'?"

"I guess you could say that," said O'Reilly.

"So, what? You get paid for staring out over the damn ocean all day?"

"I guess you could say that too," he replied.

"Well, Jesus, sign me up."

O'Reilly turned his back to the young woman and picked up the Ziter. As he did so, he glanced down at the update on his left thumbnail. *Three hours and ten minutes* until the main event. His gut tightened in a familiar spasm.

"Yes," he said, turning back in her direction with a smile, "it is a highly sought-after job. That is for sure. There are always many, many applicants."

Petra looked back at him as though trying to make out an unknown object through a frosted window.

"You know, you are one weird mother. Seriously, you live up here in this above ground tomb. You dress like a homeless friggin' street dweller. You're so outta shape you can hardly make it up the stairs. And ...oh yeah ... 'coincidentally' just as you arrive downstairs, the two 'assholes from hell' fall over in a dead heap. I mean, seriously, something's way the fuck out of line here." She concluded her biting summary of O'Reilly with an expression of self-satisfaction and a broad smile.

O'Reilly shook his head slowly.

"Sounds to me like you're looking for some truth...some answers...it's important to you, and you don't appreciate being in the dark about things. Do I have that right?"

"Yeah, Bowtie, you got that right. I am way passed being lied to and used by people. I like to get the truth up front ...know where I stand. And I am way up to here (She lifted a hand high above her head) with liars and losers. So, which are you? Own up, Bowtie. Come clean. Liar or loser?"

O'Reilly placed himself behind the only chair in the room, an ancient swivel oak affair that had once belonged to an oversized roll top desk. Having been separated years earlier from its companion piece, it now wandered the world alone. Tired and ponderous, its solid rubber casters worn thin, the old chair somehow retained a modest air of dignity as O'Reilly nudged it across the floor in the direction of his guest. Stopping directly in front of her, he nodded toward the chair.

"Take a load off, Judy. You've been through a lot today. It *is* 'Judy' isn't it? And if it is...well, oh my...you haven't been entirely truthful with me either, now have you?"

The young woman blanched noticeably. "What did you say?" she blurted.

"I'm simply pointing out that you, Judith Hooley, have not been entirely truthful with me."

Anger washed over her face as Judith Hooley (aka Petra) lurched forward and grabbed her bag still lying where she had placed it.

"You sneaky son-of-a-bitch!" she shouted at O'Reilly. "You went through my bag!"

But, as she examined the bag more carefully, she could see that its single wide strap was still pushed snuggly through the bag's copper loop, both of its snaps still securely fastened. Swiveling back in O'Reilly's direction, she demanded answers. Fiercely agitated, she was screaming now.

"Ok, asshole! ...How do you know who I am, and who the fucking hell are you anyway?"

The Kazinsky - Palucci Convergence

Scud Kazinsky had arrived on the bright beaches of sunny
Florida eleven years earlier. A high school senior on
spring break, he had been so enthralled by the open
promise of drugs, drink, sex, and thunderous music, he
chose to stay behind when all his friends returned home
in time for their graduation day. For several years, he
worked parking bicycle rentals beachside. This was
followed by a stint as a dishwasher and, eventually, a fast
order cook at the *Bottoms-Up Bar*. But, as he approached
his thirtieth birthday, Scud began to question his career
choices. Increasingly, he found himself dreaming of great
and amazing accomplishments, a new and different path
that would lead him to celebrity and success. Though
unsure just what that path might be, he was nevertheless
certain it would be overflowing with excitement, pleasure,
and big, big money.

Randolf Palucci was thirty-two years old when he first
arrived in Florida. Raised in a strict Catholic household,
Randy had been an angelic looking alter-boy until age
twelve, had graduated without distinction from St.
Margaret and Mary's High School outside of Baltimore,
and had determined at an early age *not* to accept a single
word of wisdom or advice from anyone. This included the
many earnest attempts by the sisters at his school to
instruct him in the basic message of *The Golden Rule*.

"Fuck that" he would whisper in class behind his hand.

Randy had been raised by "good enough" parents who
provided him with food, clothing, shelter and a modicum
of parental affection. But, from the time this young man

first entered his teens, he began to look around for something more exciting and dangerous than anything that suburbia had to offer. He reveled in computer blood games, World Wrestling events, zombie apocalypse movies, and comic books in which evil triumphed over good. Anxious to find his way into such worlds, he experimented with small misdemeanors at an early age. This included stealing from collection plates at church and his mother's purse at home. He spray-painted obscenities on bridge overpasses; and demanded cash from younger children at the nearby mall. Arrested multiple times before his sixteenth birthday, his usual punishment was to provide community service at a local homeless shelter. While there, he sought out the least ethical of its patrons to learn all that he could about living on the street and how best to fleece the endless flow of "marks" waiting to be plucked.

Three days before his eighteenth birthday, Randolph spontaneously abandoned his family, friends and home to seek his fame and fortune in the Big Apple. Having no marketable skills to offer "The City", he soon fell in with a group of like-minded cohorts. Quickly learning, then honing a handful of con artist come-ons, along with some slick pick- pocket skills, he soon earned enough to keep himself in pizza and cigarettes. But, after eighteen months of living on icy streets and hard mission cots, he had concluded that living in a northern city was not for him. He determined that, as soon as he was able to put together a few hundred bucks, he would escape the cold winds and harsh streets of New York City for a new home, one that could offer him endless sunshine and a steady flow of patsies.

And so, in the midst of a record-setting blizzard, when the fates intervened on his behalf, Randy was quick to respond. Coming across a well-dressed wall street-type lying unconscious in a snow drift, he took the opportunity to claim the man's valuables, along with his full-length wool overcoat. Then, with over eight hundred dollars in his pocket, a Breitling Chronomat 41 on his wrist and three stolen credit cards in his shoe, Randolf Palucci walked directly to 8th and 41st to the Port Authority Bus Terminal where he purchased a ticket to Florida, the Sunshine State.

An hour later, as he sat back comfortably in his warm cushioned seat, Randy smiled broadly in a rare moment of total contentment.

"Sky's the limit!" he said to a surprised mother of three sitting next to him.

When Training Bears to Juggle Knives

No matter how experienced a Cliff-Hunter may be...no matter how many missions they have completed or how many years they have spent in the field, it is vital that when they arrive at their final time-place destination, they be completely familiar with the customs, language, clothing, prejudices and belief systems of the period. Consequently, Cliff- Hunters spend far more time in retro-study classes than they do on actual missions. Usually, pre-mission class time required from one to three years of detailed learning and enactments before Launch Central would pull the trigger. Because there was so much to learn, and because most periods to be visited were so different from that in which Cliff- Hunters had been raised, instructors often joked that the training process was like "training bears to juggle knives ...not totally impossible, just very, very hard."

For this particular mission, his third to the same site, O'Reilly had logged two years and ten months of additional focused study. Still, even with the extensive research and preparation that goes into each mission, mistakes can be made...misinformation passed along.

A classic example had occurred to O'Reilly on his thirty first mission, a fact gathering tour of 1944 Europe. Somehow, the research section had inadvertently combined the fact files of two different decades. So, when O'Reilly had tried to impress a young airborne soldier in the town of Bastogne with his knowledge of Elvis Presley, there was an awkward and extended silence. Luckily, such a slip up had had little effect on his overall mission. It did, however, impress on him a valuable lesson...**Do Not Trust Your Training 100%**...Be prepared to improvise. If what you thought you knew turns out to be a completely misinformed or misinterpreted slice of historical intel, just "go with it and find a way."

So, it was that when O'Reilly arrived in Coca Beach, Florida wearing a pink and purple Hawaiian shirt, a red bow-tie, drab green cargo pants and a shiny pair of Florsheim brown wing-tips, he was not totally surprised to learn that his **LBQ** (**L**ocal **B**lending **Q**uotient) was below 8%. A less experienced CH might have panicked, but O'Reilly quickly found a way to carry it off. Instead of trying to tone down his strange appearance, he simply added to it. He presented himself as "that crazy eccentric loner hold-up in the old light house". On the several recon trips he had taken outside the tower, he selectively added some additional "color" to his character. Limping heavily and continuously talking to an imaginary friend seemed to do the trick. The locals often stared, but few approached him. Crazy, it turned out, was the perfect cover for a visitor to a Florida coastal town.

As thorough as the pre-mission training had been, it still had its limitations. What, for example, was a CH to do should they be approached by a persistent, overly curious local. What if a CH should become intentionally or unintentionally attached to a local? What if a local guessed the truth about them or the purpose of their mission? These and a hundred other questions were particularly "sticky" to address. Every CH was repeatedly instructed to avoid any personal involvement while on mission. The manual clearly stated in **Chapter 352,**

Article A22-23 that *"Should a CH experience any emotional, sexual, or psychological attachment to a residing local, they will disengage, distance, and retreat immediately. If this strategy fails to resolve the attachment issue, they are to abort their mission and return via the earliest possible time horizon to launch control home port. This core directive is to be carried out without exception."*

In the lengthy recorded history of Official Mission Annals, only two breeches of this policy existed. One occurred on October 24, 1929, at an observation point known as Wall Street in New York City, New York, and one on July 29, 1588 aboard a British Man-O-War outside the harbor at Calais, France. The results, in both cases, being that a true reading of the events that unfolded became impossible to determine. Some even surmised that the course of future events may have been compromised by the emotional involvement of the two misguided Cliff-Hunters.

Upon their return to Launch Central, the two hunters who had erred in judgement and broken with strict protocol, were dealt with in a predictable way. After a brief trial overseen by the *Co-founders Council*, CH2 Edward Costanzo Albright and CH3 Christina Elizabeth Gutierrez-Mann were given the option of mind execution by the state, or permanent banishment to the unimproved area of the island known as Northside. Both wisely chose option one and were "reconstituted" after a twelve second exposure to a *High Wave-Length Resonator*. Subsequently, both found employment ...Edward as a laboratory test subject at the Boffin Academy of All

Sciences and Christina as an official door opener at the Gopher Underground Transport Facility.

Like all Cliff-Hunters, O'Reilly knew full well the consequences of forming any kind of unapproved attachment to locals. Though tempted more than once, by the tears of a grieving mother or the plea of a dying soldier, he had never surrendered to that strong human impulse to help them. Now, with his career abruptly ending and any hope of a life beyond that of a Cliff-Hunter fading, his previous resolve to coldly ignore all such pleas, no longer held the same sway over him. An emotional shift of seismic proportion had begun to tremble and move within his weary heart, one that he had refused to acknowledge or give in to over the course of his long career. And as he neared the finale to this last mission, he found it increasingly difficult to ignore the feelings he had managed to suppress for nearly two centuries. This time would be different. This time, he resolved, he would allow the needs of another human being to matter.

On this, his last mission, he would present a single other sentient being with the precious gift of compassion. Yet, what he had not considered was just how difficult the actual delivery of such a gift might prove to be. Especially, if the intended recipient was one very angry, suspicious, tattooed, foul-mouthed beach creature who called herself Petra.

Subcutaneous LULU

"Oh, ok," said O'Reilly. "You want to know who I am. Well sure. No problem, 'Judy'. I'll just tell you anything you need to know. Yep. I will, by God, fill you in completely. I mean, you've been so forthcoming with me...it's only fair isn't it!"

Abruptly spinning on his heel, he turned his back to his inquisitor, picked up his 'Ziter' and looked out once more in the direction of the submarine turn basin. A few minutes later, having regained his composure, he added...

"Now if you'll excuse me, I'm going to walk through that door out onto the observation deck that surrounds this tower. So, feel free to stay right here in this room and do *absolutely nothing.*"

Judith got out the words "Well what about my..." just before the thick deck door closed behind him with a thud.

"Well you squirrely nut job!" she shouted after him.

O'Reilly felt a strong ocean breeze push against his body. Pushing back, he made his way to the four-foot black metal railing at its edge. The strong, heady smell of fish and brine filled up his lungs.

"Damn, but I'll miss this," he said.

Then adjusting the Ziter to *"full focus-scan-enhance"*, he put the unit up to his eyes and peered in the direction of a deep basin several miles further north. Having lived through so many solo missions in his career, he had long ago given himself permission to talk both to himself and to LULU as needed.

"And there she is," he said aloud. "Right on time!"

Though too far away for the naked eye to see, let alone identify, the Ziter enhanced the image of the USS Louisiana to appear to be within 87 feet. He could literally make out the rank of the enlisted sailors there on its deck. O'Reilly examined his thumbnail once again. "Two hours fifty-seven" he murmured. Then gently squeezing the middle knuckle of his left ring finger to initiate a *level 1 importance code*, he spoke in a calm and natural tone.

"LULU, update and confirm pre-event mark as 2:56 hours in 3,2,1...set.

LULU, set pre-event respective alerts at 7 minutes, 5 minutes, and 60 seconds prior to *Circle-Transport-Depart...set.*

LULU, confirm command and repeat."

Faithfully, his subcutaneous mission assistant accurately repeated the commands as dictated.

"LULU, you're the best!"

"Compliment confirmed," LULU replied.

"Atta girl," he said off handedly, then refocused his vision on the mission-event target two miles away. Previous experience had taught him that the next several hours would be a deeply emotional time for him. Still, he knew that this mission would be unlike any other. Not just because this was the only horrific event, he had visited for a third time, but different in that he, not mission control, would determine how it would end. Closing his eyes, he inhaled the warm salty air slowly, as he listened quietly to the ocean's playful waves rolling ashore. As always, they seemed to whisper something important, profound... an obscure message he had yet to decipher. Exhaling softly, he smiled, comforted in the private knowledge that he would soon learn this timeless secret message first hand.

"Death, where is thy sting?" he murmured to a distant seagull dot.

"Where indeed!" replied LULU. "Where indeed!"

Lowering the Ziter, O'Reilly shifted his view far out to sea.

"You're about to get much deeper, old girl," he said softly.

Then turning on his heel, he crossed the deck to go back inside. To his surprise, the door was now locked. Through its thickly dimpled glass he could just make out the silhouette of his uninvited guest, her look of arrogant vindication lost behind the opaque window.

"Problem, mystery man? Anything wrong out there?" she asked innocently.

"I don't have time for this," O'Reilly said in a matter-of-fact tone.

"What?" she mocked cupping both hands behind her ears. "Sorry. You'll have to speak up. Can't hear you." Her smile was now the mischievous smile of a three-year-old with a handful of stolen cookies.

O'Reilly closed his eyes as he searched for a last reserve of patience.

"You're a real treat," he murmured.

Then taking a small disk-shaped object from his right pants pocket, he attached the magnetic object to the door's ancient metal lock. Taking two steps back, he said calmly ...

"LULU ...*Activate* tool-source #5 ...80% max heat...duration five seconds ...in 3,2,1 ...start."

At once, the small object began to glow first red, then blue, then finally white as it melted its way through the lock. Its task completed, it then fell with a thud at the feet of one very confused Judith Hooley.

Gently pushing the door open, O'Reilly strolled casually through it before slowly bending down and retrieving the useful tool, now cool to the touch. He dropped the disk back into his right-side cargo pants pocket before speaking.

"We need to talk," he said gently.

Judy's eyes seemed strangely far away, out of focus.

"What the hell just happened?" she asked sheepishly. "What the..."

"We need to talk," repeated O'Reilly.

The Digital Neighbor Nexus

It took several years for Zachary Pittkiss to finally
determine just how he would destroy the world. Visions of
bursting dams, forest fires, and excessive CO_2 levels were
just a few of the fleeting considerations that entered his
brilliant young mind. But no matter how many diverse
forms of destruction he considered, each had its draw
back. They were either too limited in their impact or too
slow in achieving the desired permanent outcome...the
termination of mankind on planet Earth. So, it was with
some relief when, at the ripe old age of sixteen, Zachary
settled upon a plan that had the potential to deliver a
decisive blow to the world he had come to see as cold, evil,
and unrepentant.

His perfect plan had unexpectedly arrived as a sudden
flash of inspiration one morning at 3:00 AM Eastern
Standard Time. Propped up against three pillows, having
finished off a second bag of frosted cheese sticks, Zachary
was restlessly paging through the video titles offered up
on his notebook, when his attention was suddenly
grabbed by a documentary entitled "How to Command A
Nuclear Submarine." And in that brief, random moment,
Zachary Pittkiss knew that he had at last discovered the
best, most likely, method to terminate every last off spring
of Homo Erectus...forever.

In the months that followed, he read up on every private,
public, and in some cases, confidential file he could locate
on nuclear submarines, their weaponry, and most
importantly, their digital defenses against computer
attack. What he discovered was that nuclear submarines
maintained a sophisticated, multi-tiered system of

hacking defenses. These protected, not only the encrypted messages flowing back and forth between submarine and its land–based command center, but also included a highly sophisticated on-board system dubbed "R.E.P.E.L", an acronym for **R**epel **E**ntry - **P**rovide **E**dit Lock.

This defensive system was well thought out, well-engineered, and well maintained. It was considered by industry top guns to be the ultimate in digital attack deterrence. To test its ongoing relevance and reliability, a select group of independent agencies were periodically employed by the US Navy to attempt an unauthorized entry into their onboard computer control systems. To date, R.E.P.E.L had proven 100% effective in preventing any digital penetration to any part of that system. It was with great pride then that Vice Admiral Brubaker, head of the black budget office known as the Counter Chaff Command, had declared at a Pentagon staff meeting.

"There is nothing and no-one who has the capability to penetrate our onboard submarine command core. It would take the resources of a nation-state to even attempt to breach that barrier. And even then, the outcome would be predictable...*total* failure on their part."

As Zachary pieced together the substantial digital defenses he would face in his assault on America's deterrent fleet, he came to appreciate how very complex and seemingly impossible the task of breaking through it would be. But such a realization did not dissuade him from the mission he had determined for himself. In fact, the massive improbability that anyone could score a win over such a system did not discourage him at all.

On the contrary, it enticed him to rise to the occasion, to think outside the box, and then to think outside the box that box came in. Zachary now focused all his brilliance and intellectual prowess on one goal...find an entrance, a never before thought of way, to successfully negotiate a seemingly impossible path through smart, complex, adaptive, and layered software. A mere 48 hours later, as young Pittkiss awoke from an uneasy slumber, he realized, with an overwhelming sense of accomplishment, that his amazing brain had arrived at a solution to the problem ...an elegant and unique method that would allow him to penetrate the "impenetrable". He chose to simply call it *The Digital Neighbor Nexus*.

The approach was awe inspiring, a direct contradiction to most dark virus programs that had ever been directed at a digitally reinforced target. Unlike all other attacking software programs, his would rely not on a direct or confrontational approach, not even a sly back door entry strategy. Instead, the viral bug that he would send against the US Navy's best digital defenses would rely on a low key, almost passive, approach. Extraordinarily complex in its structure and morphing characteristics, this new assault would rely on the *cooperation* of the very protecting attributes that had been built into the defending structures.

Zachary visualized the process as being similar to that of a newly arrived neighbor in a suburban community who simply wants to borrow a cup of sugar from a strident recluse living next door. Instead of running up the man's sidewalk, pounding on his door and demanding his cup be filled with sugar, a subtler and far less combative approach could be tried. The new neighbor might begin by politely ringing his defensive neighbor's doorbell. If the door were opened to him, he might introduce himself and perhaps mention that he admired the color of the man's house, or that he had heard kind things about the man from other neighbors. He might apologize for intruding on the man's privacy or suggest they had something in common such as the need to be left alone. Whatever the gentle approach might be that was employed, it would not involve confrontation or traditional ways of asking for a favor. It would be an approach that slowly gained the trust and confidence of his neighbor over time. And even if his initial request for a cup of sugar were to be initially turned down, even turned down more than once, the hope would be that eventually the neighbor, feeling no sense of threat or violation, would agree to the request. In the end, such a careful, patient, and subtle approach would eventually be rewarded with a nice big overflowing cup of sugar.

This very same principal would be applied by Zachary in his attempt to breach the substantial defenses of a nuclear submarine.

First, his viral program would quietly arrive at the door of the vessel's computer defenses.

Second, it would politely "knock on the door" to make acquaintance with each adversary it met within that system.

Third, his program would subtly request, over the course of time, miniscule bits of information about any unguarded paths into the boat's nuclear arsenal fire control.

Fourth, a redux of this "neighborly" approach would be utilized for each subsequent level of defense.

In the end, Zachary surmised, the very digital and algorithmic components that had been assigned to keep him from gaining access would, in fact, *unknowingly assist* him in doing so. The sophisticated defenders of the submarine's ballistic capabilities would basically have given up everything for a tip of the hat and a pinch on the cheek.

Two days later, having once again reviewed all available public and classified information on America's ocean-going arm of its nuclear deterrent, Zachary Pittkiss launched his stealthy Neighbor Nexus assault against the entire fleet. His confidence was great that at least one of these floating nuclear platforms would eventually be caused to launch a devastating attack upon the world's population, thus ending it forever.

"Let the games begin," he said, then cranked up the volume on his favorite song ...

"A Whiter Shade of Pale" by Procol Harum.

Scud and Randy Seek Revenge

"Just remember," Randy would instruct Scud, "we gotta hit them when their keeper's not around and when they're too high to remember faces."

So, for almost two years, this petty crime duo had ruthlessly fleeced and beat up on any beach stray who had a few bucks in their pocket and no chance of defending themselves. They preferred to prey on the young drug addled females who had been pimped out in return for a hand full of pretty pills. Their mistake, on this day, had been to assume that the very combative Petra was simply one more such easy target, a confused and frightened beach girl who would quietly hand over all her possessions without a fight.

To date, their enterprise had paid off well enough to keep them in cigarettes, beer, and a funky one room residence at the Black Marlin Motel on the edge of town. Most of their victims had not bothered to report their mugging, knowing full well the local police patrols had little respect for, or interest in, their personal well-being. "Sogs", as law enforcement continued to call them, were considered to be the worthless by-product of the legitimate tourist trade...the residue left behind when the reputable folks had all gone home to the suburbs of Des Moines or Kansas City. And any chance that a sog's cry for help would be taken seriously, was somewhere between zero and zero times two.

Randy was the first to fully regain consciousness; his nose, mouth and ears filled with gritty white sand. For several moments, he had some difficulty remembering the events that had led up to his incapacitation. Now, as he stumbled to his feet and brushed still more sand from his hair and clothing, he felt a fierce anger rising up in him.

"Nobody does this to Randy Palucci and gets away with it...nobody!"

Then looking up at the tower, still backlit by a fierce noonday sun, he shouted one more time.

"You are fucked bitch! You and whoever else is in there with you! Fucked!"

There was a muffled moan off to his right, as Scud Kazinsky began to stir.

"What?" he asked in a raspy monotone. "What?"

"What?" repeated Randy. "I'll tell you what. You and me are gonna kill somebody today. That's what. Plain and simple." Then pointing toward the tower's peak, he added, "Blood is gonna flow. Believe it."

A few minutes later the two would-be assassins were running and stumbling their way down the beach.

"Wait up," said Scud holding up a hand. Then stopping in the shade of a stunted palm, he attempted to catch his breath. "Where the hell we goin' anyway? I mean, where the hell we goin' and what the hell's the plan?"

Randy strolled casually back toward his accomplice.

"We are going," he said through gritted teeth, "to find ourselves some firepower. And *then,* we are going back to that tower and waste whoever it is that is still inside."

"Oh," said Scud, confusion creeping across his face. "But how we gonna kill 'em if we can't get in?"

"Use your tiny little brain, Scud!" Randy shouted. "Seriously, you should try it! Look," he added in a less hostile tone, "we shoot 'em from a long way off...way down the beach...we use a high-power rifle...one with a scope...see...easy and done!"

"Oh." said Scud a second time "But where we gonna get somethin' like that?"

Randy's patience had now officially run out. Turning back in the direction he had been walking, he strode forward with long, determined steps. Calling back over his shoulder, he said two things.

"You're a fucking idiot" and "I know a guy"

Twenty minutes later, a squatty single-story ranch came into view. It was a sad little cement block structure that had endured coastal storms and the total neglect of renters since its construction sixty years earlier. Where a jalousie window had once looked out over a parched brown lawn, a jagged gaping hole and a fluttering plaid curtain now stared back. A single S.W.A.T. team tear gas canister had found its mark on the first try. A rotting front door hung loosely on a single remaining hinge that had somehow survived a police battering ram. The walls of the puce colored building were covered in the various shades and colors of Florida mold.

Cautiously approaching the building, Randy and Scud made their way around a rusting 2006 Police Crown Victoria Interceptor. Years of neglect and a daily dose of salt laden beach winds had done their work. The once proud cruiser, with its 4.6 Liter engine and its Kevlar lined front doors, had been reduced to an aging metal eyesore. What could not be seen, by those who passed it by, were the half dozen claymore mines stacked neatly within its Police Trunk Pack...a testament to the full-service mind-set of the car's owner.

Scud reached out to ring a doorbell that had not worked for three decades.

"What are you doin', fool? Just knock!" scolded Randy.

Scud began pounding the side of his fist against the loosely hanging door. From inside, there came the scuttling sounds of movement.

"Colt. Colt!" Randy shouted. "Dude, it's me. It's me and my man, Scud. You in there, man? We got business. Hey! Come on, man. It's Randy. Open up."

"Colt Savage", as he called himself, was a thirty-six-year-old self-described "arms dealer" who had worshipped weapons and firearms since he was ten years old. Having been raised by a single mom who worked two jobs, he had spent endless hours watching every cop, criminal, and war story that television could offer up. What he learned from his thousands of hours of dedicated viewing was that firepower matters, and a loaded 1911 made for an acceptable substitute for confidence, education, and a father.

The very first time he had ever pulled the trigger on a big bore hand gun, the angels sang sweetly as every peg in God's creation fell into place. Since that day, he had never looked back. He purchased, sold, cleaned, modified, and worshipped any well-made weapon that could send forth the wondrous fire power of Satan himself. He had been christened Edward Nathan Trumbly, but over the course of his troubled life he had preferred the moniker of various gun manufacturers, occasionally combining several into one. For a time, he had gone by the handle *"Smitty Wesson"*. This was followed by *"F.N. Ruger"*, and most recently, simply *"Colt Savage"*.

As small-time gun worshippers go, "Colt" had met with modest success by selling all manner of "clean" firearms to all manner of criminal types. His guarantee was simple...no serial number, no prints inside or out, and no locatable paper trail. Business may not have been booming, but it was steady. Steady enough to keep him in cheap whiskey, endless ammunition, and his daily olfactory fix of burned propellant down at the gun range. As far as Colt was concerned, every day in every way was just plain sweet, fat, and easy.

"What do you want?" he demanded from the other side of his battered front door.

"Colt, it's me. It's Randy. Remember me, man? I sold you that revolver last year...the one I found on the beach. You gave me fifty bucks. Remember?"

"The Ruger 101?"

"I don't know man. Yeah...I guess. But hey, we're here to *buy* now, man. And what we need...we need right now!"

"Really? Well, how 'bout that now?"

Randy looked over his shoulder and lowered his voice.

"Dude, we need a long-gun with a scope."

There was an extended silence on the other side of the door followed by the sound of a sofa being pushed away from the door.

"How much you got on you?"

"I got over $800 right here in my pocket."

"Where'd you two get $800?"

"Does it matter?"

"It could."

"We just got lucky that's all."

"Lucky?"

"Yeah. Well. Some drunkin' old fart tourist gave us eight hundred plus last night."

"Wow. He sounds generous. So, tell me the truth, boys. Did he also give you his watch and rings?"

"Well, maybe. Man, what if he did? Look we need to make a purchase."

"A purchase such as what exactly?"

"Colt ...like I said ...we need a rifle with a scope. And we need it fast. Could we just talk face to face...instead of through this damn door?"

"And just how bad-ass should this rifle be?" asked Colt, ignoring Randy's request.

"Bad-ass enough to make a certain asshole dead from a football field away…"

 "Well then …sure fellas…come on in…store just opened. But, do yourselves a big favor and **do not** try to grab anything in here for free. 'Cause, fellas, that would be the very last stupid thing you'd ever do on this earth. Now, I'm gonna clear some things away. And once I do, me and my favorite 1911 are gonna open this door. Then you two are gonna come through it one at a time…nice and slow. I hope you know I'm serious. And one last thing, boys… the weapon you're lookin' for costs a whole lot more than eight hundred. Three times more."

The muffled thumps of boxes and furniture being shuffled could be heard from inside. Then the broken door to Colt's weary home was cracked opened just wide enough for one body at time to slip through.

Thirty minutes later, having provided Colt Savage with a down payment of $800, Randy and Scud departed. They carried a Springfield M1A, the civilian version of the legendary M-14. Wrapping it in a colorful oversized beach towel, the two hurried off in the direction of the lighthouse. Though they retained very little of the crash course instructions they had been provided, Randy continued to repeat the rhythmic chant given to him by their salesman …

"This weapon is a gas operated semi-automatic seven point six two-millimeter scoped instrument of hell."

"We are going to so end these fucks!" shouted Randy to the sky above.

" Hey, wait up, man! This hot sand is killing me. And by the way...how the hell we gonna get Colt his other sixteen hundred?"

"Tomorrow's problem, Scud," yelled Randy over his shoulder. "Tomorrow's problem!"

A short time later, the novice assassins were ensconced behind a yellowing Sago Palm, the barrel of their sniper rifle protruding from it. Three hundred yards away, the building at the site of their recent humiliation rose stark and white beneath the bright Florida sun. Randy adjusted the 50mm objective lens of his Vortex Viper scope to achieve the best possible magnification of his target. And as the details of the lighthouse deck rails came into view, he smiled broadly. Then, modifying a sacred prayer from his Catholic upbringing, he slowly recited his own twisted version. "Hail, Petra, mother of no one, the Lord is definitely *not* with thee today. And blessed art thou *never* amongst women...because, bitch...it is time for you to die."

The Last Citizen Born of Lovers

Neil Vanguard Presley was unusual, as he had been born
the last child of the union of a man and woman and not
the enhanced final product of a digital-laser-protein soup
and a professional birth-giver. He was, in fact, the very
last citizen of Tibetland III to have arrived in this manner.
His birth, and subsequent upbringing, had been followed
closely by the nostalgia clubs such as the "Way-Backs"
and the "Daze Gone Bye". He even had several followers
as far as the Northside settlement.

"How does it feel," the interviewers would ask his mother,
"to know you are the last female to conceive a child in this
primitive manner...the last woman who will ever do so?"

"I have no words," she would reply. "I have no words at
all."

Neil continued to be the center of continuous public
attention throughout his early life. His smiling rosy-
cheeked face could be seen on the entertaining 3D pop-up
Gopher-ads that ran across the island.

*"Neil Presley learns to stand" "Neil Presley's first day at
prime-thought" "Neil Presley's favorite food."*

Quite a popular celebrity really...that is, right up until the
day that a rogue Cliff-Hunter, named Manson Emmanuel
Drucker, returned from a 20th century mission with a
Duncan Yo-Yo and an unopened can of ***Campbells
Chicken Soup***. From that infamous day forward, Neil
Presley's star began to dim. Inevitably, the time came
when few talked about him or his unique lineal
circumstances. By the time he was thirteen, few citizens

would have been able to recognize him as the final living legacy of mankind's vanishing primitive past.

Predictably, as Neil's fame subsided, his prospects for a promising future dimmed as well. His popularity among the nostalgia clubs first faded and then disappeared altogether. At thirteen, he was re-assigned to a local collective when his mother was granted a "voluntary life exit passport". And as one final indignity... a state promised scholarship to Tibetland III University was unceremoniously revoked.

Over the years that followed, Neil had tried his hand at a number of pre-slot entry positions. These various government career paths included *apprentice to a time distortion artist; cloneroom hospitarian greeter; and Northside informer*, among others. Now thirty-one, Neil found himself working second shift-B deep within the formidable bowels of the Brane-Transport Command. Having barely passed the entrance exam requirements, he was grateful to have a steady paying job at all. Upon his hire, he had been given three months of detailed technical training, eight months of intensive protocol behavior indoctrination, and a twelve-minute explanation of what would happen to him, should he intentionally or accidentally overlook any part of either.

The room in which he sat was large by island standards. It was perhaps 20X30 feet with a ceiling that towered overhead. Carved from solid rock during the early years of settlement, its walls were covered in a dull composite of copper, vanadium, and a third substance known only to a few elite Homeland scientists. Half sitting, half reclining in his extremely comfortable control chair, Neil's job was a simple one...to launch and recover Cliff-Hunters, and to monitor the constant flow of information and interface updates that flowed back and forth between them and the flawlessly functioning bank of monitors before him. Though his primary duty directive was to "call for assistance should there be any indication of a technical or human concern within the active missions", after a number of years of reclining in his comfortable monitor's chair, he had observed only a single variation from anticipated mission outcomes or designs.

Lately, his four-hour shifts felt as though they would simply never end. There were, in fact, times when even the tourmaline colored somni-stop pills barely kept him from nodding off. Still, he persisted in the very best manner he could, ever hopeful that an acceptable performance in this entry level position might lead to something more important, more interesting. And for Neil, "more interesting" meant nothing less than his eventual acceptance into the Cliff-Hunter training program.

Obviously, there were so many desirable perks in being a full-fledged Cliff-Hunter, one could hardly count them all. The most obvious, of course, was the mere fact that Cliff-Hunters lived, on average, two hundred and fifty-three years longer than the 83.2-year life span of the rest of Tibetland III's citizens. The specific reason such an extended lifespan was possible had never been scientifically determined. The phenomenon was generally accepted to be a "by-product" or "positive side-effect" of repeated travel through the various Brane layers. Recent research had, in fact, confirmed a direct correlation between the number of missions a Cliff-Hunter had undertaken and the age to which he or she would live. One confident researcher had even gone so far as to propose a formula for longevity prediction among the CH class. He put forth the proposition that **L** (lifespan) = **A** (original passive anticipated lifespan) x **T** (total number of Brane crossings) x **W** (average length of stay in weeks within a foreign brane) x **A** (alternate aging constant = .023) ...**L = A** x **T** x **W** x **.023.** So, if a Cliff-Hunter had an original estimated lifespan of 80 years, and they crossed 60 Branes throughout their career, and stayed in their destination for an average of 3 weeks, they could be expected to live approximately 331 years. (**L = 80** x **60** x **3** x **.023 = 331.2**)

As impressive as such a benefit was to most everyone, Neil was equally impressed with the idea of being able to partake of certain exquisite experiences that the average citizen could only view on the authorized docu-vid-channel or the black-market past-times-modules. Of all the enticing possibilities Neil had ever viewed or smelled via olfactory enhancers, he had narrowed his favorites down to three. His dream was to one day ...

- Touch a real live woman
- Taste a chocolate bar
- Walk barefoot through green grass

On those rare nights, when his dreams were especially kind, he imagined himself an accomplished, confident Cliff-Hunter, enjoying the wondrous exhilaration of all three. Neil had met perhaps fifty active members of the Cliff-Hunter population during his stay in the launch/retrieval room. Most he disliked. The CH5s were the worst...prima donnas the lot of them. They never gave anyone a please or a thank you, just "do this" "do that" "faster" "slower" "don't be stupid".

Still, there were a few who he genuinely admired and respected, none more than Cliff-Hunter third class Ramon O'Reilly. Besides being pleasant in his conversation, he also came across as someone who cared about the feelings of others, even a lowly mission transport-tech.

On one occasion, having found out it was Neil's birthday, O'Reilly had actually taken the time to wish him well and to express his appreciation for the constant monitoring services he provided to all Cliff-Hunters. While admiring O'Reilly as a true Cliff-Hunter role model, Neil could not help noticing in the man an abiding sadness, a weariness of soul...something about the way he carried his shoulders; how he smiled but never laughed. How, Neil wondered, could such negative feelings possibly take hold in anyone who was participating in the most revered and respected profession within the entire island nation?

Everyone Knows What They Think They Know

"Oh, so now you think it's time for us to talk? Well, good friggin' guess, Bowtie Man. How 'bout we start with just who in the hell _you_ are and what it is _you're_ doin' here. Because, darlin'...you are definitely NOT from Florida, ok!"

O'Reilly took a small step backwards and gathered his thoughts. Then smiling the smile of a Disney greeter, he began.

"Are you a fan of science fiction?"

Petra looked first confused, then irritated. "Just what the hell does that have to do with a ...?"

"No. Please," he interrupted, "just bear with me. Just answer the question. Are you a fan of science fiction?"

Petra gave out a loud, forced sigh and rolled her eyes. "Ok, fool...let's play. Yes. Yes, I am a fan of science fiction...but not all of it. OK? Not that lame ass shit where every other character is flying around or melting metal with their eyeballs. I'm like a fan of just-maybe-that-could-happen sci-fi. You know...a story where some believable egg head scientist discovers a way to read minds or use the full potential of his brain, or figures out how to ..."

"Travel through time?" asked O'Reilly.

"What?"

"Travel through time," he repeated. "Would that be one of the sci-fi plots you might buy into?"

Petra revisited her look of irritation. "Yeah I suppose...sure."

"Well, that's just excellent," said O'Reilly.

"Excellent?"

"Yes. Because, that makes everything I have to tell you...well, more likely to be believed and accepted by you."

"You, Bowtie Man, are the strangest fuck I have ever met. And believe me when I tell you...I have met some truly strange fucks, most of them right down here on this beach."

O'Reilly subdued a smile.

"Can I ask you something, Judy...I mean before I share the truth of who I am?

"It's still 'Petra' and sure ...no problem. Just as long as it doesn't involve *your* pecker or *my* private parts. Got that?"

O'Reilly quietly stared at the young woman for more than a few seconds before asking his question.

"Why do you use so much profanity in your speech? I mean, you seem above average in intelligence and are at least average in word compilation, and yet your conversations are laced with multiple profanities. Not that I haven't heard them all before. But usually I've heard them from angry sailors, or politicians or a serial killer or two. But you...well...you have the rare distinction of being the most profane speaker among the entire menagerie."

It was Petra's turn to stare now.

"Well first of all, that's a stupid fucking question. You just wasted a golden chance to learn something about me. Second...I will bet you a fuckin' Benjamin that your sailor, your politician, and your serial killer friends did not live the life I have. They have not gone through what I have gone through. They have not done what I have had to do...just to survive. And I'll bet you Benjamin number two they were all white fuckin' males...a herd of greedy idiots who all had it pretty damn good, while all the while convinced, they were somehow suffering. I bet they all were sure they were not getting their fair fucking share of anything of value. I will bet you that they were white fuckin' men with a chip on their shoulder and a permanent hard-on...just waiting for a chance to fuck the world and everyone in it." Petra's face was now flushed, both hands doubled up into fists.

"Oh, I see," said a contrite O'Reilly. "Sorry. Just curious."

"Yeah ...'just curious'" she said. "So how 'bout we just cut to the chase. And in 25 words or less you tell me who the hell you are; what the hell you're doin' here; and why the hell I should care in the friggin' least!"

"Fair enough," said O'Reilly.

"Now you're down to 23," Petra said without a smile.

O'Reilly took a deep breath before speaking. "I am a Cliff-Hunter traveling across co-occurring branes and time to study catastrophic events in order to, hopefully, one day safely reconfigure them."

"That's 24," she said.

"Well no…actually, 'Cliff-Hunter' is hyphenated," he replied.

Petra's demeanor did not soften.

"So, you're telling me that you're what? A time traveler?"

"Yes. Pretty much …I am *that*," said O'Reilly.

"And you're here doing research?"

"Yes."

"And you're here studying some terrible event that's about to happen."

"That is correct," said O'Reilly with a nod.

"Well, that's great. That's just great…terrific. Not only are you one more crazy fuckin' white male, you're fuckin' crazy in a brand-new way!"

"No," protested O'Reilly. "What I just shared with you is something I have never shared with anyone in the last two centuries. I swear to you. Everything that I have told you is absolutely true."

Petra took a long slow step backwards. Then calmly, and without taking her eyes off the strange man before her, she pulled a lethal looking dagger from her bag. Inching carefully in the direction of the stairwell, she said coldly.

"Do not take even one small step in my direction or I will bury this blade in your ribs."

O'Reilly tilted his head to one side.

"If it were only that easy...I mean, normally I would just say 'Sure...Go...Leave'." But here's the thing. I have been doing this a very long time ...longer than you can imagine. And I have, for a number of reasons, determined that this mission will be my last. And, while I have stood by in the past and allowed millions of souls to perish in a sudden cataclysm of volcanic lava, or tidal wave, or napalm...I have determined that, this time, I am not going to let that happen to at least one sentient being. And, I am sorry to apologetically report that, that sentient being just happens to be *you*."

Petra frowned and shook her head violently from side to side. "All of which means what?"

"All of which means, I am not going to let you die a meaningless death here on the white sands of this Florida beach."

Petra stopped her retreat to the stairs. "What in God's name is wrong with you?"

"Wrong?" A relaxed smile washed across O'Reilly's face. "Well, nothing's wrong now, Judy ...now that I've finally made a decision to do something that requires some courage and real backbone. No. There's nothing wrong with me. Not now. You see, Judy... young foul-mouthed beach woman...I am weary. I am worn out. I have been lonely, and I have walked alone through a thousand moments in time, through twenty-three separate civilizations here on Earth. And the truth is...my time is up. And to be perfectly honest ...I am relieved and grateful. So, nothing matters to me now, except that I send you away from here and the devastation that will shortly transpire. At the very least, I will die knowing that you will have received, at minimum, a few more days or months of life to work things out...to get an informed clue before The Homeland Council determines what is to be your final disposition. And, in this way, I will have experienced a very thin and temporal slice of what I imagine it might mean to be human."

Judy looked dumfounded. "So...you're telling me what?"

"I'm telling you that, should you leave this lighthouse, you will die with everyone else on this beach in only a few short hours. I am telling you that, though I have never saved any other human soul in my several centuries of living, I am about to save yours. Not because I enjoy your conversation, or because you light up a room when you walk into it, but simply because it is one small, one miniscule good thing I will have done in an extended lifetime of blind service to duty and homeland. I am telling you that I am transporting you to another time, to this earth-world's future time. I am saying...asking...that you put your very sharp knife back in your bag and prepare for your upcoming journey to my homeland...Tibetland III."

 "Holy fuck!" Petra blurted out, "You're serious as a heart attack!"

O'Reilly smiled broadly for the first time in many years.

"Ms. Hooley, you are very welcome," he said.

65

Max Installs the End Times

"Excuse me, commander," said Max. "Now that this whale is safely parked, I really need to get to the head. I feel a little nauseous."

Patterson scanned Max's demeanor. His affect did appear slightly different from his usual distant presentation. An aura of mild distress now surrounded him, one that had never shown itself before.

"Sure, Max," said Patterson. "Seaman Baxter here will see that you find your way. There's a crew head one deck below."

"Baxter, would you escort Max to and from the head."

"Yes, Sir," responded Baxter. Then turning abruptly toward Max, he instructed. "Follow me below, Sir."

Thirty seconds later Max stepped off the crew ladder, nodded at his helpful guide and moved toward the head door a few steps away.

"No locks on it, Sir," said Baxter. "Sub life, Sir. No privacy. No secrets."

"Just one big happy family, huh sailor?" replied a smiling Max.

Baxter smiled back. "Well, something like that, Sir."

Max closed the door behind him and set down his tool kit. Looking up, he studied an aluminum vent cover in the nearest wall. An unexpected wave of emotion swept over him. For the first time in many years, perhaps since he was a young man, an overwhelming flood of joy filled up his heart, his eyes filling up with tears of gratitude. He paused for just a moment in order to regain his composure and steady his focus. Then reaching into the tool kit, he produced a Phillips screw driver before climbing up onto the toilet. Then quietly, lovingly, he removed the twelve pan head metal screws that held the air vent cover in place. Once accomplished, he carefully deposited them in the front right pocket of his jeans. Then, with the careful concern of a mother for her infant, he removed and lowered the cover to the deck beneath him. Still balanced on the toilet, now standing on tip toe, he reached as far as he could into the dark vent cavity. After several frustrating attempts, he finally felt what he had been searching for...a primary detonating charge and its timer magnetically and faithfully clinging to the inner vent wall. Pulling the unit into the light, he began to examine it for any signs of corrosion or functional degradation. The unit had held up surprisingly well, with no apparent signs of impairment. Nevertheless, and ever cautious, Max pulled a small sheet of extra fine sandpaper from his back pocket and methodically polished the twelve battery contact points upon which so much would depend.

As he worked away at his dark project, one which finally promised fruition after years of meticulous planning, strong emotions once again challenged his concentration. And as he carefully placed six brand new D cell batteries in the waiting slots of his device, a wave of relief and delight began to spill out of him. Childlike in his demeanor, Max giggled like a school boy in love as he whispered to the polished aluminum walls around him.

"Time to wake up, ladies. Time to rise and shine. Max has your candy...six shiny new D cells. It's time to do your thing for Max and God ...Hallelujah and Amen!"

"You ok in there, Sir?" asked a worried Seaman Baxter.

"Almost done," Max shouted over his shoulder. "Starting to feel better already, son. Way better now."

The Art of Knowing Nothing

For the first time in a very long decade, Petra did not know what to say. She was at once surprised, disbelieving, and intrigued. Finally, with a half laugh and just the right amount of impatient disgust, she lowered the knife and pulled herself up to her full five-foot three-inch stature.

"Well now...that is some story there, Bowtie Man. It's got all the ingredients that a good science fiction plot should have. Seriously. And your delivery is spot on. I mean, you genuinely sound like you believe all that shit your own damn self. And that, when you think about it, is kind of more worrying than if you didn't. You see my point?"

O'Reilly turned his hands palms up and shrugged. "I do see your point," he said.

"Tell you what, Bowtie. I'll put this knife away, if you first just move back across the room toward that deck door. And then stay there until I say you can move your sorry ass. Got it?"

"Got it," said O'Reilly, as he ambled back across the room. "How's this then?" he asked as he reached the broken door.

"Good enough," said Petra, as she slipped the stiletto back into her hand bag.

"So, what now?" asked O'Reilly. "You do remember we are very low on time, right?"

"So now you answer some very specific questions. After which, *I* decide what happens next."

"OK. Fair enough…except, how about this…Every time I answer one of your 'very specific' questions about *me*, I will also include something very specific about *you*."

"Whatever," Petra sneered. "Here's your first question."

"Go for it, Judy."

"Why in the hell should I believe a single fucking thing you tell me?"

O'Reilly paused. "Well, let's see. You've already witnessed several events that have taken place in your presence, events for which you have no plausible explanation. I'm referring here to the sudden incapacitation of your two attackers just outside this building, and to the melting of the lock on the door behind me." Smiling, he gestured over his shoulder with his thumb.

Petra looked unconvinced. "Question number two…"

"Whoa," said O'Reilly calmly. "Did you forget? I now get to tell you something about you?"

"Knock yourself out," she said with cold contempt.

"OK, well, let's see. You are not from Florida. You are from Springville, Illinois. Your mother died when you were approximately four years old. You were raised by your father, who did his best to steer you on a proper path, but who, nevertheless, failed you in several important ways. Though you are very bright, having an IQ that is 2.5 standard deviations above 'normal', you dropped out of high school before graduating. You have worked as a waitress, a parking attendant, a motel service maid, and as a reluctant party escort for older men. You believe in God, but you aren't sure why. You still believe that, one day, something good will happen to change your unhappy life. You got your first tattoo when you were sixteen. It is a small colored one that depicts a butterfly hovering above a saffron colored flower. It is located high up on your right hip, as you wanted it to remain a secret...something about you that no one else would ever know unless you chose to share it...Next question, please"

Petra looked shaken. A low gurgling sound escaped from her throat as she tried to gather her thoughts...Finally, she pulled herself together and pointed her finger accusingly at O'Reilly.

"I don't know how the hell you know what you know about me. I mean maybe you've been following me around and I didn't even know it. Maybe you've been asking questions about me...going online. I don't know. But I've still got questions for you. You got that? I've still got questions"

"Got it," said O'Reilly. "You've still got questions."

"Question number two...If you're from another place in time, how the hell did you get here...travel here?"

O'Reilly didn't hesitate. Speaking in a calm and even cadence, he said "I traveled here from my homeland, Tibetland III. It is located on this Earth, but further into the future. I traveled via discreet Brane Tier 223 Protocol on a common thread transfer pattern. This simply allows a body to jump from one brane to another multiple times. And in so doing, to choose specific moments and locations in which to 'arrive'. In order to successfully arrive in any Brane, an enormous amount of information must be gathered, filtered and accurately deciphered. This requires exceptionally robust computing capacity...a capacity which the scientists of my homeland perfected hundreds of years ago. It is impressive to be sure. But there is one caveat. There is no room for error, not the slightest...or a body can end up playing tag with a tyrannosaurus rex ...That's an old Cliff-Hunter joke by the way."

Petra shook her head fiercely "And you expect me to believe this bogus busload of bullshit?"

"Nice alliteration there, Judy. And, yes, I am hoping you'll believe me...But if you can't right now ... maybe you will after you hear what I tell you next."

"Which is?"

"OK, here it goes. But remember, you agreed to hear it ..."

Then, turning away from her, he gazed out over the grey ocean one more time. In a low and measured tone, he began to recite what he knew to be true.

"You go to the library ...often. You read books on history, government, science, as well as major works of literature. You feel better about the world and your place in it whenever you've spent time in this way. You have a strong desire to learn more about many things. However, your positive feelings do not last. It seems that most nights, before you place your head on your pillow there in your tiny little rented room, you drink a full tumbler of cheap red wine, swallow an over-the-counter sleep aid, and cry yourself to sleep. There is a well-worn stuffed bear named *Crumbles* who sits on the pillow beside yours. You have disturbing dreams that often wake you. On such occasions, you turn on one of the shopping network shows and learn about the limitless number of possessions you do not own. Oh, and you have a recurring dream that you're a tall and very kind nun."

Petra backed-up slowly to the wall behind her and pressed her backbone against it for support. Then, as though her legs were slowly melting beneath her, she slid in slow motion to the slatted wooden floor beneath her.

"Why are you doing this?" she asked without looking up. "Who are you and why?"

O'Reilly took several tentative steps in her direction before slowly bending down on one knee.

"Judy, I am only telling you these things, so you will believe me. I am telling you these things so that you will accept the truth in time to save yourself from what is going to happen in very short order."

Petra looked up with a dazed stare. She tried with great effort to refocus on the strange male who was speaking to her now. Moving her head from side to side, she simply said, "I'm lost here, Bowtie Man."

"Yes. I can understand why that might be. But, Judy, we don't have the luxury of time for you to completely sort it all out. Not right now. You're going to have to trust that LULU and I will keep you safe and get you where you need to go. Even if you don't understand the details of all that is about to happen, you need to draw on that reservoir of strength that I know is inside you. You've got to take care of yourself, stand-up for yourself one more time. Alright, Judy? If you can just do that, then we'll do the rest, OK? Trust us. It'll be alright."

Petra coughed once, as though clearing something distasteful from her throat. Then taking a long, even breath, she made eye contact with O'Reilly.

"Who the fuck is LULU?" she asked.

Neil Presley Bids His Hero Forever Good-Bye

Though protocol forbad non-mission conversation with a Cliff-Hunter, once they were within thirty minutes of launch/ departure, Neil could not help himself. He had to ask.

"Are you alright, Sir? I mean, Commander O'Reilly, you seem a bit pre-occupied."

"Pre-occupied?" O'Reilly echoed back.

"Yes, Sir…as though something was wearing heavy on your mind."

"It shows does it?" O'Reilly asked with a forced smile.

"Yes Sir…it does" said Neil. "And to be honest, you've seemed kind of sad or something for a while." Then, fearful he had overstepped the rules of discourse, he backtracked. "Not that you haven't performed with top notch skills, Sir…I mean, you always get the goods…You always…"

"Stop!" shouted O'Reilly raising a hand. "Stop." He repeated in a quieter tone. "You don't have to try to please me. You're not in trouble. In fact, your observations are dead on."

"They are, Sir?"

"Neil, do you know how many missions I have completed and how many years I have been going and coming from this launch facility?"

"Not really, Sir."

"Well, let me ask you this. How old are you?"

"How old, Sir?"

"Yes. How old?"

Neil shrugged his shoulders as though giving up common knowledge. "I turned thirty-one last month, Sir."

O'Reilly leveled a fixed gaze on the curious launch-tech."

"Well then, let me put it this way. On the day you came into this world, I had already been playing this game for over one hundred and forty years."

"One hundred and forty...?"

"Yes, one hundred and forty years, Neil. And that is a long, long time to be brane hopping."

"Sir, may I say that you don't look older than thirty-eight...forty tops."

"True enough. I'm a forty-year old Cliff-Hunter with a two-hundred-year-old heart. And to be honest with you, Neil, my soul...that concept that is not supposed to exist...my soul feels more like a thousand."

Neil shifted uncomfortably from foot to foot. "Sir, I apologize. I was way out of line. It's not my place to ask you questions or get you thinking about things that are painful. I hope you can just maybe not report our talk to command, Sir. I don't think they would..."

"Don't worry, Neil," interrupted O'Reilly. "It won't be mentioned at all ...not a chance."

Neil looked relieved. "It won't, Sir?"

"Nope," said O'Reilly. "It won't be in my final report because ...Neil ...there will *be* no final report."

"No report?"

"Nope. No report. No recovery. No 'mission accomplished'."

"Sir?"

"Neil, did you ever hear the expression 'Death where is thy sting?'"

"No, Sir."

"Well, it's something someone said a very long time ago...something written down on paper by a writer of plays...an observer of life."

"What does it mean, Sir...if I may ask?"

O'Reilly left the question unanswered. Then fishing around in the breast pocket of his transport fatigues, he produced a triangular translucent pod-tab. Then extending his hand in the direction of one very puzzled launch-tech, he said calmly...

"This will get you into my pod. There's not much to show in there for two hundred years of ..." He stopped abruptly before continuing ..." but if you see anything there that you would like...well, it's yours, Neil."

"Sir?"

"I wouldn't take more than a few items though, security would be all over it if more than that were missing."

"I don't understand," said Neil. "You're supposed to return here in five years and two months."

"If it were me…that is, if I were you," O'Reilly said with a crooked smile, "I'd look under my rem-cot. Check out a box marked 'memorabilia'. Just a thought, Neil…up to you really."

"I don't understand," Neil repeated with genuine distress.

"It's pretty straight forward, tech Presley. This mission is my *last*. It is my final transport. It will be the end of my endless journeys…so very many journeys…all of which that have led me …blindly …absolutely *nowhere*."

Neil was visibly shaken. He protested the very best he knew how.

"Sir, you can't do that. It's against protocol…all protocol. It's against everything that you stand for…everything a Cliff-Hunter lives for. It's wrong, Sir. It's…"

"It's long overdue is what it is, Neil. It's long overdue."

Then slowly reaching out, he placed the shiny pass-tab to his pod in Neil's left hand before grasping his right.

"Thank you, Neil. Thank you for noticing that I'm not invincible."

Then stepping forward onto the launch/ recovery circle, CH3 O'Reilly nodded confidently in Neil's direction.

"Count me down, Neil. And don't worry...not even a little. It's all going be just fine."

Thirty-three seconds later, CH3 Ramon O'Reilly found himself standing on the one hundred and first interior step of a very old lighthouse in 21st century America. Mission coded as "Indigo Tower", this bleached dinosaur of a building stood as an aging testament to both the ingenuity and the frailty of all manmade technologies. Once the shining savior of storm-tossed ships, it was now the occasional backdrop for a curious tourist's selfie.

Opening his eyes, O'Reilly straightened to his full height.

"Don't worry even a little," he repeated aloud. "It's all going to be just fine."

That Place Where Heroes Go
By Neil Presley

There is a place where heroes go

To drift and melt like flakes of snow

Where sleep at last repeats their name

Without reproach or hero shame

...That place where heroes go

Neil's Dilemna And the Dreams That Follow

Neil Presley had been standing in the same spot for more than twenty minutes, transfixed and frozen by the unimaginable conversation he had just had with certified Cliff-Hunter, Ramon O'Reilly. The piercing smell of half burned carbons still hung in the launch/ recovery chamber, as did CH3 O'Reilly's final words. ...

"This will get you into my pod. There's not much to show in there for two hundred years of...but if you see anything there that you would like...well, it's yours." And then... "It's all going to be just fine."

Slowly, the shock of recent events began to wear off. And as the final minutes of his shift drew closer, Neil began to consider the implications, the choices that O'Reilly's words had placed squarely on his shoulders. To begin with, launch and recovery protocol clearly required that all support personnel are to report any unusual or non-compliant behaviors exhibited by Cliff-Hunters before or after their assigned missions. The regulations were unambiguous in this requirement, and equally unambiguous in describing the consequences that would be administered to any who ignored it. These would include "forfeiture of employment and related benefits", "reassignment to a Northside re-education facility", and perhaps worst of all, "forfeiture of one's right to a voluntary life-resignation."

As the shift-end reminder chirped, Neil pulled sequentially the three primary levers that would place the launch unit into its sleep/recharge state. Then, walking slowly from the polished chamber, he followed a 100-

meter-long hallway out to the facility's guarded entrance and into the days fading light. A frigid blast of cold air bit at his ears and nose as he looked out over the vast manmade landscape stretching out below him. Here and there a dome shaped solarium or village resident complex protruded from its frozen surroundings, the evening sunlight dancing from their frost encrusted plexi-shield covers.

As always, Neil descended public elevator 14-A to the heated Gopher relay-station three stories below. Gophers were basically heated cocoons that resembled an above ground ski lift. They were an inexpensive and energy efficient way of moving island personnel to and from their neighborhoods. Powered by steam, chains and pulleys, they resembled more closely contraptions from the 19th century rather than the 27th.

Neil held out his hand as a young government newster placed the Daily Homeland Progress Report in it. This mandatory one-page bulletin was required reading for all citizens, and one could be randomly quizzed about its contents by any other citizen. The consequences of not knowing something as tedious as the monthly projection for artificial tofu production could, for example, bring a written reprimand from Homeland-Center and perhaps the loss of one's annual coastal ice-fish pass. Repeat violators had even been known to lose their semi-annual artificial intercourse visitation privileges.

Twenty minutes later, Neil was comfortably tucked away in his tiny 8 X 12-foot pod. While, a small pot of artificial coffee brewed slowly over a methane-hydrate (fire ice) flame, Neil pulled off his heavy frost-proof boots and pulled on a pair of heavy wool slipper socks he had won in a craft fair drawing two years earlier. Because they were made of a non-artificial material, they were a particularly prized possession, not to mention especially comforting in their own right.

Turning up the intensity of the pod's single overhead gleamer, Neil reached into one of the boots he had just removed and produced the triangular tab given him by CH3 O'Reilly. Slowly rolling it over in his hand, he studied every aspect of its shape and markings. It was translucent in appearance, but when held up to the light, the almost invisible tracks of intersecting information paths could be distinguished. Sequentially, along the tab's three edges were: the owners Identifying profession; Homeland ID Code; and Pod Location Numbers.

Neil suddenly found himself in the dark and confusing waters of indecision. Nothing in his carefully orchestrated life had prepared him for anything so different, so unexpected...so challenging. He felt as though he were an eight-year-old once again...but an eight-year-old being asked to explain the universe or to assemble a three-stage transport drone without instruction or tool. In short, he was overwhelmed to the point of agitated discomfort. And as the sun lazily set below the horizon of Tibetland III, he found himself rocking back and forth on the edge of his fold down cot. He found himself talking aloud to Jerome, the artificial parrot that hung above his polished metal toilet and who carried on basic conversational responses as requested. He found himself crying into the night, unable to come to terms with the uninvited changes that had arrived unannounced in his life. For several long hours he tossed and turned, struggling with the implications of what such changes might bring and what part he would play in them.

Finally, just after midnight, confused citizen, Neil Presley, slipped slowly over into sleep. But it was a fitful sleep, one filled with twisted dreams, restless spirits, surreal images, and a foreboding sense of imminent danger. Then, just as daylight broke, something else arrived, a vision not wrapped in the heavy weight of worry.

It was a bright and distant ball of dreamed light, a shining beacon that slowly floated toward him. And as he lay there half conscious, half asleep, a distant clap of thunder filled his tiny pod. With it a series of primitive images burst forth, a fleeting parade of long dead ancestors. Some battled wild animals, some navigated treacherous seas. But all who appeared before him communicated, without a spoken word, how they had lived and how they had died in the dignity of deed and the valor of duty. One by one, they showed themselves, each shaking their heads in exaggerated disapproval. Then silently each evaporated into the ether from which they had come. Such are the hidden truths of our souls, that on occasion they arise to guide us to a new and better path.

And so, when the pale sun rose once again over The Homeland, Neil awoke with a sense of self and of mission that had never previously entered his consciousness. Amazed to have such thoughts and unfamiliar determination pulsing through his body, he lay in his bed for some time. Staring at the low ceiling overhead, he found himself suddenly laughing aloud. Then reaching beneath his pillow, he produced the tab given him by Cliff-Hunter Ramon O'Reilly.

"Jerome," he said to his manmade parrot, "today our world begins!"

Decades later, accounts of Neil's sudden awareness would often be recounted by his followers in a somewhat grander fashion.

"Awoke he then, a determined and singular-minded seeker of the unknown...a bold soldier, indifferent to despair, oblivious to foul consequence, and forever dedicated to discover that which might be the truth of his life...of all life. Such was the miraculous transformation of this untutored citizen of the realm, that surely only divine intervention can be assumed or granted explanation. So, did it then come to pass, that Neil Presley, a child of human parents born, awoke as a new man, one who follows his heart, his intuition, and that higher calling known as truth, that gift which is forever sacred. Such are the miracles that arrive, when least expected. Such are the events that have created and sustained the world itself...miracle upon miracle...we rejoice, our daily prayer a simple one... Thanks be to the "Four Books of Knowing" that transformed disciple into saint ...Thanks be to him who has led us out of fearfulness and into the light of what might be."

[Authorized History of "The Neil", 3ʳᵈ revision]

The Final Redemption of Zachary Pittkiss

Zachary had chosen on that Saturday to walk to a nearby park. It was his intention to clear his mind of all things extraneous to his primary life goal...the best and most efficient way to end the world. True, he had already conceived and set in motion a morphing algorithm hack that he believed would be capable of eventually penetrating the multi-layered programs and defenses of a U.S. nuclear ballistic submarine. What was concerning him now was just how long his program was taking to make its way into the well defended launch control system. Three months had already passed, since his stealthy intruding program had knocked on the door of the submarines first tier defenses, and six weeks since it had successfully "schmoozed" its way into the second tier. How long, he wondered, before he could finally gain full control of the submarine's launch codes and target guidance trajectory systems.

Zachary sat quietly and alone on a tired wooden bench. He overlooked a flat stretch of park filled with screaming children and doting parents. Off to his left, a young man flung a swirling Frisbee over the head of a manically barking border collie. As he continued to watch and listen, a warm ocean breeze lightly touched down, its invisible hand swaying a hundred thorny rose bushes nearby.

"I don't care!" said Zachary aloud. "I don't care!" he repeated. "I don't care if all of you laugh and sing beneath a perfect sky. I don't care if the air smells sweet or the angels sing. My plan is in place! Your destiny is assured! So, save your energy for your final prayers, if you even have time for that...You will get what you asked for. You will suffer in proportion to your sins. And your sins, children of this broken planet, are many and great!"

Having concluded his tirade, and feeling anything but calm, Zachary stood up and turned to leave the park. As he did, a swirling purple Frisbee slammed against his right temple. Initially stunned, he dropped to one knee, both eyes involuntarily filling with tears. As he struggled to clear his head, he felt the wet rough surface of a dog's tongue on his face and the concerned whimper that went with it. Slowly, as his vision cleared, he could make out the ridiculous nose and eyes of a dog's furry face. As his senses slowly returned, he quickly gathered up information from all around him. He became aware that the Border Collie that had just a few minutes earlier been concerned only with catching and retrieving a plastic disk had, without direction or coaching, completely shifted his focus onto the victim of his sport. Ignoring the Frisbee which lay there beside the bench, his primary concern was now the well-being of a total stranger...a sentient two-legged being who had nothing whatsoever to do with the game he loved or his canine life to date.

Struggling to his feet, Zachary accepted the profuse apologies of the dog's owner who was now standing before him.

"No worries," he said as though nothing of significance had happened. Yet, the truth was, something very inexplicable had indeed taken place. It was as though Zachary's amazing brain had been cracked open like a raw egg and all its preconceived concepts of the world and his place in it had simply spilled out at his feet. Something profoundly moving, even frightening, was now taking place there among the billions of cells and synapses of his amazing gray matter. For the first time, since the death of his parents, he looked out over his immediate world without the angry, opaque filter of disdain and suspicion. Instead of leaving the park as he had planned, he stayed on through the rest of the day. And as he sat and watched and listened, something strange and unfamiliar began to stir within him.

For the first time in his young life, he recognized something he had never recognized before…a subtle, and sometimes not so subtle pattern, a viable and fundamental connection that flowed among all living things.

"And though sometimes imperfect, sometimes cruel," he reasoned aloud, "it is, nevertheless, there and indestructible."

The implications of this unsolicited discovery were immense for him. For what it implied…what it meant was that living creatures, whether dog, cat, moth or man, are part of a living fabric.

"And," he surmised, "if that is the case…then…then no person, creature, or living entity is ever completely alone. And if that premise is true, then it logically follows that I am not alone either. The primary variable," he concluded, "would simply be the degree to which the invisible connections are weakened or strengthened, acknowledged or ignored."

Zachary smiled, giddy with his bold new discovery. "Can it be that simple?" he wondered. Could he, with the preposterous assistance of a canine and a swirling plastic disk, have stumbled upon the scientific solution to his own personal suffering? Could the relentless pain of loneliness and sorrow he had always felt be lessened, even overcome, by just reaching out to others and by strengthening the constant universal connection already in place?

"Yes," said Zachary to his own question. "Yes. I believe it can."

And so, as he left the park that day, he felt a lightness of being he had never felt before. He sensed the limitless possibilities of a world capable of kindness. And quite extraordinarily, he determined to use his considerable genius for something other than revenge, or to inflict pain upon a world he had misread and misjudged for years. Breathing deeply and easily as he walked, he began to formulate what he would do to correct the dark strategy, the evil treachery he had set in motion. He briefly imagined several ways in which he could redirect the full energy of his being to strengthening the loving bonds that joined all men...bonds that needed only encouragement and proper resources of spirit and soul.

"First things first" he announced to a metal light pole beside him. "It's time to recall and shutdown the project. *Digital Neighbor Nexus,* I now declare you officially deceased."

Consumed by rushing thoughts as he walked, Zachary nevertheless stopped at the busy intersection near his home to confirm that he would be crossing with the appropriate pedestrian signal. Then, as he moved into the street...as he took his third step inside the chalk-white crosswalk lines, a stolen Mazda Miata, driven by a teenager his own age, struck him full on at sixty miles per hour. And just as suddenly as his recent life-changing awareness had arrived, the living essence of the most brilliant young man to ever have walked the earth...departed from it.

Many miles away, within the digital calculating heart of the USS Louisiana, the *Neighbor Nexus Project* ground on with relentless determination. Constantly schmoozing, updating, modifying, speculating and drawing new algorithmic conclusions, it continued its quest to gain final and full control of one of the deadliest war machines known to man. Perhaps if the spirit of Zachary Pittkiss could have mystically looked down upon the dire events that were now about to unfold, he would have provided a pithy commentary of simple elegance ...a counterbalance to his original angry Manifesto Poem.

Look - See - Step...Carefully

We live our lives postponed in fear
As though we live ten thousand years
But the truth of things
*Is simply **that***
Sometimes we leave without our hat
So, find it soon
That truth you need
And look both ways
For teens that speed...

Two Quarts of Wisdom in a Ten Ounce Cup

"Well, ok then, Judy," said O'Reilly. "Let me just tell you who my LULU is. Ready? LULU is the name of the subcutaneous learn/assist unit that was originally integrated into my body's nervous and muscular systems approximately one hundred and thirty years ago. 'L.U.L.U.' is actually an acronym for 'Lifelike Under-derma Learning Utility'. She...I prefer to think of the unit as a she...has an extensive array of discovery and external effect capabilities. She senses and comprehends everything that my five senses register. She has math calculating and algorithmic capabilities that are one hundred and fifty times faster than the super computers of your current earth time. She can calculate the weight and composition of any object within one hundred miles. She can determine if any object has the potential to be a threat. This would include explosives, firearms, germs, toxins...or a loose plank on an aging pier for that matter. In short, LULU is my second consciousness. She is my 24/7 constantly awake and alert warning system, one that can quite accurately decipher the brain and body histories of those around me. This ability, known as 're-pathing', gives her the means to invisibly tap into the memory storage component of those nearby, and to accurately surmise their personal histories. By combining an individual's history with their current physical and emotional vital signs, she can accurately determine immediate intent within an error component of plus or minus 1.3%. LULU has been upgraded seven times since her initial installation, her most recent configuration having been installed just three years ago. So, Judy...I could go on. But, hopefully, you get the picture.

LULU comprehends all that is taking place around me...whether it is a gust of wind, an erupting volcano, or a young woman with an ice pick hidden in her bra. One way or another, I'm going to know about it."

There was an extended silence that followed, as Petra processed her thoughts. Then, with a look of pretend disdain, she said "It's not a bra, Bowtie Man, it's a halter top."

"Noted," said O'Reilly.

"So how exactly does LULU communicate all this to you? I don't hear anything."

"It's a neural relay thing...complicated. But, just think of it as having someone softly whispering in your ear."

"So...it's like a whisper?"

"Yes. Like a whisper...unless the world around me is noisy. In which case, LULU's volume compensates, or does a buzz-in on my thumbnail."

"Show me," she said, crossing her arms defiantly.

"OK," said O'Reilly with a slight hesitation. "LULU, thumb display ... activate please. Books of the bible, slow scroll." Then approaching Petra cautiously, O'Reilly turned his left thumb in her direction.

"Mathew, Mark, Luke, John..." it read.

"Damn! … And, can LULU say things out loud? You know, so other people can hear her?"

"Well, actually, yes she can. However, it does require that I stand relatively still while she scans and calculates all surrounding surface densities. Once that's accomplished, she can then project and bounce energy pulses off them. The result being that her voice resonates throughout the room as though those listening were standing inside some sort of vintage speaker cabinet."

"Show me," said Petra abruptly.

"Sure," said O'Reilly. "LULU…Open channel-chamber voice response please. Recite a simple poem of your choosing …3-2-1 and start."

The low seductive voice of a female could be heard…far away at first, then gradually growing louder.

"Mary had a little lamb. Its fleece was white as snow. And everywhere that Mary went, the lamb was sure to go."

"LULU …stop," said O'Reilly. "Repeat poem. Change name to Judy."

"Judy had a little lamb. Its fleece was white as snow. And everywhere that Judy went, the lamb was sure to go."

Petra, recovering from the full-throated voice that had just enveloped her, announced, "Well, that's cool as shit!" "Seriously."

Then turning toward O'Reilly "Can *I* ask her something? Can *I* ask LULU something?"

"Yep," he said. "But first, I have to provide permission. LULU, add voice response connectivity for Judith Hooley, aka Petra."

"Request acknowledged. Connectivity granted." replied LULU.

"Go ahead, Judy," said O'Reilly. "Ask away."

Judy thought carefully about what her question might be. A full thirty seconds passed before she finally cleared her throat and began.

"It's a two-part question, LULU. First, when was this lighthouse built? And second, what was Bowtie Man here...I mean, CH3 O'Reilly ...what was he doing at that time?"

"Answers retrieved," said LULU three seconds later.

"Reply one: *The congress of the United States of America approved construction of this lighthouse in the spring of 1860. Work was completed in April of 1863.*

Reply two: *CH3 O'Reilly was, at that standard earth calendar time, fulfilling his twelfth month of study at the Academy of Past Histories -Tibetland III. He was actively learning the events, customs, prejudices, and language patterns required for pre-Civil War deployment to Fort Sumter, South Carolina, United*

States of America...End of answers, Judy Hooley. Standing by."

"Cool as shit!" said Petra for the second time. Then, striding out into the middle of the large windowed room, she stepped inside its brightest patch of sunlight, before carefully reaching into her halter top. Smiling the defiant smile of a middle school child caught with contraband, she then produced an ice pick wrapped in a thin strip of leather. Tossing the implement at the wing-tipped feet of CH3 O'Reilly, she shrugged her shoulders.

"Tell me something wise," she insisted.

"Something wise?"

"Yeah. Something that's wise...something you've picked up over your two centuries of stompin' around in other people's lives. What exactly have you and LULU learned about anything...I mean the two of you being fucking masters of the universe and all."

O'Reilly looked down at his brown wingtips. "How much wisdom do you need?"

"Oh, I don't know...maybe ten or twelve juicy slices of the stuff. Yeah...ten slices. That would work."

"Alright," said O'Reilly thoughtfully. "Ten slices..."

"Oh yeah," added Petra "and all that needs to come from *you*...not from skin deep wonder woman."

"I see. Well, ok. How about I give you ten tidbits...ten conclusions I've come to believe after so many years of service."

"Great. Surprise me."

O'Reilly cleared his throat as his eyes looked up and to the left. "Let's see...Oh ...OK...

1. Everything is exactly as it appears, and nothing at all as you perceive it.
2. One should not believe everything one believes.
3. "Never retreat, never surrender" is a great saying, but a self-defeating life strategy.
4. On average, 83% of all human activity is simply some form of distraction, apparently designed to avoid addressing the more profound questions of existence.
5. There is life after death...just not in the same brane in which you die.
6. Everything breathes, including gravity, light, and time.
7. *Déjà vu* moments are simply out of sync, identically occurring, events from two or more touching branes.
8. Absolutely everything that takes place in the universe is recorded *without judgement* somewhere in time.
9. The best things in life are, in fact, free...sorry, but it turns out to be true.
10. The correlation between wishful thinking and the positive actual outcome of a wished-for event is rarely greater than .13372.

O'Reilly returned his gaze to Petra. "And there you are, Judy. Ten slices of wisdom as promised."

"I think you mean ten slices of *bullshit*," replied a skeptical Petra. "Jesus, Bowtie, can't you do better than that?"

"Actually …Judy …yes I can …**Number 11** …The *truth of things* frightens humans more than it calms them"

"Whatever."

"Whatever indeed," replied a smiling O'Reilly.

As she often did, when confronted with unwanted information, Petra closed her eyes and hummed the melody line of a vintage song popularized in the previous century. Inexplicably, she had found it calming since the very first time she had ever heard it.

"Your song is 'Love Me Tender'" said LULU without being asked. *"It is a song performed by the so-called entertainment 'King'"*.

"Yeah, well who asked you?" said Petra. Then fiercely staring down O'Reilly, she voiced her concern … "OK. So, let's say I believe you and your time warp tale even a little bit. What the hell does that mean for me exactly?"

"What does that mean?" repeated O'Reilly.

 "Yeah…suppose I do believe your crazy ass? So, what does *that* mean for me? What happens next? Where do we go from here?"

"Simple enough, Judy. We just go to where we've always been."

Petra rolled her eyes with exaggerated contempt.

"Does it bother you at all that half of the things you say sound like a friggin' bumper sticker and the other half like a quote from a self-help book?"

"Well," said O'Reilly with a mischievous smile, "all I can say to that is...*Have A Nice Day.*"

The Rules of Souvenir Gathering

Four hundred years earlier, when the Cliff-Hunter program was first initiated, it was made clear, to all who participated, that there would be no transport of contraband from any visited time point to the present. Objects of any kind were strictly prohibited from being brought back to Tibetland III. The primary fear was that, by permanently removing an artifact from any past-time event, there could be an unpredictable altering of events yet to come. Originally, the punishments and consequences of any unauthorized "time smuggling" were explicitly laid out on page 13 of the very first *"Manual of Time Transport"* ever issued. Nevertheless, the overpowering attraction of certain exotic items from the past was simply too much to pass up for some Cliff-Hunters. As a result, many capable Hunters were demoted or punished in severe and public ways. However, about 150 years into the study program, it was determined by the *Science Council of Time Transport* that, if a horrendous earth changing event were imminent, it would matter not at all if a small artifact or two were retrieved just before the event took place. *The Council* determined that a modest number of items could be brought back by Cliff- Hunters without initiating dire consequences. However, there remained six specific exceptions, six absolutely forbidden types of contraband. These were first published in revised *Manual of Time Transport #22.*

1. No item can be of fissionable material
2. No item can be explosive in nature

3. No item can weigh more than 8.039 kg
4. No item can be located more than 1000 meters from the original Arrival/ Departure Circle
(**Corolary 16A**: No item shall be intentionally moved to comply with stated 1000-meter rule of requirement number 4)
5. No life-form, whether carbon based in nature, or evolved from other than a carbon-based genetic platform
6. No recordings, regardless of format, commonly represented as "entertainment" (refer to *Label Definitions Section* of current *Retrieval Compliance Guide # A150-R-C10* for specific examples) notably artifact productions referred to as *Rap Music, Reality Shows, Political Message Speeches, or Religious Call-In Telethons*

[Only the retrieval of contraband described in **Exception #6** originally carried with it the threat of Capital Punishment]

Upon the return of a Cliff-Hunter, he or she had the option of keeping the legal artifacts they had brought back or donating the items to the **National Museum of Historical Preoccupations**. Under no circumstances were Cliff-Hunters permitted to sell or profit from their retrieved items.

Over his extensive career, CH3 Ramon O'Reilly had retrieved a total of 136 separate artifacts, 96 of which he had donated to the public museum. The remaining 40 were scattered about his living pod or carefully tucked beneath his rem-cot.

Those beneath his cot, being especially prized, were carefully wrapped and stored within a colorful silk pillowcase, its raised embroidery reading simply *"Pearl Harbor Hawaii"*.

The Accidental Bifurcation of Neil Presley's Soul

In the days that followed CH3 O'Reilly's departure from Tibetland III, Neil Presley experienced a personal psychic transformation of seismic proportions. Whereas, he once thought only about the world immediately before him, dreamed of nothing beyond the annual **Homeland Founder's Holiday**, he now spent much of his day daydreaming about the possibilities of...well...something else. Ever since his amazing and disturbing talk with Cliff-Hunter O'Reilly, he had been haunted with a series of questions that seemed to have no real answers. And even though he could feel the exciting pulse of possibility moving through his veins, he was, at the same time, beginning to question his path forward. The initial flush of excitement that had washed over him when he had first held the Tab to CH3 O'Reilly's POD, had abated. While still excited about the prospect of unforeseen wonders that could await him, he also began to consider the practical consequences of any non-sanctioned future choices he might make. Questions arrived and haunted him daily.

- Should he not tell his immediate Launch Administrator that one of their longtime Cliff-Hunters had determined to voluntarily resign from life while on a mission? And what if he didn't and the Council then discovered that he had known this to be so, even before the mission started?
- But if he were to share what he knew with his Administrator, would he not then forfeit his one chance to do something unique...something outside his carefully planned daily cycle?

- What would the POD of a Cliff-Hunter look like?
- If he were to somehow actually make it into CH3 O'Reilly's POD, would there be anything there worth bringing back to his own?
- What if he were discovered in an off-limits *Cliff-Hunter Living Facility*? Would he not lose his job...be banished from Homeland...sent to The Northside...or something even worse?

With every day that passed, new questions arose. New fears stirred. And yet, there was a niggling unrelenting voice from somewhere deep inside, some primitive instigating awareness that insisted he do something new...something unexpected...something foolhardy and dangerous. Where, he wondered, does such a voice come from? It certainly did not come from his six years of basic homeland schooling, or the various low-level jobs he'd held over the previous ten years. And it did not come from family or friends, as he had neither. "Where then?" he would ask, "Where does such a voice come from? And why will it not let me be?" And was so often the case, artificial parrot, Jerome, could provide only minimal comfort and advice.

"Neil, my friend, you should get a good night's sleep followed by a hearty breakfast. Everything looks more hopeful in the morning. Always remember...you are important to the Homeland and all members of the Science Council ...who will always make sure all your needs are met."

Not surprisingly, as the weeks wore on, Neil became increasingly confused and agitated. Should he continue to live his life unchanged, safe within the world he had known for three decades...a predictable life as prescribed and managed by the Homeland hierarchy? Or should he chance a radical leap of faith that could literally cost him everything, every single benefit he now enjoyed ...safety...food...warmth? And, of course, the *semi-annual* state sponsored AI-escort visits. Neil Presley had become a man torn in two.

"Why," Neil would ask himself at the end of every day, "does it all have to be so hard to figure out?"

And for only the second time, Neil expressed himself in verse. It was a short and unsophisticated poem, but nevertheless, one more vital seed of creative thinking that was destined to grow and come to fruition in his lifetime.

The Glow of Snow
By Neil Presley

The snow is meant to fall on us
And melt there into water
But we've been bred to be too cold
For such a slushy slaughter
And so, it seems, we're made of ice
Not too smart and way too nice
Frozen more than once or twice
Time for our souls to melt

Eighteen Things You Need to Know...
And Other Understatements

"What happens now," said O'Reilly calmly, "is that I will provide you with some basic instructions about the transport journey you are about to take."

"Transport journey?" asked a perplexed Petra.

"Yes, I am going to provide you with some very specific information that will assist you in arriving safely in my Homeland."

"Which is some time in the future, right?"

"Exactly."

"How far in the future...'exactly'?"

"Oh...well...that would be five hundred and seventy-three years...and a little"

"Oh...OK...just 'five hundred and seventy-three years'?"

"And a little," corrected O'Reilly.

Petra laughed abruptly. "Christ, Bowtie, you know I only came down to the beach today for a burger and a beer."

"Yes, well...sometimes things change...suddenly...they just do."

"Right. And that's supposed to make everything just fine, huh?"

Ignoring the comment, O'Reilly continued.

"So, first you need to know why you can't stay here. Then, you need to know just where it is that I'm sending you. And finally, you will need to know the specifics of the transport process. And since time is running out, I suggest we get started."

"Sure," said Petra. "Why the hell not!"

"OK then. Let's begin...

LULU, please prepare three brief summaries. They are:

- current submarine threat to immediate area
- Tibetland III historic overview
- specific departure protocols Judy will need to know"

Three seconds later LULU replied. *"Information compiled."*

O'Reilly nodded and smiled at Petra. "Ok, LULU, commence summaries...begin."

LULU's throaty voice filled the room in a calm, matter of fact tone.

"Here are thirteen separate informs for Judy, aka Petra.

CURRENT THREAT TO IMMEDIATE AREA:

- *A nuclear submarine, the USS Louisiana, is presently maneuvering in a turn basin north of this location.*
- *It has been boarded by an emotionally and mentally challenged man named Max Sturg.*
- *This man has placed high explosive C-4 charges on board the vessel.*
- *These explosives will detonate in **fifty-six minutes** and **thirteen seconds**.*
- *The commander of the damaged submarine will make a determined, but unsuccessful, effort to sail his vessel far from the populated shoreline before its onboard nuclear reactor achieves melt down status.*
- *Before complete meltdown occurs, a secondary compromising attack...digital in nature and originated by a young male known as Zachary Pittkiss...will take place. Overcoming an odds projection of 43 to the 7th power (271,818,611,107), this attack will successfully penetrate and override the submarine's weapons/launch/control system.*
- *A random unguided launch array of all but two nuclear missiles will then immediately initiate.*
- *One such missile, a Trident D5 455-kiloton W88/Mk-5 warhead will achieve a minimal altitude above the Atlantic Ocean shoreline before detonating 2.3 kilometers above this lighthouse structure.*

- *This single burst explosion will result in the immediate death of 1,956,319 humans within the projected blast radius.*

TIBETLAND III OVERVIEW

- *Tibetland III is an autonomous island nation that came into existence following a catastrophic nuclear weapons exchange and a resulting extreme climate warming. Originally part of the Himalayan Mountain chain, this island nation represents the only known land mass remaining on earth. Tibetland III, referred to by its citizens as "The Homeland", was founded and developed by a contingent of extremely gifted scientists who created a strategic pre-event plan to retreat to the highest peaks on earth. Within thirty-six months of today's cataclysmic event, devastating flood waters will engulf the planet. Eventually, eleven of the twelve originally surviving islands will be enveloped and lost. Only Tibetland III will remain.*
- *Politically, Tibetland III was originally founded as a benevolent Factocracy and is currently overseen by a Council with DNA directly traceable to its original founders. Unlike other countries throughout the history of man, Tibetland III is governed by what is known as the Preference for Immutable Facts Doctrine. This doctrine clearly spells out the necessity for...*
- *Scientific facts to take precedence when deciding upon any matter affecting the nation and its*

citizens. It points out, with uncompromising clarity, the foolish and dangerous nature of relying on outmoded icons and instruments of governance previously embraced by past failed civilizations.

As summarized in the pre-amble to The Doctrine "Such naive and emotionally based methods have been tried countless times throughout the history of mankind and they have repeatedly been found wanting."

DEPARTURE PROTOCOL FOR JUDY HOOLEY (AKA PETRA)

- *Subject should remove all metal body jewelry and make her way to interior lighthouse step number 101. It can be easily identified by a red launch circle in its center.*
- *Subject should stand in the center of the circle and hold all transportable possessions close to her body.*
- *Subject should gently exhale once just prior to transport.*

Delivery of requested summaries completed," added LULU.

O'Reilly looked over at Petra. "Well, what do you think?"

"'What do I think?' Are you nuts? I *think* you and your 'subcutaneous' girlfriend had just better be a bad dream brought on by too much sun on a hot Florida day. Because

108

I *'think'* I don't want to go zoom-fuck-flying into the future. I would *prefer* to live out my pathetic sad-girl life right here on this stupid frying pan of a beach. I *'think'*...no, make that I fucking *pray* that you are just a stupid-ass nightmare...and it's three o'clock in the morning and I'm in my bed in my room...and I'm about to wake up to take a piss any second now. That's what I *'think'*, Bowtie Man."

"Oh well then!" said O'Reilly thoughtfully. "That's all so very interesting...really...and colorful as well. But, beyond all that childish and wishful blather, how do you feel about the instructions LULU just gave you. Do you have any questions?"

Petra glanced around the room in a defiant glare, lips pursed. Then calmly walking to the work table near the deck door, she picked up the Ziter-1000 unit by its woven glass strap. Swinging it violently in a wide circle overhead, she let out a piercing screech not unlike the gawky Sandhill Crane.

"FUUUUUUUUUUUUCK!" she screamed as she launched the instrument across the room.

LULU instantly contracted two of O'Reilly's major right-side muscle groups, causing him to swivel safely to one side just as the two-pound object hurdled passed his head. The Ziter-1000 completed its trajectory by slamming against the wall behind him, then fell with a muffled thump to the hard wood floor.

"Well, that was playful!" he said. Then walking slowly over to it, he gently picked it up and checked for damage.

"Good news, Judy. No harm done. One tidbit for thought...These units are drop-tested from a height of 1000 feet onto a Composium metal surface with a Mohs factor of 10. So...lucky us ...no need to worry...the unit's just fine." Then, lovingly, he looped the cherished instrument around his neck. "You really should be more careful with other children's toys!"

Petra spun 180 degrees and faced away from him. Bowing her head, she spoke slowly over her shoulder.

"You know what, Bowtie...You live your life the best you can. You do whatever you have to do to eat and stay alive. You avoid people, because people always only want to take something from you. You wait for a break ...any break that'll take you out of your shithole world. You wait, and you wait and you fucking wait some more. But the break never comes...just more of the same...more of the same old same." Then, reaching out with both arms, she leaned forward, palms against the work table.

"I don't feel right, Bowtie Man. I..." Her voice faded to a whisper. "I don't..."

As she struggled to complete her thought, her vision began to shrink into a pinpoint of greying light. And as that too disappeared, both knees buckled beneath her. Then, not unlike the Ziter-1000 a few moments earlier, she collapsed abruptly to the same hard wood floor. When she came to a short time later, O'Reilly was kneeling over her gently slapping her face.

"Come on, Judy. Wake up!"

"What?" she mumbled feebly.

"LULU informs me that you suffer from an Isle of Langerhans affliction. So, you need to drink this."

"Drink what?" she asked with confusion.

"It's orange juice. Just drink it. We need you on your feet and ready to go."

For some reason known only to her, Petra half giggled...half groaned. "Sure" she said "Sure. Why not?"

Carefully pulling her to an upright sitting position, hc held the small carton of juice as she slowly drank.

"Tastes good, nurse," she said wryly.

Five minutes later, Petra was fully vertical and leaning heavily against O'Reilly.

"That happens sometimes...especially when I get too nervous. Usually, I catch it in time ...find something sweet somewhere."

"Well, I'm just glad you're back. We need you to be totally present in a very few minutes."

"Right," said Petra, suddenly recalling she was to be transported to an unknown world and a future time. "Yeah. Wouldn't want to miss that, would I?"

"You sure you can stand on your own now?"

"Yeah, Bowtie. I got it. I'm way good at that."

O'Reilly lowered a supporting hand from her shoulder. Not about to take any chances, he asked...

"LULU, is Petra fit to continue?"

"Confirm 85.3% fitness and rising," responded LULU.

"Great," said O'Reilly. Then meeting Petra's eyes straight on, he added... "Look, I know this is a lot to take in in such a very short time. But it's important that you listen carefully now from here on out...that you believe what I say...what LULU says...about your situation. Because, if you don't...if you just get angry or ignore what we tell you...if you get it wrong...your part in this...well, Judy, your life is over.

Petra cleared her throat. Pausing for a moment, she then moved one step closer and asked bluntly ...

"So, why so much concern about 'sweet little 'ol me'? Why not just leave me here to die with everyone else? Then you and your chatty girlfriend could just beam yourselves on back to tomorrow land. So, what gives?"

O'Reilly's expression softened briefly as though he were about to share something personal. Then, refocusing on the Ziter-1000, he pretended to be re-checking it for damage.

"LULU," he said calmly, "would you please reply to Judy's question?

"Confirm request" said LULU.

- *CH3 O'Reilly has no intention of leaving this mission zone despite anticipated/impending blast.*
- *After 173 years of repeated missions similar to this one, CH3 O'Reilly is no longer capable of suppressing his emotions ...i.e. concerns for those left behind.*
- *CH3 O'Reilly has grown weary of watching you personally perish ...He is currently thinking...*

"OK, LULU," O'Reilly interrupted. "Stop please. I've got this from here."

Letting go of the Ziter-1000 still hanging from his neck, he looked reluctantly into Petra's eyes.

"'I am currently thinking', Judy Hooley, that I do not want to watch you die one more time. So, please...remove your metal jewelry, including the nose ring, and prepare yourself emotionally for your pending transport."

Roar Like A Lion or Live Like A Lamb?

Neil Presley had never considered himself a brave man. In fact, there had been times in his life when he found himself fretting over the most unlikely of hardships. How, he wondered, would he cope if he should say or do something in public, or worse yet at work, that would imply he was not a loyal believer in *Homeland Doctrine* and its many related protocols? What if he accidentally caused a Cliff-Hunter mission to fail? Or, what if he inadvertently expressed excessive emotion while being monitored during a "Fact Refresher Course"? And while most of his concerns were unlikely to ever actually take place, this did not prevent him from worrying about the consequences such wayward actions might bring down upon his head.

So, it was something of a surprise to Neil when, for the second time since CH3 O'Reilly's departure one month earlier, he found himself increasingly consumed by a wave of daring possibility. The provocative voice within him had returned and was now growing louder and more insistent with every passing day. Increasingly difficult to ignore, it became ever-more specific about just what it was that he should do next.

"Neil Presley," it said, "you need to achieve much more from this life. Do not continue to live it as you always have. There is more to learn, to see...to *feel*! Do not settle for the breadcrumb hints of life you've been given. Stand up. Move forward. Walk now, knowing you will one day run. Live your life as you never dreamed possible. Die, if you must. But 'do not go gently' without reaching out for more. And when you experience danger, sorrow, hurt, and pain...as you surely will...remember this. Though these four companions may arouse trepidation within you, in the end, they are simply the foretellers of future rewards, of greater things to come. These companions need never be feared. They simply and always arrive first to prepare the way. So...Neil Presley...now is your time! Let this be the day you enter a brand-new world. Embrace the **Three Practices** and you will prevail...all will be well.

- *Breathe deeply.*
- *Nourish hope and faith.*
- *Never doubt the journey you have chosen, unless you have chosen it solely based on fear."*

"So, what do you see?" Scud demanded. "Can you see them? Can you see her? Is he there?"

"Hey! Cool it, dickhead...wouldja?" snarled Randy. "I'm lookin'."

Peering through the black Vortex scope, Randy could now clearly identify O'Reilly, but only from the neck up.

"I can see *him*," he reported. "But she's too short. The angle's too sharp."

"So, what now?" asked an anxious Scud.

"Well, for now...we're gonna end **his** ass for good."

"Well, what about her?"

"Oh, I think she'll get the message. She can just think about it real good for a while. Then we'll deal with her another time. Sometime when she doesn't expect it ...make her suffer just a little bit longer ...or maybe we'll off her ass tomorrow. But, she's not gonna know when ...is she?"

"Yeah...a little bit longer," repeated Scud.

"Now listen up," Randy said sternly. "Once I pull this trigger, we gotta get our asses out of here in a hurry. I mean fast. But listen up. We're gonna *walk*, not run, away from here. We'll split up then. You go down toward the beach and I'll head toward the motel. We'll meet up there and figure out our next move. Got it?"

"Yeah, I think so," said Scud. "I go down to the beach and then head back to our room."

"That's right," said Randy "And one other thing...***Do not*** talk to **anyone**!"

"Right. Don't talk to anyone."

LULU's voice suddenly filled the lighthouse room. *"Alert Notice: Seven minutes until transport depart. Repeat Alert Notice: Seven minutes to transport depart"*

"Alert notice acknowledged, LULU," said O'Reilly.

"Seven minutes?" Petra repeated.

"Yes. Seven minutes, Judy ... Seven minutes until you transport. We need to make our way to the circle."

LULU interrupted a second time. *"Alert. Immediate Threat: Weapon identified...Vintage combat weapon ...caliber 7.62mm ...335 meters southwest this location."*

"Down!" shouted O'Reilly and he pulled Petra to the floor with him. "It's probably you're beachside pals. Looks like they don't appreciate being told "No."

"What's the plan then?" asked a stunned Petra.

"The plan is to stay low, beneath their line of sight. They can't hit what they can't see."

"Shit!" declared Randy. "He just disappeared…ducked down out of sight. I can't see him now. Son of a bitch…I think he knows we're here."

"How could he know that?" asked Scud. "How would he know that?"

"How would I know how he knows that? yelled Randy. "But I'll be damned if I'm leaving here before they both shit their pants."

Then, with a piercing scream of raw anger, Randy squeezed off all twenty high power rounds in rapid succession. Eleven of the 168 grain projectiles impacted the lighthouse at a speed of 2712 feet per second; the remaining nine arcing harmlessly out over the ocean.

Now That We're Dead, The Pressures Off...

"We've got to get you to the stairwell," said a concerned O'Reilly. "You've got a bus to catch."

Petra looked surprised. "What about _you_?"

"Don't worry about me, Judy. This bus is not my ride...kind of tired of public transport."

"Jesus, Bowtie! What the hell was that? A hero speech from a cheap cop movie?"

"Hey. Let's not chat about this right now, OK? Let's just get you down the steps to number 101. So, stop talking, stay low, and follow me."

"Yeah. Sure, bossman. Lead on!"

And as the two of them clumsily duck-walked toward the stairway passage, eleven deadly projectiles slammed home. Six of the shots were absorbed by the iron lined brick walls below them, the remaining five punching through the thick panes of glass overhead. Of those five, four buried themselves harmlessly behind vintage tin ceiling tiles. The final round, true to the laws of unexpected consequences, struck a vertical steel support, causing the lead-antimony slug to shatter into three lethal chunks of shrapnel. Had LULU been asked beforehand, she would have calmly explained that the odds of any such projectile striking her main control core just below O'Reilly's left wing were ...well ...astronomical. And yet, that is precisely what happened.

119

"Oh, Jesus," said O'Reilly. "That one found me!" Then rolling slowly forward, he sprawled belly first onto the floor, a rivulet of bright red blood rolling from his wound.

"Holy fuck!" screamed Petra. "You're shot! You're bleeding!"

"Yeah," said O'Reilly through gritted teeth, "I know."

"What do I do?"

"Use a cloth. Press hard. Keep pressing. Stop the flow."

Petra looked around frantically for a cloth of any kind. When none could be found, she leaned forward and violently ripped the lower back of O'Reilly's shirt from him. Then wading it into a ball, she pushed it onto his wound and leaned hard against it.

"Can't LULU help?" she shouted. Can't she stop the bleeding somehow?"

O'Reilly formed his words slowly and with great effort. "Ordinarily...yes. She could help. But I think the shrapnel took out her control core. Maybe she can hear us, but I doubt she can help."

"So, do we really need her now? I mean...we just have to get down the stairs and stand in the circle, right?"

"Not quite," said O'Reilly, his voice growing weaker. "Still need a position beacon for Homeland to lock on to."

"And LULU does that?"

"Yeah. She does that."

"So, now what the hell do we do?"

"One chance," O'Reilly whispered before abruptly blacking out.

"Oh no!" Petra shouted. "No you don't, you ridiculous bastard!"

Still applying pressure to his wound with her left hand, she lifted his right hand with hers. Then, uncertain just why...she bit down sharply on the tip of his little finger.

Both eyes instantly popped open.

"Now that we're dead," said a delirious O'Reilly, "the pressure's off us for a while."

"Whatever," said Petra. "Just please tell me how we can get a signal or something out. How can we get your people to lock on to us?"

"Ziter-1000," O'Reilly muttered. "Back-up locator. Ziter-1000. Flip the cover. Press red switch three times... then hold long."

"Got it!" screeched Petra. "Now hold on. We're goin' for a walk."

"No!" insisted O'Reilly. "You go. Go now. Just a few minutes left. Go. I stay...never meant to go back. Will end it here. This time...will end it here."

"You will, huh?" mocked Petra. "Well, I don't fuckin' think so, Bowtie Man! Now get your legs under you 'cause we're goin' down those stairs...got it? We're goin' down those stairs right now, and I can't carry your damn ass."

The Ziter-1000 suddenly started to glow. *"Alert Notice: Five minutes until transport depart. Repeat Alert Notice: Five minutes until transport depart"*

"Alright, damn it. Why is this Ziter thing talking now?"

"LULU ...a download. A LULU download," grunted O'Reilly.

"Christ! So, Bowtie ...you gonna help me out here or not?"

"Too late, beach girl," whispered O'Reilly, as he passed out for a second time.

"Alright then...if that's how you want it. We'll just fucking do it the hard way."

Then, grabbing onto the collar of his bloody Hawaiian shirt, Petra began dragging him in the direction of the stairs. Three minutes and forty-five seconds later, she had successfully dragged, bumped and wrestled CH3 O'Reilly down to step number 101. Then marshalling all the strength left within her small frame, she pulled him half way to his feet. As she did, O'Reilly came around just long enough to partially straighten his legs. Remembering LULU's instructions, Petra now struggled to position them both within the red launch circle. Standing behind him, her left arm wrapped around his chest, she frantically stretched out her right arm to locate the Ziter-1000 still dangling from his neck. Locating it at last, she managed to flip open a small protective cover with her thumb, before confirming the red beacon button beneath it. An excruciating forty-five seconds later, the Ziter-1000 announced its final warning.

"Alert Notice: Thirty seconds until transport sync-depart. Repeat Alert Notice: Thirty seconds until transport sync-depart"

One short half-minute later, the final countdown began. *"Awaiting transport lock-on in 5...4...3...2...1...Lock-on sync commence.*

Petra began pressing the glowing red button exactly as O'Reilly had explained to her.

"One. Two. Three ...and hold!" she recited out loud. Then steeling herself for whatever might happen next, she clenched her jaw and waited. But there was not the slightest change in sight or sound.

"Shit!" she screamed, her echo bouncing up and down the stairway walls. Again, she pressed the button precisely as she'd been instructed. And again...no response.

Hanging her head in despair, she now closed her eyes tightly and, for the first time in many years, prayed a simple prayer. "Please, God, help us," she whispered. Then, repeating the sequence one more time, she held the switch down as tightly as she could. "Please, God, help us," she repeated.

Suddenly, a distinctive high-pitched hum filled the stairwell. Barely audible at first, it grew in intensity before morphing into alternating physical sensations of hot and cold. Still clutching the Ziter in her right hand, Petra now wrapped both arms tightly around her semi-conscious charge. Then, as a blinding flash of orange light filled the stairwell, and a distant thunder rolled toward them, all previous trepidation instantly vanished. In its place ...a vaguely familiar sensation of well-being.

"Am I dead now?" she wondered. "Am I dead now forever?"

Many decades earlier, O'Reilly had programmed LULU to recite poems of her own construction, ones that would summarize, in a creative way, their most recent mission. She would then automatically recite her poem during their brief, but intense, jump-transport back home. This mission was no exception. And as always, anticipating the worst, she had backed-up her latest poetic work in the storage bank of the Ziter-1000. So it was that, out of the confusing darkness, Petra suddenly heard LULU's calming full-throated voice recite the following.

The Indigo Tower Waltz
By: L.U.L.U.

We dance with our demons
On the ballroom floor
Kiss all the angels
And ask for more
We pick up the slipper
Though we're not quite sure
If we should be Petra-fied

"Yeah? Well ...who the fuck asked you anyway!" shouted a defiant Petra. "Who asked you anyway?"

Always Neil Before A Prayer

Neil Presley remained confused and uncertain about many things. But, of one thing he was very certain. Something had changed within him, something profound and unexpected. He now found himself thinking about a myriad of possibilities, a thousand different ways in which he might change his life ...everything from the time he went to bed to the way in which he looked at the morning sunrise out over the frozen ocean. It was an exciting, exhilarating, and occasionally terrifying time, this new vision of all things in his world. It was as though he suddenly could not help but notice the subtlety of things, the small and not so small differences among his peers...among all living creatures for that matter. With very little effort and no clear understanding of the important journey he was about to take, common launch-tech Neil Presley, had miraculously awakened from a lifetime of slumber.

"I can't wait," he said to Jerome, "to see what Commander O'Reilly left for me. I've got to find out soon."

"Patience is a virtue of all great citizens," replied Jerome.

"So I've heard," Neil replied.

Then tearing off a glean sheet from its tablet, he used his pointing finger to thermal-jot the steps he would need to take if he were to make his way to O'Reilly's pod and retrieve whatever exotic objects he might find there.

- Pretend to be sick at work
- Leave early
- Wear clothing from Commander O'Reilly's locker
- Use Commander O'Reilly's pod-tag to board Gopher transport
- Exit Gopher tunnel two stops before reaching main station in Cliff-Hunter Village
- Walk calmly to the address on pod-tag
- Enter pod
- Locate a few amazing items
- Reverse above steps and return to my pod
- Replace Commander O'Reilly's clothing the following workday

Pausing momentarily, Neil thought deeply for a moment before adding

Do Not Fail!

The Tibetland Founder's Club and Their Noble Well-Intentioned Plan to Save Humanity and Never Do Evil in a World that Has Never Not Known It

In the earliest decades of the 21st Century, the governments of the world began to reluctantly acknowledge that there was a serious earth problem unfolding. The piecemeal scientific data that had arrived for decades, now poured in with convincing evidence that the viability of the earth as a future oasis of life was in serious doubt. In response, most of the larger, wealthier nations began to make modest efforts to curb activities that would contribute to ongoing global warming and the inevitable rising of ocean levels. Projections of just when the more serious consequences of man's interaction with nature might arrive were commonly considered to be somewhere in the mid twenty-second century.

However, the larger and more influential corporations of the world continued to stand by a much more optimistic analysis. In a confident public news release statement, by thirty of the world's largest corporations, their position was once again made quite clear.

"While we will continue to monitor with due diligence any future climatic changes that might occur or be cause for concern, we remain optimistic that the various steps already taken by the governments of the world will successfully offset any extreme threats to the nations and peoples of our planet."

And so it was that, in response to such distorted re-assurances, a handful of gifted like-minded scientists began to consider the serious implications of climate change and to consider a radical survival approach in addressing its threats to mankind's very existence. Gathering and communicating as a single entity, they carefully evolved a very different theory regarding climate, ocean levels, and the very survivability of humanity. What they determined to do next would be considered by future generations as the high chance risk that saved mankind from extinction. Undoubtedly, the most prestigious and dedicated scientists within this radical scientific club, were its founding members...Ezekiel Faux (Fox), Jokum Nordvig, Tom Bitt, Teresa Apple-Gate Suarez, Lukas Warmer, Terrence Breitlit, and Abigail Overlord. It would be their theories, leadership and fundraising skills that would eventually provide a handful of surviving men and woman on planet earth a second, desperate, and final chance to get it right.

Over a period of two full decades, this determined group built upon its membership, recruiting the very best minds available. Eventually its rolls swelled to over five hundred dedicated members, the breadth and expertise of their talents ranging widely to include every major scientific field and endeavor. The diversity of its knowledge base extended from nuclear fission to animal husbandry; from solar energy to public transportation, from archeology to zoology, from digital computation to behavioral interaction. And while this wildly diverse group arrived from a host of varied backgrounds, all were united, without equivocation, in the firm belief that planet earth had entered a dangerous historical moment of existential importance...a final last chance for humanity to survive.

Motivated, they worked tirelessly to beg, borrow and liberate the funding, support, or physical materiel they would need to regenerate a world covered in rising waters. Tirelessly operating out of their respective countries, the members slowly built up a war chest of more than eighteen billion Euros. And with every passing year, additional plans were drawn up and acted upon in order to prepare for what they believed would be a cataclysmic natural event of incalculable dimensions. After much deliberation and thorough study, the Goa Club, as they came to call themselves, adopted what they considered a workable, if monumental plan.

They purchased outright, one of the world's largest ocean-going oil freighters, the "Princess of Tides", and rechristened it the "Noah Grande´". They then converted two thirds of the ship's cargo into customized storage units for passengers, crew, and such important items as a distillation system; extreme weather clothing; machining equipment; mining equipment; cables of every kind; a digital library of scientific studies, large solar arrays; portable heating units; recycled lumber from a defunct coal mining town; two-way radios and their batteries; large rapid charging lithium batteries; generators; one thousand pounds of fruit and vegetable seeds; one million completed works of art (music, paintings, literature, movies) from forty-four nations; dyes; cloth; and blueprints of small buildings/motors/ toys/ and several dependable hand-held weapons ...to name but a few of the extensive store of supplies and materials they deemed critical to establish a new self-sustaining earth settlement from scratch. The remaining one-third of the vessel was then filled up with its originally intended cargo...oil. It was reasoned that a ready supply of energy could be utilized to initially heat and power the many projects required to establish a new and thriving community.

In short, they included in their inventory, every item they collectively conceived would be needed in order to start over. Inevitably, they reasoned, something would be omitted that might prove necessary, even critical, to their reboot of civilization. Any such omission could be addressed on-site, provided they carried with them the tools, plans, and machinery required to manufacture such items. Without a doubt, the massive blueprint of this rarified, well-funded mix of scientists and "professors of possibility", was barely comprehensible, an effort on a par with the Pyramids of Egypt or the Great Wall of China. And in the final year of preparation, the group determined that an inspirational motto should be adopted...one that would inspire current and future generations. Following a contentious debate, in which several hundred suggestions (to include such pearls as "WE THINK BIG" and "WAKE UP AND SMELL THE FUTURE") were considered, an acceptable motto was finally chosen by a simple majority...one that expressed the official ethical mindset of this grand endeavor's founders:

"Forward Together - Beyond Fear Hate and Evil".

Their new society would be based on the principles of science, kindness, and tolerance. Such were the Herculean dreams of Tibetland III's founding men and women. But, like so many dreamers before them, and all those who envision a perfect society, the Goa Club underestimated the eroding effects of time and human passions on even the strongest and committed of ideals.

Let Us Never Fall, Like Kukenaam, to Dark Waters Far Below

"Few evil leaders start out that way/ It's just what happens/ When love don't stay"

(Pop song lyrics, circa 2019, Cleveland, Ohio, as performed by the band **'Righteous Wrong'**)

The intricate plans of the Goa Group had always been centered firmly around the concept that only science could save the physical earth and lead mankind to the purer essence of something better. Most of the group's membership believed with absolute resolve that the failure of previous civilizations had simply been their reliance on non-scientific decisions. They had trusted political debate, or religious tradition, or a single strong-minded leader to sustain their governments and protect their citizenry. In such scenarios, human emotion was consistently substituted for fact-based data. In this way, all previous cultures had inevitably succumbed to the strongest of mankind's emotions in the same way. Fear, greed, jealousy, prejudice, lust, arrogance, ignorance and wishful thinking had supplanted common sense and indisputable science. The outcomes had proven predictably consistent over time. Cultures embrace a set of clear values. They rise to wealth and power. Eventually, original values give way to the baser emotions of its population and governing bodies. Nations then overreach in ways that cannot be sustained, their cultures spiraling down into chaos and oblivion.

For these reasons, it was determined by the group that whenever the time came for them to establish a new world governing body, whether it be in twenty years or one hundred, that body should be an institution based on knowledge, science, fact, and irrefutable evidence. It should be staffed by only the most highly educated and reasonable minded among them. In this way, they felt certain that the survivors of mankind's follies, could be spared future suffering and despair. This salient group concept was perhaps best summarized in Abigail Overlord's impassioned final speech before the Goa Group steering committee.

"We must embrace science, fact, and indisputable knowledge over all other forms of knowing. The world in which we are about to enter cannot afford the luxury of sentimental dreaming, wishful thinking, or misguided compassion. If we are to succeed in creating a home that is sustainable...one which provides its citizens with well maintained, peaceful and predictable life outcomes, we must never fall from our highest ideals. Unlike that towering waterfall, Kukenaam, we must not drop precipitously into the dark and unknown waters far below."

So just as this amazing gathering of geniuses had planned for the physical needs of their future world, they carefully constructed the ethical, moral, and intellectual standards to which they would conform and by which their great experiment would be conducted. Priority would always be given to that which could be clearly proven or surmised through factual evidence. All other sources of knowledge would be considered secondarily, if considered at all. This time, they vowed, the world would enjoy an orderly presence that would last for limitless centuries to come. This time, the *truth* of things would reign supreme over the naïve and self-destructive *hope* of things. The future of mankind would be carefully and thoughtfully placed on a self-correcting path of accomplishment and sustainability. Life would go on. Humanity would thrive. The factual truth of things, would at last, prevail.

On a chilly October morning, in the three-story brick residence of Ezekiel Faux, the founding members of the Goa Club met to finalize details of the maiden voyage of the *Noah Grande ´*. As always, the meeting itself, and any matter discussed within the group, was wrapped in strict secrecy. Not even family members of those attending were provided with the slightest clue as to the topic of the meeting or the long-term goals of the group. In this way, for two decades, the unique organization had avoided public scrutiny and the ridicule of naysayers. Simultaneously, they worked with determination to market their concept to the world's wealthiest entrepreneurs. Their selling point was a very simple one.

"If you substantially contribute (minimum of €600 Million) to the *Last Chance Initiative*, you and your family will be guaranteed passage on the *Noah Grande'* when it sails at the hour of mankind's self-inflicted demise."

Members of Goa's original steering committee had been surprised and encouraged by the robust positive response they had received from so many billionaires around the world. And while approximately eighty percent of their 'clientele' were citizens of either China or the United

States of America, other smaller nations were modestly represented by the financially elite within their respective cultures. The total number of such paid-up ticket holders and their families would total 330. The number of Goa Club scientists and their loved ones would eventually peak at 551. The number of skilled craftsmen and physically fit workers required to establish a new settlement leveled off at 1321 (this figure included no more than one family member per worker). As a matter of routine, all persons who were primary to the mission and would eventually board the ship, were screened for criminal history, communicable disease, acceptable IQ scores, and basic coping skills when under pressure. Those who managed to navigate this maze of requirements were rewarded, in addition to their salaries, with a single 400 troy ounce gold bar of .999 percent purity (to be delivered upon the ship's departure) and a chance to escape the horrific fate of their neighbors and the world at large.

 As the Goa Club's founders finalized their extensive plans for a "shake-down" cruise to test the real-life viability of their master plan, all its future sailing members were notified in advance that they were invited to test out the facilities and onboard resources of the great ship. If there was any difference in the tone of the invitations, it was simply that all founding members were *required* to be onboard, all others merely encouraged to take part. The goal being to adequately assess the functionality of their planning to date, and to determine what changes might be necessary to assure the mission's future success. In the end, the final tally of shake-down cruise participants was as follows.

Founding members and guests	=	**497**
Paid-up financial elite and guests	=	**273**
Craftsmen/ workers and guests	=	**836**
Ship's full complement	=	**1606**

To ensure compliance with the organization's policy of privacy, the entire adult population of those sailing were required to sign legally binding *Contracts of Non-disclosure.*

Having formalized the upcoming dry run of the *Noah Grande'*, all attending Goa Club members shook hands with their host, Ezekiel Faux as they departed his home. All were now more confident than ever in the future success of the first ever launch of their great vessel of hope; the path of their efforts a clear and certain one.

In just ten short months, a bottle of champagne would be cracked across the stern of their massive vessel, and the first phase of their historic plan could be checked off as *completed and on schedule.* At last, a scientific hedge against any future worldwide calamities would be firmly in place. The Goa Club and its supporters would be primed, ready, and very much willing to step into the breech. They would, with luck, and more importantly, science on their side, be able to create a new world order ...one based on logic, fact and irrefutable knowledge. A happier group of brilliant scientists would have been hard to find anywhere.

Exactly ten months and three days later, the newly christened Noah Grandé, quietly slipped from its moorings. Quite coincidentally, as the ponderous ship, now fully loaded with passengers, crew, cargo and high spirits, departed its California port, one Maxwell Goering Sturg was making his way to a Florida shore, his recent treachery aboard the USS Louisiana soon to unleash a devastating series of horrific events upon the world.

Three thousand miles away a cantankerous captain, named Ulysses P. Gunther, turned to his first mate. And as the Noah Grandé cleared the shoreline, he made the single worst assessment of his life.

"Diago," he said," I've captained every kind of ship there is, but I've never seen a bigger ship of fools than the one we're on!"

Gumption Gone Wild...
The Rise of Neil Presley

Neil's artificial parrot sang him awake just as he had requested. At precisely 05:15 hours, Jerome broke into song. "We get up" he screeched cheerily. "We get up. We get up when we are called...and we need to be called only once!".

"Jerome," Neil screeched back, "turn off. I'm up now!"

Though it was fifteen minutes earlier than his normal wake up time, it was not so early that it would arouse suspicion when he left his pod for work. The closed monitor cameras on the streets and transport line would simply see an earnest citizen trying to get to his job slightly earlier than usual. None of the thirty-minute variance alarms would have been triggered...no inquiry generated from Central Oversight.

Gliding silently along beneath the deep frostline overhead, Neil casually glanced at the other three passengers packed into Gopher 23...a teenage nurse from St. Abigail's Healing Center, an aging ice cutter bundled up in standard issue thermal-keep coveralls, and an angular twenty-something male proudly wearing the enforcement shoulder emblem of the Britelit Police Academy. Three stops and seven minutes later, he arrived at the vertical elevator that would take him up to the surface entrance to his workplace.

Once inside the guarded facility, he stealthily made his way into the Cliff-Hunter prep room where he located CH3 O'Reilly's locker. Just as he had hoped, the same pod-tag that would soon open O'Reilly's locked home pod, also worked flawlessly to open his departure locker. As the opaque plastiplex door swung open, Neil was nearly overcome by his first ever look at the private "kit" of a long serving Cliff-Hunter. Talking himself back into the moment, he carefully removed the full length CH3 hooded overcoat hanging there. Like a mother experiencing her newborn for the first time, he gently touched the long gold braid that looped across and under one shoulder of the coat. As he did so, the passing image of Cliff-Hunter O'Reilly briefly flashed then faded before him. Closing the locker door quietly, he walked quickly to his own locker in the adjoining anteroom. Opening the door of his own locker, he carefully placed the commander's coat inside. "Mission accomplished" he whispered to the empty changing room. Then glancing down at his trembling hands, he turned and walked in the direction of his launch-retrieval work space.

Throughout the rest of his workday, Neil tried to maintain a natural appearing composure, to go about his day to day chores with the same level of interest and low-key humor as he always did. Thankfully, no launches or retrievals had been scheduled for the day, and so his shift was not in danger of being altered. Still, as the morning dragged on, he began to have some doubts. "Who in their right mind" he asked himself "would intentionally enter a Cliff-Hunter's pod for the purpose of retrieving historic artifacts to which he has no legitimate right to see, let alone possess?" Though increasingly anxious, he nevertheless martialed his courage and approached his supervisor. Complaining of nausea and diarrhea, and

139

having never complained of illness in the past, he was granted an early release from his duties and sent home.

As he approached his locker, Neil felt an exhilarating surge of energy pulse through his body. For the first time in his life, he was about to confront established governmental policies and protocols. He was about to take dangerous steps, steps that he would never be able to retrace once made. It was not difficult to imagine the consequences of his actions, should he be found out.

First, he would immediately loose the several bonus privileges he enjoyed as a launch/ retrieval tech. The increased caloric diet, the subsidized pod heating unit, and the semi-annual robotic-female visits...would all instantly disappear. Second, he would be suspended from all work-related duties; be required to live on the most basic of food rations; be forbidden to leave his pod until his trial. Third, upon his most certain conviction, he would be deported at once to the Northside mining settlement. No appeal or pardon would be possible.

Emerging from his workplace, a particularly fierce blast of cold wind penetrated the medium layer of clothing he had purposely chosen that morning. Looking around in all directions, Neil reached into the modest sized duffle tucked beneath one arm.

Pulling out a heavy dark blue overcoat, he slipped into it, flipped up its hood, and carefully fastened its classic double row of gold buttons. From a deep inside pocket, he retrieved a sturdy set of government issued snow goggles. As he straightened the coat's bright gold braid, an unexpected sensation of confidence and warmth swept over him. "We get up when we are called," he said with a frosty breath. "And we need to be called only once!"

Neil left his goggles and hood in place as he boarded the familiar Gopher that would return him to his authorized neighborhood. He avoided looking out any of its portals, as status-cams were strategically placed all along his return route. Burying his face in the latest Daily Homeland Progress Report, he tried to breathe very slowly and to recall the various steps of his plan. He found himself repeatedly reaching into the pocket of his borrowed Cliff-Hunter coat to be certain that the O'Reilly pod-tag was still safely stowed.

Just as planned, Neil stayed on the Gopher as it passed his usual stop, exiting the transport two full stations before the Cliff-Hunter Village. He then walked at a moderate pace along the heated ice-free paths that led to the central pod complex. Approaching an external elevator, he entered it with the distinctive surefooted gate that most Cliff-Hunters display when in public. To his relief, the elevator was empty and remained so for the whole vertical ride up to terrace-floor seven.

Looking down one more time at the pod-tag, Neil verified that CH3 O'Reilly's pod number was indeed 1236BAT14.

As he approached the substantial door to the commander's residence, the tag in his hand began to glow and pulse with increasing speed. Even before he had reached out for the doors latch, the crisp metallic sound of a retreating lock could be heard.

"Pure cool," said Neil. "Classy cool."

Then brushing a layer of accumulated snow from his shoulders, he stepped cautiously across the glowing threshold. A series of low intensity lights slowly began to glow throughout the pod, precisely as they had been programmed by its long-term resident. A pot of real coffee began to brew in the small kitchenette attached to the living area. Seeping from the surrounding walls came the sound of a female voice and accompanying orchestra. *"Long Ago and Far Away,"* she sang. "A t*wentieth mid-century performer known as Jo Stafford"* announced a hologram as it slowly scrolled before him. Neil stood transfixed by the foreign, yet pleasing, stimuli arriving from all corners of the pod.

"So, this is how the other half lives," he said with genuine wonder.

"More precisely," observed a young female voice, *"this is how Commander CH3 O'Reilly lives."*

"What?" asked a startled Neil Presley. "Who's talking?"

"To refine your observation, I am explaining that this is the residence of CH3 O'Reilly. And to further clarify, I wish to explain that I am now complying with the encrypted Pod-tag access permission he has granted you. Please know, Neil Presley, that you are entitled to all benefits and embellishments embedded in this pod. Also, **CHV3 directive 2136-BAT** allows me to respond to any questions you may have. Therefore, on behalf of Commander O'Reilly and this humble service assistant, consider yourself extremely welcome!"

"Well thank you, spooky voice," Neil muttered cryptically.

*"You are entirely welcome, Neil Presley. Also, you may call me '**assistant**', 'Zarita' ...or simply 'Z'."*

Neil stood quietly in place as he tried to comprehend the new world into which he had wandered. He noted with rapt interest the exotic sights, sounds and smells so unlike those of his austere and much smaller living pod. As he tried to take it all in, his eyes were quickly drawn to a handmade blanket of ancient origin. The blue, red, and yellow work of art hung along the largest wall, its design putting forth a powerful presence. Its bright colors and geometric patterns made it somehow inviting and irresistible. Reaching out to touch its roughly worked surface, he noticed a large rounded object sitting just below it. It appeared to be a dented metal head covering of some
sort. Crudely painted lettering covered both sides. *"Sex Love & Rock n Roll"* read the first inscription; *"Home in '68"* the second.

Neil placed the palms of both hands on its surface, as though looking into a crystal ball for the first time. As he did, the haunting beat of a long-ago song began to slowly arrive from the surrounding walls. *"Neil"*, said Z, *"I hope you enjoy this related musical enhancement by Mr. Marvin Gaye. It is entitled 'What's Going On'"*.

Enthralled, Neil listened with wonder to the words that filled the room.

"Mother Mother...There's too many of you crying. Brother, brother, brother...there's far too many of you dying."

A sudden wave of unexplained sadness swept over him, and as he gently removed his hands from the object, the music from five centuries earlier slowly faded into silence. Struggling to shake off the subdued mood that had engulfed him, Neil inhaled slowly several times.

"Coffee is brewed and now ready," said Z. *"There is a cup beside the brewer."*

"Well, thank you," said Neil. Then moving toward a stainless-steel appliance across the room, he picked up an ancient beige restaurant cup and filled it with a steaming black liquid. Taking a tentative sip of the brew, Neil let out a throaty grunt of satisfaction.

"Oh my, God!" Zarita, this is amazing. Is this real coffee? Is this what real coffee tastes like?"

"Yes. Real coffee."

Neil took several more loving sips, and with his eyes still closed with delight said "Z..."

"Yes, Neil?"

"Z, what are the different smells that I'm getting from all around this room? They're really different."

"Neil," she replied, *"there are three primary olfactory antagonists currently being generated. The first is a spice called ginger, a favorite of the commanders. The second is incense, an organic substance that releases aromatic smoke when burned. The third is the simulated smell of marijuana."*

"Marywanna?"

"Close, Neil. Also known as Cannabis, this psychoactive drug was derived from the Cannabis plant and often used by 20th and 21st century citizens of North America for both medical and recreational purposes. Additionally, it was very popular among United States of America soldiers deployed to South Vietnam...a Southeast Asian country that bordered the South China Sea."

"Oh," replied Neil.

"Do you wish to know more about this topic, Neil?"

"No. That would be enough for now. Thank you, Z."

"De nada," replied Z.

"What?"

"Not at all!" came the reply. *"Not a problem!"*

For the next hour, Neil moved slowly about the accommodations of CH3 O'Reilly. Fascinated by a dozen different artifacts, he carefully examined each one. Now and then he would call upon Zarita for an explanation of an object's purpose or history. Most of these explanations did little to help him comprehend what he was looking at, as he simply lacked the reference points and historic understanding to place the information in context. Every explanation seemed to raise more questions than it answered. Each new fact and revelation just seemed to lead to more questions. Still, the experience was incredibly moving for him. More importantly, Neil began to grasp, for the first time, just how limited his learning had been...how little he comprehended of the world outside his own. He began to experience the disquieting sensation of floating in time, disconnected from past or future. Not surprisingly, this feeling of disconnection brought with it a growing sense of loss and regret. At the same time, he could not deny that it also brought with it a powerful surge of curiosity, wonder, hope and more than a little confusion.

"You seem to be perplexed by your new surroundings," observed Z.

Neil smiled and nodded. "Well, Zarita, at the risk of sounding totally ignorant, let me just say that ... I am struck dumb by just how much I do not know ...how very much I do not know!"

Commander Patterson struggled to regain control of his boat. Within two minutes of the initial explosion, he had received enough feedback from crew and onboard systems to confirm that it had suffered severe damage. And as the frightening minutes passed, three things became increasingly apparent.

1. The reinforced shell surrounding the nuclear reactor had been breached
2. The ship's electrical systems were now functioning on back-up generator power only
3. Maximum power to the props was less than 10% and falling

Uncertain of the extent of the boats damage, Patterson now complied with standing orders. Steering it away from the populated port area, he pointed it in the direction of the open waters of the Atlantic. If the boat were in real jeopardy of sinking, he wanted to remove any possibility of nuclear spillage within the turn basin, minimizing any threat to port residents or coastal inhabitants. The plan was a simple one. Steer the wounded Louisiana to the deepest waters possible. Assess the full extent of the damage. Place Coast Guard and US Naval resources on stand-by status for the probable evacuation of the boat's crew. Pray to God for deliverance.

Twenty-three minutes later, Patterson's beloved "Louise" had cleared the mouth of the basin. Chugging along at 7 knots, all seemed to be going according to plan. Within two hours, the boat would once again be over deep water, and all immediate threat to civilian life would be abated.

Relaxing only slightly, Patterson glanced over at a clearly shaken Seaman Dowd.

"Don't worry, son," he said calmly, "this is all just going to be an exciting tale you tell your grandchildren."

Dowd nodded tentatively. "Yes, Sir." Then, surprising even himself, he added ... "Request permission to exaggerate when I tell that story, Sir."

"Permission to exaggerate granted," replied a bemused Patterson.

It was now 1303 hours. The Florida sun was at its fierce summer apex as the commander authorized what would be the boat's final message.

*Sierra Oscar Sierra, **Msg-Priority-Full Urgent***
to: Shore command and related relay hub station 13/
USS Louisiana now full clear Florida coastline/ extreme
damage primary propulsion unit/ will continue on
last conveyed course to designated rendezvous and
assisting vessels/ est. arrival: 1500 Hours
End Msg-Final"

Murphy's Law is a common, overly used adage. "Anything that can go wrong, will go wrong," office workers say when the printer runs out of ink at a crucial moment. "Anything that can go wrong, will go wrong", hairstylists observe when an intended hair coloring turns orange instead of red. "Anything that can go wrong, will go wrong", declare high school coaches when the team bus breaks down en route to the big game.

But the *Murphy's Law* phrase is rarely invoked by commanders of the Navy's devastatingly destructive warships. The phrase simply seems too whimsical, too pat and glib, to be considered in connection with a floating weapons platform of unimaginable power.

Even so, what happened next aboard the Louisiana was probably the most glaring confirmation of that overused adage one could imagine. When Max Sturg's carefully planted charges had simultaneously ripped through the heart of the boat, penetrating the core of the nuclear containment pod, it laid bare the units vital control rods. Within minutes, the super-heated core began to melt through the thick metal shielding beneath it. And as it slowly cut its way toward the boat's outer skin and the ocean depths beyond, it incidentally severed and disabled the boat's sophisticated hacking deterrence system that wound through the deck beneath it. Its digital defenses compromised, the system now passively looked on as a sophisticated algorithmic saboteur reached out and shook hands with the launch/ guidance system below decks. The esoteric calculations of a deceased teenage genius had finally prevailed. And that, as they say, was that!

As alarm sirens began to blare, a chilling series of announcements echoed throughout the doomed vessel.

"Weapons Armed - Targeting Confirmed - Consecutive Array Selected - Launch Countdown ...Start"

Thirty-two seconds later, a stunned crew stood by helplessly as the first of 24 Trident II D-5 ballistic missiles lifted from its tube. Inexplicably, it would explode overhead in just fifteen seconds, but not before all but 2 of the remaining 23 had followed in rapid succession. From as far away as Orlando and Jacksonville, the pale blue sky of the sunshine state was suddenly chalk-marked with the thick white trails of outbound missiles.

Then, in an ever-darker twist of fate, the guidance systems onboard the missiles began to recalculate their global positioning. Incredibly, all 22 incorrectly determined that they were, not ten miles off the east coast of Florida, but one hundred miles west of North Korea in the Sea of Okhotsk. With the graceful precision of lithe ballerinas, the missiles course-corrected themselves to impact what they believed to be mainland Russia. Whether or not their electrostatically-supported gyro navigator (ESGN) systems had collectively failed, or some other digital interface had malfunctioned, would never be determined. Whatever the cause of the malfunction, the outcome was predictably horrific. At 3:13 PM, Eastern Standard Time, on a Friday afternoon, The United States of America was mercilessly attacked by a massive barrage of ballistic missiles...22 weapons launched by its own naval forces

Though no major US cities received a direct hit, many of the warheads landed within several hundred miles of major population centers. California, Washington, Oregon, Colorado and Montana received the brunt of the attack. Immediate impact casualties totaled over twelve million, with that figure doubling within a week due to radiation, burns, and physical trauma injuries.

Within seventeen minutes of the initial burst, the President of the United States was abruptly evacuated from the White House by helicopter. Within twenty-nine minutes of the attack, he was onboard Air Force One circling high above the still intact eastern seaboard of America.

Looking very stern and genuinely shaken, the President leaned forward in his chair, hands passively clasped above the embossed presidential seal atop his desk.

"General," he said, "talk to me. What do we know? What the hell just happened?"

"Well," replied two-star general Alexander Creedmoor, in the greatest understatement of all time, "apparently, something that *could* go wrong...just did!"

Jesus, Freddy, Shakespeare and Joe
All Go Home in a Gaudy Bag!

Neil was aware that he had only a few more minutes in which to choose the several objects that CH3 O'Reilly had authorized him to take. But, given the number of fascinating choices openly displayed in the commander's pod, it was becoming increasingly difficult to decide which three or four objects they would be.

"Zarita," he said, "Commander O'Reilly gave me permission to take several objects from this pod."

"Yes," she replied, *"I can confirm that."*

"Yes, but I've got a problem. I mean, I've never seen so many interesting things in one place before. I'm confused. I need some help."

"A recommendation?"

"Yes. Exactly! What would *you* suggest would be some good choices for me?"

"Neil Presley, as you appear to be in an emotionally transitional period, I suggest that you retrieve the several items that the commander has stored beneath his rem-cot. Inspirational and instructive, they could prove a sound choice."

Neil looked mildly uncomfortable.

"A transitional period?" he repeated. "And how would *you* know what *I'm* going through emotionally?"

"Here are the four primary observations that confirm the validity of my conclusion. They are, in order of relevance...

- *Eye movement*
- *Heart rate*
- *Physically displayed patterns of uncertainty*
- *Also, you are choosing high risk behaviors today, the type of behaviors which are totally absent from your past status profiles."*

"You can see my past profiles?"

"Yes. I can see and retrieve them all."

"Well, of course you can. Why not? And you think, because of these four things you *think* you know about me, you somehow know what it is I should take from here?"

"Yes, Neil. I do think that."

A brief silence followed as Neil considered Z's confident observations.

"So," he said finally, "tell me what I'm looking for."

"That would be a box marked "memorabilia" beneath the commander's rem-cot."

"Right." said Neil, and he steered his steps in the direction of a small curtained alcove. Pulling the curtain aside, he looked down at a standard rem-cot with its heating/

cooling/ vibration dials. But unlike his own, this one was equipped with a mattress perhaps three times thicker.

Beneath the rem-cot, Neil" said Z.

"OK already. I'm looking!" said Neil as he lowered himself onto one knee.

Then reaching under the cot, he carefully pulled out a dog-eared cardboard box of considerable weight. Carefully removing its cover, Neil looked down in wonder at a brightly colored silk bag and its gaudy embroidered scenes of tropical island life. "PEARL HARBOR HAWAII" it read in bright red stitching. Dropping onto both knees now, he impatiently shook the bag's contents onto the heated floor tiles. Four books of various sizes spilled out before him. Picking up each one in turn, Neil read the book titles aloud. "Freddy And the Perilous Adventure"; "Holy Bible – KJV"; "The Complete Pelican Shakespeare"; and "The Hero with A Thousand Faces". Flipping gently through the pages of each book, he was overcome by the wondcrous mystery of so many words. Then focusing on a passage from the heaviest book, he slowly read the random lines.

"Thunder and lightning. Enter three Witches.

WITCH 1 - When shall we three meet again
                In thunder, lightning, or in rain?
WITCH 2 - When the hurly-burly's done,
                When the battle's lost and won
WITCH 3 - That will be ere the set of sun."

Looking up from the book, Neil shook his head. "Zarita, why would you recommend these kind of old books? They don't even make sense. I don't understand them. Why would you recommend these?"

"Let time be your friend" she replied. "Take them with you. Take all four. Commander O'Reilly would want you to have them all, I'm quite certain. They have several common themes. But you will need to look at them carefully. Study them carefully. Trust that they will take you where it is you need to go. Read them over until you understand them. Do not give up."

"Yeah, well reading old books that I don't understand is not exactly what I was looking for. I mean, I wouldn't even know where to begin."

"Let time be your friend," repeated Z.

Neil was not particularly happy with the objects, his first ever contraband from life beyond his pod.

"Zarita," he said, "I have to be honest. These books are not what I was hoping for. And I really don't see the point of my dragging them back to my pod."

"Ironically," said a confident Zarita, *"the very fact that you do not see the potential value of these books to enhance and improve your life, argues strongly for your need to take them with you."*

"Sure!" said a disgruntled Neil "Why not! Look. I'm putting them all back in the bag. Look. I'm picking them up. And now, look. I'm taking them all with me."

"An excellent decision, Neil. ¡Bravo!"

Neil made his way to the pod door, the heavy silk bag

thrown over one shoulder. Hesitating there, he turned back
 to look at the room one last time. Taking in the exotic sights and smells, he smiled and shook his head.
"Sorry, super pod," he said, "but I've gotta get back to my tiny little pod, and I've got less than thirty minutes to do it. So, I guess you could say that, right now ...ti*me is **not** my friend.*"

"Humor!" observed Z, "I get that. Also, have a safe journey to your home, Neil Presley."

Latching the door behind him, Neil stepped out into the ever-present cold. Ignoring the elevator, he began his long descent down a heated stairwell. When he finally emerged onto the ped-walk below, he was no longer recognizable as Neil Presley. Having pulled his hood up and his snow goggles down, he was now simply a respected Cliff-Hunter out for a brisk evening walk. Seven stories overhead, the lights of the "super-pod" first dimmed, then disappeared completely.

"What in the hell is a hurly-burly?" he muttered.

When Three Weeks Equals Five Years and Curiosity Calls Your Name

From the very beginning, Tibetland III's cadre of brilliant scientists was impressive. And over the five centuries of the country's existence, they had contributed immeasurably to the safety, comfort, and order of this final bastion of humanity. Whether reproducing inventions from a previous era (i.e. - led lighting, solar collectors, transition lens goggles) or pioneering unimaginable breakthroughs (i.e. - time travel, supplemental subcutaneous assistants, precious mineral transmutation), the list of their achievements was an impressive one. Even so, five centuries of study and debate had yet to unequivocally answer the dilemma of *Age Retardant Time- Travel Effects*. Most suspected it had something to do with the several "jumps" that were required by travelers as they hopped from one parallel occurring brane to the next. A few hold-outs deferred to the Theory of Relativity. But just what the specific and provable cause of age retardation might be, remained a puzzling, open question.

Nevertheless, though the primary cause of that process was yet to be discerned, the reality was apparent to all...especially those who experienced it. Time moved differently for anyone who traveled back through it. A rough formula for the effects of this disparity was...1 day of "beam-back" time equals 86.9 days of Tibetland time. Thus, when a Cliff-Hunter returned from their standard three-week mission, they would discover that their friends and all current events had aged approximately five years. This being consistently the case, few Cliff-Hunters ever chose to marry or even become attached to pod pets. The disparity in the aging processes was simply too painful for all concerned.

Neil Presley's life and his way of experiencing the world had changed dramatically over the five years since Commander O'Reilly's departure. From the moment he retrieved and began to read the "*Four Books of Knowing*", as he came to call them, he began to slowly question many of the established givens of his government. Initially, Neil had begun reading only Freddy and the Perilous Adventure, a child's book about a talking pig. But as time went on, his curiosity overcame his reservations, and he began to read the other three books daily. And when he had finished lightly reading all four of the books, he felt compelled to go back and re-read them more carefully. He found himself pondering over the meaning of words and phrases from both the Holy Bible and the Works of Shakespeare. But as time went on, and he discovered the value of introductions and footnotes, the mysteries of these books began to slowly reveal themselves. As they did, he also began to experience subtle, and then, profound changes in his life. He found himself looking for alternate answers to common questions. He developed a skepticism to pat, long-standing answers, preferring to consider alternate possibilities. And with every re-read of the precious *Four Books*, Neil became less certain of the predictable world around him and more and more likely to question his passive place in it. There appeared to be no limit to the new questions that arose for him and haunted his nights.

- Why must every decision be based solely on facts?
- Should not emotions count for something?
- Why is it that the leaders of Tibetland III had not appeared in public for over a century?
- Why are the citizens of the homeland discouraged from interacting?
- Why is there never any discussion of the possibility of a spiritual aspect to existence?

These, and a thousand other questions, now roiled up his imagination, kept him from a sound night's sleep, and caused him to reconsider his place in society and even the universe itself.

As these many changes began to take hold, Neil felt for the first time a full range of human emotions. In place of an ever-present sensation of mild despair, Neil now began to experience alternating waves of hope, fear, euphoria, regret, anger, longing, despair, confusion, and joy.

Not a single day went by that he didn't notice something new or consider the larger questions of existence. Somehow, against all odds, Neil Presley had evolved into a thoughtful, feeling, questioning poet-philosopher...a deeply concerned citizen of the universe. Predictably, Neil's newfound awareness made it increasingly difficult for him to go about his day to day as though nothing had changed. With each new day and every familiar book chapter revisited, Neil found it more and more challenging to function at his job and in the compliant community surrounding him. Something would have to give, and he knew it. Expressing the frustration of his predicament, he wrote the following poem.

That Is the Question
(A Poem by Neil Presley)

Freddy was a clever pig
Who always did quite well
Unlike the others in his world
Where the working critters dwell
And Jesus was a carpenter
Who worked in wood and souls
While Shakespeare's lusty royals
Just died in stacks and rows
But Joe Campbell's ancient travelers
Struck out in search of more
And journeyed far to find their star
Their own fate to explore

Never Underestimate the Power of Dumb Luck

Neil awoke early, as he had for the past five years. He said good-morning to faux parrot Jerome, drank a steaming cup of simulated coffee, and pulled out one of the *Four Sacred Books* to read and enjoy. Flipping through *A Hero's Journey,* he stopped abruptly to reacquaint himself with a few favorite passages.

> *"You enter the forest*
> *at the darkest point,*
> *where there is no path...*
>
> *If you follow someone else's way,*
> *you are not going to realize*
> *your potential."*

It reminded him of one of the other sacred writings from "Freddy and the Perilous Journey", and how Freddy the talking pig had bravely taken on many frightening adventures, one after the other.

"I guess," he said to Jerome, "it all comes down to choosing to do something that is not easy or a sure thing. At least, that's what I'm getting out of it."

"And you are rarely wrong!" squawked Jerome. "It just sounds right."

"Yeah, well...in case you haven't noticed, Jerome ...you *always* agree with whatever I say. So, pardon me, if I'm not completely reassured by your reassurance."

"Yes. I see what you mean," said Jerome cheerfully. *"And, of course you're right. Your observation is truly a good one. Well done."*

"Jerome," said a weary Neil, "I'm going to ask you to reset yourself now and to *mute* yourself for the rest of the day. Would you do that for me please?"

"Yes. Of course, Neil. And let me just say what a good choice you've made ...commencing reset now to 24-hour MUTE"

When Neil stepped out of his pod twenty minutes later, he was dazzled by the tall blue skies overhead. Though clear skies were not unusual on T-3, todays seemed particularly beautiful. And had it not been for a single lonely cloud floating far off above the horizon, it would have been flawless.

Twelve minutes later, Gopher 23 had delivered him to his workplace. Changing quickly into his flame-retardant coveralls, he made his way to the polished metal chamber in which he worked. During the previous two months, he had successfully launched 2 and retrieved 3 Cliff-Hunters, most of whom had demonstrated that cold and aloof demeanor that defined their profession. On such occasions, Neil found himself reflecting on the one CH who had never treated him with disdain, the Cliff-Hunter whose secret he had kept for the past five years. And as painful as that secret had been, Neil shared it with no one. Only he knew, with certainty, that his hero would never be returning to Tibetland III.

Neil glanced down at the flashing hologram calendar in front of him. *"Scheduled for return this date ...0815 hours*

...CH3 Ramon O'Reilly". A poignant spear of sorrow pierced Neil's chest as he reflected on the loss of such a good man. And in only thirty seconds, the entire Launch/Retrieval Center would finally know what he had known for so long. A good and kind man would not be coming home.

"Jesus wept," said Neil to the empty room in which he stood ... "John 11:35".

Neil's reverie was not to last. It was suddenly interrupted by the unmistakable whine and whistle of an incoming CH-Retrieval. Forgetting about ear protection, Neil glanced over at the self-adjusting time-space-elliptic monitor that had clearly locked onto a returning signal. As the chamber's temperature plummeted below freezing and an orange glow began to slowly pulse through it, a shaken Neil Presley struggled to remember his duties. Recovering his senses at last, he verified that the three-foot receiving circle in front of him was clear of all obstructions and that the oxygen level within the chamber had temporarily increased by 17.3%.

The monitor's urgent warnings began to blare ...

"Attention! All organic personnel stand clear of circle-site. CH retrieval now in progress. Attention! All organic personnel stand clear of circle-site. CH retrieval imminent."

Neil, now a somewhat shaken retrieval-tech, looked on in wonder as the intrusive sights and sounds of the event grew in volume before slowly fading and finally disappearing altogether. The vision that then presented itself was one he struggled mightily to comprehend. A full

163

thirty seconds passed before he could identify just what it was that he was now seeing before him.

"So!" shouted an angry female voice, "are you gonna stand there like a fucking idiot or are you gonna help us?"

"What?" replied a rattled Neil. "What?"

"Jesus! Help us for Christ's sake! Bowtie's hurt bad!"

"I can't do that just yet," said Neil timidly.

"You what!" boomed Petra.

"Per protocol ma'am ... miss, I can't approach the circle-site until you've been scanned and cleared."

"And just what's that supposed to mean?"

Neil shrugged sympathetically and nodded in the direction of the chamber's only angular corner. As he did, a squatty looking robotic unit began moving in the direction of the recently arrived travelers. Stopping within three feet of the arrival-site, it began to slowly circle the couple ...not once, but three times.

"What's this fucking thing doing?" demanded Petra.

"Please be still," said Neil. "Please. It's just a scan & resolve unit. It's looking for any kind of foreign matter, living or otherwise that could pose a threat to Tibetland citizens or for its current host."

"Oh yeah! Well, how 'bout I put my foot up its friggin' scanner. How 'bout that!"

"It's almost finished," Neil reassured her. "Almost there."

"And then what?"

"Well, if nothing is found, the scan-resolution unit returns to its corner and you're both cleared for full arrival."

"And if it finds something?"

Neil never got a chance to answer Petra's question, as the scan-resolve unit abruptly moved closer to Petra, a lime green beam of light now sweeping the full length of her body.

"Hey!" she shouted. I feel something. One of my arms and one leg are starting to burn funny. Come on, dumb-ass. What the hell's goin' on?"

"Oh, well…I think the unit has identified something on your person that it does not like. I think it's addressing that concern."

"And just what the fuck does that mean?" demanded Petra.

"Well, I'm not sure. But I think it's removing all those drawings on your body."

"Whoa! Whoa! Whoa! Those are *my* tats. They cost me a lot. Those need to stay. You hear me. Those need to stay!"

Neil shrugged for the second time. "That's not something I can change," he said apologetically. "The unit is programed to scan and correct whatever it determines to be a threat…not sometimes …but always. There's nothing I can do."

"Well, how in the name of God are my tats a threat to anybody? Tell me that."

Neil looked in the direction of the busily scanning unit.

"Scan-Res #12," he said, "please display nature of current identified threat."

A hologram print-out immediately appeared overhead...

- **Vintage ink-based skin applications covering 11% of body surface**
- **Threat to community – 0%**
- **Threat to wearer – 7% chance of liver/ 5% chance of kidney damage over average female lifespan**
- **Treatment initiated: Removal ink-based skin applications**
- **Exception – removal lepidoptera applied ink image not required – threat to organ functions negligible**

Five minutes later, having removed the cross-body bag swinging from Petra's neck, and its scanning duties completed, the unit returned to the chamber's angular corner, and placed itself once again into a *dormant-recharge* state.

"Hey, dumb-ass!" shouted an angry and impatient Petra. "Get us the hell out of here and get us some help!"

Working together, a nervous Neil Presley and a still-fuming Petra pulled, pushed and carried an unconscious Ramon O'Reilly to one side of the chamber. Still pressing firmly against his bleeding wound, Petra now made direct eye contact with her first acquaintance from a future world.

"Who are you again?"

"Me? I'm Neil …Neil Presley. I'm a tech. I'm a launch-retrieval tech."

"Well good for you, Elvis."

"Elvis?" repeated Neil.

"And I am just totally relieved to see we're in such good hands," she continued.

Mistaking Petra's cryptic words for a genuine compliment, Neil spoke up …" Well, thank you. I always try to do my best."

Petra shook her head violently. "No! …dumb-ass. That was not a compliment! Just try to focus. This man is bleeding out fast. He needs help. And I mean right now! So, Elvis… unless you have a suggestion on how we make that happen, do not open your mouth again!"

Neil looked stunned. He had never been spoken to in such a demeaning manner. "Well," he stammered.

"Well what?"

"Well, there *is* a first aid scan-kit by the door."

"Oh well then!" snarled Petra. "How 'bout you mosey over *there* and bring it back *here*!"

"Well, yes. I'll do that. I mean, I'm doing that."

Scurrying across the chamber, he quickly retrieved the 2-foot x 2-foot emergency assessment/ treatment kit hanging on the wall. Placing it carefully beside O'Reilly, Neil snapped open its latches.

"What is all this?" asked Petra.

"Well, it's an analysis and reversal kit. You place this...he held up a flat metallic disk...on the injured person and the extent of his injuries display nearby."

"Great. So, then what?"

"Well, depending on the read-out, you take one of the matching treatment packets and follow the instructions."

"Alright. So, fire up the damn thing and let's get some help going here."

"Right," replied an obedient Neil Presley. And he placed the shiny disk just under and to the left of O'Reilly's heart.

Twenty-eight seconds later, the small unit buzzed loudly and then displayed a hologram read out of the patient's vitals and condition. Flashing in bright red letters was the phrase ...

"**Patient condition critical-urgent.** Three of three vitals in red zone. Treatment confirmed: *Apply packets three, five, and seven as directed, and in this order*".

Reaching into the small kit, Neil retrieved the three packets. Turning each one over to read their printed instructions, he began to apply each in its turn.

Packet 3: Firmly place and hold *packet 3* pad on bleeding wound for five minutes or until bleeding stops

Packet 5: Place <u>adhesive side</u> of *packet 5* pad on back of victim's neck. No pressure required

Packet 7: Shake *packet 7* vigorously before applying. Place green side of pad directly over victim's heart - Remove pad after 30 minutes

Approximately 40 minutes later, all packet interventions having been properly applied, CH3 O'Reilly began to stir. Looking up, he struggled to focus. He could just make out the concerned expressions of Judy Hooley and his tech friend, Neil.

"Guess I'm still not dead," he said weakly.

"Well," said Petra, "don't push it. The day's still young."

Then glancing at Neil, he added "She's mellowed nicely ...used to be so bitchy. Can you believe it?"

"Yes," said Neil earnestly. "Actually, commander, I can."

Within ...Within ...Within ...
A Brief Report Card on The Dead

- At the very moment that Petra and CH3 O'Reilly materialized before Neil Presley, a single nuclear weapon above the surface-running Louisiana suddenly detonated. And within thirty seconds ...five centuries in the past ...the populated community surrounding Cape Canaveral, Florida, United States of America, disappeared from the earth.
- Within forty seconds, local casualties approached two million.
- Terrorist, Max Sturg, had just tuned in the CNN network and was awaiting an important *Breaking News* event he was certain would take place any moment.
- Would-be assassins, Scud Kazinsky and Randolf Palucci, had arrived back at their cheap, grimy digs where they were sharing a large bottle of malt liquor in celebration of their recent deeds.
- Colt Savage was replacing the recoil spring on a tricked-out Kimber 1911 pistol.
- Captain Patterson and the crew of the USS Louisiana were standing together, stunned into silence by the grim reality about to unfold.
- Within one hour, twelve million citizens of the United States had died.
- Within one week, a savage, undeclared nuclear conflict had erupted.
- Within one month, four billion innocent souls had perished from the earth.

- Within one year, an additional two billion had died of disease, hunger and local violence.
- Within ten years, and inexplicably, the vast amounts of water (three times that of the surface oceans) that had been stored deep within the planet in the mineral brucite, slowly reconfigured itself into liquid H2O and began to flow inexorably upward, seeping into existing oceans and most remaining land mass.
- Within one hundred years, most dry land had disappeared beneath a massive deluge of ancient water.
- Within three hundred years of the Louisiana event, the only known planet survivors (approximately 5500) lived on a single island, a former towering peak from the roof-top mountain ranges of Tibet.
- Within four hundred years, for reasons debated by Homeland scientists, the Earth began to cool. Occans were once again beginning to freeze over. Only a thin circle of ocean-surface at the equator still remained in liquid form.
- Five hundred plus years after the initial destructive event, Tibetland IIIs population numbered approximately 11,000, as the remaining inhabitants of planet earth clung determinedly, precariously, to life.

"Take her with you," O'Reilly said to Neil. "Take her with you. Hide her in your pod. If I make it, I'll meet you there."

"Take her with me?" Neil looked both terrified and intrigued.

"She can't stay here. If they find her here...If they find her here..."

And then he was gone, unconscious once again.

Petra grabbed Neil's arm and pulled his face close to hers.

"What's a pod?"

"It's where I live."

"And what about Bowtie here? What happens to him now?"

"Well," Neil said thoughtfully, "I guess, per protocol, I call a _Zebra-12 alert_ and then a rescue unit will come and take him off to the Hozpit."

"And they'll take care of him there? Good care of him there?"

"Sure. That's what they do. He'll be fine. Now that he's stabilized ...I think he'll be fine."

"You _think_ he'll be fine."

"Well ...yeah ...most likely."

"So, what do I do in the meantime?"

"Well ...um ...you can't go outside looking like that. And you can't stay here."

"So ...what does that leave?"

"O. So, here's the thing ...There is one place you could hide. But you're not going to like it."

"And, just why would that be, Elvis?"

"Because it's really small and dark."

Before sending out the medical alert, Neil led Petra out of the chamber and into the changing/ locker room attached to it. He opened up his 3' X 2' X 6' locker and removed a large grey parka, two heated snow boots, and a polyester sweater with the stenciled phrase *"Past-time is my pastime"*. These he placed in the furthest, darkest corner of the room.

Petra pointed at the open locker door.

"And so, you want me to climb in there?"

"Yes," said Neil. "Yes I do."

Petra glared fiercely at her new future-world acquaintance.

"Are you kidding me, dumb-ass? Only an industrial strength idiot would crawl in there."

Neil looked flushed and shaken. He struggled to gather his thoughts.

"It's not ideal, I know. But there's nowhere else, and it wouldn't be for very long."

"And how long is 'not very'," asked a skeptical Petra.

"Maybe an hour ...or maybe two. Long enough for the Zebra team to come and go. I'll probably have to go with them too ...answer a lot of questions."

"Well, that just sounds like the perfect grand plan there, Elvis. And can I open this coffin up from the inside?"

Neil hesitated as he shifted from foot to foot.

"Well, actually, no."

"And there's no other option?"

"No other option," confirmed Neil.

Petra struck the locker door full force with her fist, causing Neil to jump backwards.

"Fine," she said crawling into the locker. "Five hundred years later and the world is still a joke ...and I'm still the punchline."

"Don't worry, Miss Petra," Neil reassured her. "I'll be back as soon as I can. Then we'll figure out how to get you to the pod."

"Ah yes, the 'pod'. Can't wait ..."

"Neil carefully closed the locker door behind her."

"One last thing there, Elvis," she shouted through door.

"Yes?"

"Just this. If you don't come back for me ...whatever the reason ...I will get out of here and I will find you and you will die an old fashioned 21st century death ...You got that."

"Yes. I've got that, Miss Petra. Completely got that. And I will be back for you."

*****

The Hozpit trauma team had never seen such a puncture wound before. But they did correctly surmise that the extent of soft tissue and organ injury suffered by CH3 O'Reilly had been limited due to the projectile having lodged itself in the central core unit of the L.U.L.U. The primary issue for their patient was extensive blood loss. "Notably" they wrote in their report, "the initial first aid measures taken by the retrieval transport-tech, had clearly saved the CH3's life."

The treatment plan, upon which the medical team agreed, was as follows ...

- *Complete restoration of healthy blood levels*
- *Full repair/ replacement of malfunctioning LULU core hardware*
- *A mental health evaluation with selective – phased - magnetic intervention as might be required to preclude any PTSD symptoms*

- *A mandatory three-month interim rest period,
  post discharge*
- *Bi-monthly routine follow-up visits until a full-
  healing declaration could be officially proclaimed*

Providing the patient responded to treatment as
anticipated, his Hozpit stay was scheduled to be no more
than fourteen additional days.

Neil was first interviewed by the Hozpit staff to gather any
medical related information they deemed helpful. He was
then intensely interviewed by TS12 detective, Grācius Filn
of the **B**ureau of **D**angerous **A**nomalies. Like all BDA
agents he had arrived wearing black pants, black leather
half-coat, string tie, and a bowler hat. The detective's
primary concern being that, for the first time in 75 years,
a Cliff-Hunter had returned from a mission with serious
injuries. And for the first time *ever,* a CH had done so
with life-threatening injuries, and quite possibly
unconscious.

"Does that make sense to you, Neil Presley, ...I mean *at
all?* How exactly does a Cliff-Hunter, who is unconscious
and losing significant amounts of blood, manage to stand
himself upright in a circle-site, engage a back-up Ziter-
1000 program, and return to Homeland at his scheduled
arrival time? How, Neil? How could he do that?"

Neil, though nervous and agitated, and having never been
interrogated by any investigative arm of Homeland, did
his best to portray composure and present a convincing
look of bewilderment.

"Gosh, officer, that's exactly what I've been wondering. I mean, when I saw him come through the portal all weak and bleeding, I thought ...how is he even staying on his feet?"

"So, he *was* upright when he arrived in the retrieval chamber?"

Neil hesitated ever so slightly. "Yes sir. He was ...he was wobbly, but upright."

"And nothing and no one was supporting him?"

"No sir," said Neil with sincerity, "nothing and no one."

Detective Filn did not look totally convinced. In fact, he looked very skeptical indeed. But after asking the same question multiple ways, and having received the same answer, he released Neil from further interrogation ...at least for the time being.

A full four hours had passed since Neil had placed Petra into his locker. Arriving back in the facility, he now dreaded the confrontation that would follow. Lightly tapping on the locker door, he inquired softly.

"Petra, it's Neil. ...Neil Presley. You ok in there?"

But when there was no response from inside the locker, Neil grew concerned.

Raising his voice, he said "Petra ...It's Neil Presley. Are you ok? I'm going to open the door now. So, hold on. Here we go."

Then lifting the latch, he tried to slowly ease the door open. But his efforts were abruptly interrupted by the full weight of his stowaway crashing through the locker door and falling limply into his arms. Neil was overcome by the suddenness of the event ...not to mention that he had never held another human in his arms, let alone a living warm female.

Carefully placing her on her side on the floor, he raced to retrieve the parka he had stowed earlier in the room's furthest corner. Then wrapping her carefully into the parka, he began to rub her hands, and gently slap her face. A few minutes later, she stirred, but only slightly. First one eye and then the other slowly opened.

"I need food ...sweets ...I need something sweet!"

Neil knelt over her, transfixed, unsure how to carry out her instructions.

"My bag," she said. "My bag ...candy bar ...my bag."

Jumping to his feet, Neil ran to the control room, where he quickly located the crossbody bag that the resolution unit had confiscated. Then darting back to the locker room, dropped down beside Petra. Fumbling through the worn surplus pouch, he felt around for the life-saving food she had requested. His hands touched a comb; a pack of Kleenex; a tube of sun protection; a packet of condoms, and a weighty metal object he could not identify. Finally, his fingers contacted a rectangular object in a waxy paper wrapper. He pulled it from the pouch and read its large yellow lettering ...

"Snackers...The Perfect Chocolate Treat".

178

Tearing off the wrapper, Neil's hand shook as he held the sugar delivery system up to her mouth.

Petra could, at first, barely nibble at the bar, her body having lost all strength. But slowly and with much effort she fought her way back. Within five minutes, she had regained enough strength to take the bar from Neil and to begin feeding herself. Within ten minutes, she was sitting up. And a short time later, with more help from Neil, she was standing on her own.

"Are you ok now?" Neil asked with genuine concern.

Still weak, but smiling her familiar defiant smile, Petra peeked out from the oversized parka in which she was still wrapped.

 "Fuck you, Elvis ..." she said. Then pausing for a moment, she added "and also ...thanks for saving my ass."

Looking down and away from her gaze, Neil's cheeks flushed bright red.

"Sure," he mumbled to the floor tiles. "Sure."

The Perils of Domestic Life
(A Boy, A Girl, A Manufactured Parrot)

Petra arrived at Neil's pod still wrapped in his oversized parka. She was grateful to be alive and that her fellow traveler through time was safe and recovering at a medical facility. What she was not grateful for was that she had no choice, at least for the moment, but to hide out in the extremely modest digs of transport-tech Neil Presley.

"Where's the rest of it?" she asked Neil as she crossed the threshold.

"The rest of it?"

"Yeah. The rest. Not that this isn't a lovely little closet, but come on, Neil ...Please tell me you don't live here fulltime, year-round, 365."

"Why would I tell you that?" he asked earnestly. "I mean, I *do* live here year-round ...I've lived here for more than twenty years."

"Jesus! I always thought the future would be a perfect place ...everybody fat and warm and happy ...kind of glowing like they lived in heaven. But this ...this place is actually smaller than the one room toilet I live in."

"Sorry you feel that way. Sorry it isn't bigger. But it isn't the smallest pod on the island either. Mine is a little bigger than most because I work as a transport-tech. It's kind of a perc that comes with the job."

"Yeah," said a skeptical Petra. "That's what they told you, isn't it?"

Neil tried to change the subject.

"Let me take the coat, Miss Petra."

And as his guest peeled off her bulky grey covering, Neil reached down and pulled up a thin poly-grate square in the floor. Then taking the damp clothing from his guest, he placed it carefully in the heated bin beneath them.

"It'll dry out pretty fast in there," he observed.

But Petra wasn't listening. She was already standing in the center of the pod slowly taking in everything within it.

"What's that?" she asked.

"That," said the pod's proud resident, "is a container of the best tasting cookies there could ever be."

"Oh yeah? What kind of cookies?"

Neil looked confused.

"What do you mean?"

"I mean what kind? Are they sugar cookies? Chocolate chip? Oatmeal raisin? Jesus, Elvis, there must be a thousand different kind of cookies. Didn't your mother ever tell you that?"

Neil looked particularly stung.

"No," he said softly, "she never did. And as far as I know, there is only one kind of cookie a person can make …and that's what these are."

Petra could see that she had hit a nerve. And for the first time, in a very long while, she felt a twinge of what passed for empathy.

"So, what kind of future-cookies are they then?" she asked.

Neil's demeanor lightened slightly.

"Those," he said, "are cocoa-sim-oil cookies. Would you like one? …Lots of vitamin D."

Petra smiled and wrinkled her nose at the same time.

"Thanks. But, I'm gonna pass."

In the half-hour that followed, Petra examined every article and item under Neil's roof. Kind, and impressively patient, he answered every one of her many questions as she pointed at the various objects.

"That's a health-patch monitor. That's a lock defroster. A mood-booster scan light. A cough-stopper collar. A sound-negator."

And what exactly would someone use a sound-negator for?" asked Petra. "Seems to me it's damn quiet in here already …like a tomb with lighting."

"Well," said Neil thoughtfully, "that's true enough …the part about it being quiet in here right now. But sometimes, when one of the big storms set in, the winds can howl for days. That's when it sounds like there's a wild animal outside your door trying to get in. Makes it hard to sleep."

"And that's when you plug in your trusty sound-negator?"

"Yes. That's when I would do that."

"And who's this then?" asked Petra staring at a foot-tall artificial parrot.

"Well," stated Neil smiling, "that is Jerome."

"And what does Jerome do? Is he your room-mate ...sorry ...pod-mate?"

Neil shrugged his shoulders before explaining.

"Jerome? He's a little bit of everything, really. He keeps me company. Answers questions. Remembers things that I forget. Offers suggestions. Corrects me if I get a fact wrong. Sings. Recites. Keeps a history of my life. Oh, and tells jokes."

"But can he dance or core an apple?" asked Petra with a devilish smile.

"No," replied a very serious Neil Presley. Jerome has no locomotion capabilities. He is a stationary resource companion."

Petra tilted her head to one side and looked over at her host.

"Joke, Neil. Joke."

"Oh," he said with sudden awareness. "I get it now. Humor. I'll simply have to take your potential for humorous commentary into consideration in the future."

"Right, pod-man. You do that."

Then stepping closer to Jerome, she asked "How do you get him to talk?"

"You just ask him anything. And sometimes you don't even have to do that. He just volunteer's information."

"Really? Well, let's see what he has to say to his new pal, Petra."

"Hey, Jerome ..."

"I am listening" came a scratchy reply.

Petra smiled over at Neil before continuing.

"Jerome, how old are you and where did you come from?"

"Pardon me, new entity, but before I can reply, I will need permission from Neil Presley, my charge and advocate."

Neil leaned in the direction of the mechanical bird.

"Permission granted, Jerome."

"Granted to which level, Neil?"

"Well, I suppose level 3 of 4, thank you. And, also, the new entity is called 'Petra'."

"Very well. Appreciated times three," said Jerome. A short silence followed, then ...

"To answer your question, Petra ...I was conceived and completed in sub-hangar 26 over 12 years ago."

"Can you be more specific there, Jerome?"

*"Of course. I was completed 12 years, 1 month, 13 days, and **...mark ...** 57 seconds ago."*

Petra smiled. "Nice. And why did they call you Jerome?"

"Not so, Petra. I was, in fact, not named Jerome until I was dispatched and installed here. Neil then chose my name."

"So, did you have a name before that?"

"Yes," replied Jerome. *"I was known among my creators as* ***'Self-Aware Animated Companion Pack 1327TQ'.***"

"Rolls off the tongue," observed Petra.

"I prefer Jerome," replied the parrot, *"by a factor of magnitude"* he added.

Petra suddenly giggled ...something she had not done for a full decade.

"Tell me, Jerome."

"Yes?"

"Is there anything that you can tell me about me? ...Something I might not even know."

"Yes," said Jerome. *"I can do that. Do you wish for me to tell you now?"*

185

"Well, duh!" said Petra. "Yes, now."

"I cannot tell you a lot about yourself, not yet. But I can give you my salient first impression."

"Well Jesus! Ok. Just do it. Spill the beans wouldja!"

There was another short silence followed by a staccato, matter-of-fact tone that Jerome utilized when delivering straight forward information. He believed it helped his listeners distinguish fact-based observations from mere speculation.

"You are, in both speech and demeanor, quite rude and disrespectful to Neil Presley, your host."

Neil rolled his eyes and looked upward, as though looking for an escape hatch.

"Sometimes he says too much," he observed.

"Your parrot's a fucking jerk" said Petra as she backed away from it."

"That," observed Jerome *"is factually incorrect."*

When Fishing' In the Deep, Deep Waters
of Who Knows Where

BDA agent, Grācius Filn, defying the request of the ward-nurse, was now sitting at the bottom of the patient's bed as he stirred and looked around.

"Hello there, princess," said Filn with a smarmy smile. "Looks like you're back from the dead."

"Yeah," grunted a still groggy Ramon O'Reilly.

"Well let me get right to it, Cliff-Hunter. How exactly did you get your ass from _way back there_ to _way up here_ ...your being all shot-up and unconscious and all?"

O'Reilly did his best to clear his head of the spiders and webs still clinging to it. Carefully picking up a glass of warm water from the nightstand near his bed, he finished it off without stopping. Then, just as carefully, he placed the glass back on the stand.

"I'm sorry," he said. "And you are who?"

"I," said his fierce looking visitor, "am BDA agent Grācius Filn. And I am here to further explore the circumstances of your recent arrival back here in our homeland."

"Oh," said O'Reilly "That's a relief! I thought maybe I'd died after all, and you were the guy they sent to bury me."

Filn was not amused.

"Not a joking matter, CH3 O'Reilly. There are questions. Lots of questions. Questions you need to answer. Comprende?"

With great effort, O'Reilly pulled himself up onto his elbows.

"Yes. Yes, I do. I 'comprende' all over the place. And I would be glad to answer your questions another time ...sometime when I'm out of pain and maybe even rested."

"No. I don't think so. I've got questions that need answers now. And you've got those answers. So, I suggest we get started. Not tomorrow or the next day. Now!"

O'Reilly smiled generously. Then reaching over with his right hand, he tapped the nursing call-dot on his left wrist three times.

A few seconds later a very large, frowning nurse, named Veldora, appeared bedside.

"The pain is back," said O'Reilly wincing with conviction. "And this gentleman here wants to keep on asking me questions. It just seems too hard, nurse. Too hard."

"I'm going to have to ask you to leave, sir," said Veldora without looking at the agent.

"I can't leave yet," insisted agent Filn. "This man still has not answered my questions."

This time Veldora turned to face him full on.

"Well, you need to listen up. While this brave Cliff-Hunter is here in this facility, he is due the courtesy due every member of his profession ...Not to mention that, per protocol *med-reg 112-46A*, a patient's physical care and well-being takes precedent over any other governmental requirement ...until such time as he has recovered sufficiently to be discharged. So, if you would be so kind as to leave my patient's room, I would appreciate it very much."

"But ..." began Filn.

"'But' nothing. Just leave, and I mean right now!"

An angry, disgruntled agent Filn placed the small recording utility he had been holding back into the pocket of his black overcoat. Standing up, he walked slowly to the door. Then turning toward O'Reilly, he simply said, "It's coming for you, Cliff-Hunter. It's coming."

O'Reilly eased himself back down into his bedsheets.

"Catch you later, sheriff," he said under his breath. Then before drifting off beneath the dreamy-soft blanket of his new meds, he added "Thank you, nurse Veldora."

What O'Reilly dreamed next was not like anything he had ever dreamed before.

> He was standing in a wide meadow, surrounded on three sides by carefully constructed stone walls. When he tried to locate the top of the walls, they seemed to disappear into the grey clouds overhead. At first despondent and worried, he looked over to notice that there was no wall on the fourth side of the field ...Relieved, he picked up a large grandfather clock, and walked clumsily toward the

open space ...As he neared the edge of the field, images beyond it began to come into focus ...He could see roads and paths leading off in all directions and, in the distance, the flash of cannons beneath a group of rugged mountains ...Overhead, a large black bird circled and squawked ...Convinced that the narrowest of the roads might lead him to the mountains, he now began his long trek along it ...The stark road proved void of sound or life ...Finally, after walking many miles, he began to make out the silhouette of a woman walking toward him. Wrapped in brightly colored rags, she moved steadily in his direction. Freezing in place, he waited patiently for her to arrive ...But as she approached him, she did not slow down or stop ...Instead, the young woman simply slipped silently on passed him ...Shaken and disappointed, he called after her ...

"Wait! Where are you going? Where are you from?"

"I am from the caves among the mountains," she replied ...

"But where are you going?"

"I am going to the three walls ...Going there to tear them down. If you wish, you can come with me this time. And there is good news. Your ancient clock will not be needed there."

190

"And how do you know you're even on the right path?"

"I know" she said with unguarded arrogance, *"because **you** are on it."*

Only half-awake, O'Reilly could feel that his bed clothes were wet with sweat, his heart racing with an unnamed anxiety. In that moment, a vision of a petite young woman flashed before his eyes. She was standing defiantly in the middle of a burned-out structure, a proud look of defiance upon her face.

"I am not Judy and I am not Petra," the young woman said. *"But you already know that, don't you?"* she laughed. *Then r*eaching out and touching his arm gently, she simply said *"Adios, dearest Ramon."*

Fully awake now, and hoping to switch off the picture, O'Reilly closed his eyes tightly. And when that did not work ...when a feisty one hundred-and-twelve-pound female refused to disappear ...he reached over calmly and pressed the call-dot again. A few moments later the door to his Hozpit room slid quietly open, its frame filled with the massive presence of his guardian angel.

"Trouble sleeping, sweetie?" asked Veldora.

...And Occasionally a Revelation

Although she would never have admitted it, Petra was
more than a little impressed with all that she saw around
her ...a thriving future world carved from frigid
mountains, its efficient life-pods gouged from frozen soil
...manmade parrots that could carry on a philosophical
discussion about life and death, or simply remind you
where you last placed your favorite socks.

 But, as impressive as such technical accomplishments
were, even more impressive to her was the way in which
her host treated her day to day. It was behavior unlike
that of any man she had ever met. And for the first time in
her many unhappy encounters with the opposite sex, she
felt safe in the presence of a man, comfortable enough to
fall asleep without a sharp object in her hand. Her feelings
toward this unfamiliar kind of man alternated daily
between pity and admiration, and she seemed uncertain
just how to respond to him. Was he weak and nonsensical
or gentle, kind, and admirable? And just how _does_ a
woman respond to a man who has lived his entire life in
such a protected, even cloistered, way? She marveled at
his total lack of experience with females and his
discomfort in her presence. It was impossible to overlook.
And though she was quite aware of the power this gave
her over him, to her credit and surprise, she did not wield
it against him. Instead, she found her speech and
demeanor slightly moderating for the first time in her
adult life. And as the days passed, the way in which she
spoke to him began to slowly change, until she found
herself displaying a few of the behaviors that she would

have previously ascribed to one of those "gooey women who want to darn your socks and lick your face".

"What's happening to me?" she would occasionally ask the pod's resident counselor.

"You do seem troubled," Jerome would reply.

And every morning, when Neil had left the pod for his workday, she would turn to Jerome with a pithy observation.

"He's really only twelve isn't he." ...or ... "What a naïve bumpkin." ...or ... "Nobody could possibly be that innocent."

Jerome's reply was always the same, an avid defense of the human for whom he had been programmed to admire, advise and protect.

"A truly admirable man is citizen Neil Presley."

******

One full week after moving into Neil's pod, which Petra insisted on calling "the apodment", the couple sat facing each other across a tiny pop-up eating flat. Neil had just placed a toasted slice of protein *go-bread* on her plate and had filled up their hand-carved wooden cups with artificial coffee.

Petra leaned slightly forward on her pop-up stool.

"Can I ask you something, Elvis?"

"Yes," said Neil as he carefully sipped the hot brew, "of course."

"Well, just this ..." She gathered her thoughts." What do you think of your life here?"

"What do you mean?"

"I mean what do you think about living in such a cold place without neighbors or ...visitors of any kind? Because, since I've been here, I haven't heard you mention anyone, except maybe Ramon O'Reilly. You don't seem to have any friends or acquaintances and you don't go anywhere or do anything except work, eat, and sleep."

"So ...?"

"So, how do you feel about that? I mean, don't you ever get lonely or want to do something interesting? Don't you ever want to go someplace or try something new? How exactly do you put up with all that sameness every single day?"

Neil placed his cup of coffee down on the food-flat. He looked genuinely troubled, as though he were wrestling with a decision of some importance.

"I ...I don't think it would be helpful to talk about it," he said.

"You don't? But why not? Don't you ever think about those things? Don't you ever wonder about any other kind of life?"

Neil shook his head slowly side to side. "It's probably better if I just keep my thoughts to myself."

"Oh, come on now. Loosen up willya... I'm not gonna tell anyone what's really going on inside your head."

"I know," said Neil "but ..."

"Oh, never mind 'but'. Look, let's ask Jerome what he thinks."

Then turning in the direction of the parrot, Petra asked "Jerome, should Neil share with me his thoughts about his life here in friggin' Frostland III?"

There was a momentary silence before Jerome responded.

"Neil," he said finally, *"may I reply to this question which is of a personal nature?"*

Neil cleared his throat, looking more than a little uncomfortable.

"Well, of course, Jerome. Feel free."

"Confirmed," said Jerome. *"My reply is simply this, Miss Petra. If Jerome chooses not to share his most private thoughts with you, it may be that he is concerned about what you would think of him ...and that you would judge him to be a foolish or unwise man. He may also have some concerns that his sharing any unsanctioned thoughts with you could possibly place you in harm's way."*

"Oh," said Petra somewhat taken back by the specifics of the reply. "I see. So, Neil ...is Jerome right about all that?"

Neil looked up from his coffee cup to make rare direct eye contact with his guest.

"Well yes, Miss Petra, much of what Jerome says is truth based. There really is no reason why you should get in

195

trouble for something that I might be thinking. I mean, things are already hard enough for you here and ..."

Petra reached across the small table and touched his hand.

"That's sweet, Elvis," she said. "You're looking out for me. But really, you need to know ...I can handle myself just fine. In fact, I am the least helpless woman you're ever gonna meet."

Neil looked down at Petra's hand still lingering on his. It was an exciting and terrifying sight, one that caused his hand and forearm to feel numb and disconnected from the rest of his body.

Petra smiled while trying to reassure him.

"It's ok, Elvis. You're not going to die from a woman's touch. You'll be fine."

"Angels and saints," Neil mumbled beneath his breath.

"What?" asked Petra.

A flustered Neil Presley looked up. "That's one out of three" he said.

"One out of three what?"

"Wishes," said Neil softly.

"Wishes? One out of three wishes? What? You wished that someone would touch your hand?"

"A woman," he said as his voice trailed off.

"OK then …Well there you are. One wish down. So, what are the other two?"

Neil's level of discomfort began to climb once again.

"Well," he said slowly, "one of them is to walk through warm grass in my bare feet."

"Wow! Great! How 'bout that! That one's gonna be kinda tough though …it being minus a gazillion degrees outside. And the third one?"

"The third one?"

"Yeah. What's the third wish?"

Neil looked first at his toast and then at his coffee cup, "to taste real chocolate."

"Really. That's it? That's all you want?"

"Yes," Neil replied, "to taste real chocolate. I've heard Cliff-Hunters talk about it and it just sounds truly amazing."

"Elvis," said Petra, in a rare moment of compassion, "you're breakin' my heart, man."

His discomfort now nearly unbearable, Neil addressed his guardian parrot.

"Jerome, could you sing us a song please?"

"Yes, Neil, I am most certainly able to do that. However, may I also suggest that, during this evening, you confide in Miss Petra some of the recent projects on which you

*have been working. I present this suggestion for the
following two reasons.*

1. *I have appraised Miss Petra and have determined
   that she is both a trustworthy and loyal
   acquaintance.*
2. *Also, I believe it would be emotionally healthy for
   you to share with, at least one other human
   being, what you have been contemplating and
   worrying about over the recent period of 5
   years."*

Neil's gaze returned to Petra. She was smiling widely.

"OK, Elvis," she said, "Jerome said it, not me ...so spill!"

Over the next two hours Petra listened as Neil provided
her with a brief history of his life and the significant
events that had started with CH3 O'Reilly's planned final
journey back in time. He explained how, as a young man
he had enjoyed some celebrity as the "last child conceived
by the union of a man and woman". And as he shared his
story, and the recent changes that had begun to take place
in his life, he became increasingly animated.

"And that," he exclaimed "is when I found the four sacred
books. That is when I discovered William Shakespeare.
That was the very moment I began to understand more
about the world, and my place in it, than had ever been
explained to me."

Occasionally, Petra would interrupt to ask Neil for
clarification on one of his statements.

"So, you've been reading these same four books over and over for five years?"

"Yes," replied Neil, "I surely have."

"And so now you've come to believe in God and in self-expression and in taking chances? Is that what I'm hearing? Do I have that right?"

"Yes, but not taking just *any* chances …just those chances that might be called for if circumstances demand it …if progress of the heart is to be honored."

"You mean taking a chance like …oh, I don't know …hiding a stowaway in your locker or smuggling that stowaway back to your apodment. That kind of chance?"

Neil flushed for the ten thousandth time since Petra's arrival.

"Yeah …like that."

Aware now of her host's pre-occupation with his four specific books; his complete fascination with the works of Shakespeare, and his naïve understanding of the world, Petra was smiling when she said…" Elvis, you're my favorite nice guy and Bardolater.

******

Later that same night, by the light of his thermal-glow-ring, Neil recorded the following poetic summary of his momentous evening. It was a poem that later followers would faithfully record in the sacred *Book of Neil*.

How to Cook a Frozen Heart
By: Neil Presley
(The Book of Neil: chapter 2 verse 12)

Take a little fear
Add a little hope
Stir in a little courage
Untie a little rope
Turn up the heat of strangers
In a fragile bowl of kind
Prepare with all your fingers crossed
While ignoring doubters blind

...Serve and enjoy

"Beyond This Portal...Good Things Happen"

O'Reilly was only mildly surprised when nurse Veldora informed him he would be leaving Hozpit care a full week early. From the start he had suspected the scheduled LULU software upgrade procedure might not happen. He was, after all, a Cliff-Hunter who had been on the very cusp of involuntary retirement for some time and was now under scrutiny for returning from a time mission under extremely suspicious circumstances. And the recent visit from Grācius Filn had confirmed to him that his future movements would be carefully monitored once he left the Hozpit. It was just a fact of life in Tibetland III ...the authorities were constantly on the alert for any exception to standard patterns of behavior. It would only be a matter of time now, until they discovered the truth of the matter ...and took him into custody.

Veldora smiled, believing she was bringing him good news.

"Tomorrow morning at 0700 you will be officially released from medical oversight. That Mr. Filn has officially requested a meeting with you before you leave the facility. He said it would be a routine matter."

"Well, I certainly appreciate all that good news," said O'Reilly. "But I wonder if you happen to know where we stand on my LULU upgrade."

"Oh that ...yes ...well ...During your several surgeries, the doctors did install the latest LULU hardware ...a much more robust version, they tell me."

"And the LULU software?"

"Well, I understand that has been postponed to sometime in the future."

"So, the software won't be downloaded during my stay."

"No. Not at this time. But I'm sure it will be provided to you within the next month or so. They're probably just waiting for you to heal up 100% ...so as not to cause you any additional stress. I'm sure they're just looking out for you, being overly cautious."

O'Reilly nodded as if agreeing, but his mind was already spinning full speed as he struggled to understand the implications of these latest developments. He knew for a fact that it was not standard procedure to install LULU hardware without simultaneously installing and testing its software ...usually within twenty-four hours. He also knew that it was highly unusual for a member of the feared BDA to be included in a patient's discharge planning. And finally, to have his medical stay shortened by a full week could only mean that someone had overruled the doctors. Someone upstairs was more concerned in getting answers than they were about his full recovery. They wanted specific information, and they wanted it now. They wanted to know just how it was that a Cliff-Hunter had managed to complete his mission and navigate his way home while unconscious and with his primary beacon-locator disabled.

If there was one thing that O'Reilly had learned from his numerous missions spanning several centuries, it was the skilled art of *escape and evasion.* More than once he had been forced to outwit suspicious local authorities or escape angry townspeople. More than once, he had had to use creative methods or the small powerful tool (the coin shaped "melter" he carried in his belt buckle), to find his way to safety and eventually back to Tibetland III. And now, it looked as though the time had come for him to utilize those same skills, though smack in the middle of his own homeland. Giving himself a short pep talk, he closed his eyes and recited the short poem he had created for himself years ago.

> "You know what to do
> To see this thing through
> Be one of the bold
> Be one of the few"

This he repeated seven times slowly. Then taking a drawn-out breath, he patiently waited for the best moment to initiate his plan.

At precisely 0015 hours he slipped quietly from his bed. The nursing staff had just completed their midnight rounds in which patient vitals were recorded. Unless one of the patients now rang for assistance, it would be another 2 hours and 45 minutes before they returned for their follow-ups.

Thinly cracking open the door to his room, he could see three nurses at their station far down the hall. His first impulse was to dart across the narrow hallway to the stairwell near his room. But he knew that rapid movement was what the human eye had evolved detecting. For purposes of raw-survival, the species had had to identify distant threats before they became close-up threats. So, biding his time, he waited until all three nurses were facing away from his room before slowly strolling across the hallway.

Still shaky from his recent lack of movement, he held on to the stairwell railing as he descended to the floor below. "This is not the time" he lectured himself, "to lose your balance and tumble down these hard, angular steps". As on all Hozpit floors, the one beneath his maintained an unlocked soiled laundry room. It was far from the patient pods and the nurse's station and was where the medical staff would deposit the uniforms and protective gear they had worn during their shift. The intent was to minimize any contact between their contaminated clothing and their patients, staff, and visitors. O'Reilly once again waited for the precise moment when nursing would be pre-occupied, and the hallway empty. When that moment finally arrived, he made his way along one of the white-washed walls and into the room. Quickly rifling through a mountain of discarded clothing, he found a grey-green uniform he had seen the physical therapy staff wear. Though slightly large for his frame, he pulled the two-piece pants and shirt on over his short hospital gown. Finding no shoes, he pulled on four sets of the adult booties he had seen the surgical teams wear. Finding a nearly pristine face mask, he tied it around his neck. Fully clothed now, he made his way back into the stairwell.

Thirty seconds later he was standing in the small lobby of the building. Casually scanning the area for something warmer than the light uniform he had "liberated", he located a thickly insulated "loaner" parka hanging near the front entrance. Placed there for use by emergency personnel who might have to temporarily venture into the cold outdoors to assist incoming patients, it had been designed to ward off even the most frigid of temperatures.

O'Reilly slipped into the parka, flipping its insulated hood up over his head. And as he exited the Hozpit main entrance, he looked up and read the carved platitude overhead.

"Beyond This Portal...Good Things Happen"

Busy Bees in Boots and Gloves and Those Who Sell It from Above

With every day that passed, Petra found herself feeling less threatened by her surroundings and more than a little grateful for her socially impaired pod-mate, Neil Presley. She had even grown somewhat fond of his outspoken artificial parrot, Jerome. This, despite its uncanny knack for accurately depicting her character and mindset. However, with every passing day she also found herself increasingly baffled by the world around her and confused how such a strange land and culture had come to be.

"Pardon my ignorance, Elvis, but I just don't get it. How is it possible that so many people live here on this god forsaken glacier? How did they build the homes they live in? Where do they get the food they eat? I mean seriously, Elvis …What the hell?!"

"Well," her host explained, "to begin with, Tibetland III is not built on a glacier. It is built on solid ground, solid frozen ground."

"OK. Fair enough. But what about all the rest? How exactly did you build everything I saw when you brought me over here? I mean, I saw buildings and see through domes and …not to mention that friggin' underground ski lift thing we rode here on. Come on, man. You gotta help me out here. How exactly did all this come about?"

Neil hesitated briefly before speaking up.

"You have questions, a lot of questions. And while I have *some* answers, I think you need to hear the story of our beginnings from a better source than me."

Then turning toward Jerome, Neil asked politely. "Jerome, would you be so kind as to provide Miss Petra with Homeland's standard 'History of Tibetland III' package and answer any questions she might have?"

"That," said Jerome *"is no problem at all. And, tell me, Neil, is now an appropriate time to begin?"*

Neil glanced over at Petra who nodded.

"Yes," said Neil. "Please begin."

"Well, Miss Petra, perhaps you would like to take a seat at this time, as this presentation will continue for a total of six minutes and thirty-seven seconds."

"Thank you, Jerome," replied Petra. Then lowering herself onto one of the pod's heated grates, she sat cross-legged, upright, and expectant ...much like a girl scout experiencing her first campfire.

Jerome's voice was suddenly very matter-of-fact, not unlike a news broadcaster delivering the day's stories.

"I would first like to summarize my method in delivering specific portions of our nation's history in the manner to follow. First, I will report the information as the neutral third party I am. Next, I will make no attempt to include all events, but will limit my verbal report to the salient moments of progress that took place when the founders of Tibetland III first arrived. Finally, I will make no interpretations of the founder's personal motives other than to state what may be the commonly obvious.
... I now begin.

- *Ship Noah Grande arrived in the newly formed mountain harbor we see below us as the waters of our world were rising. (This was even before our planet's deep earth supply of Brucite inexplicably released its stored water...the equivalent of all the oceans of the world ...three times over)*

"Whoa! Whoa! Whoa! shouted Petra, "Just what the hell's 'Broo-Site' and what's that got to do with rising water?"

"Briefly," replied an unperturbed Jerome, *"Brucite is the mineral form of magnesium hydroxide. As such it consists of 50% water. Sometime after the world's all-out nuclear exchange, and many miles beneath the Earth's surface, enormous amounts of this mineral began to release their entire store of H2O. Some ascribe this anomaly to powerful sonic vibrations that repeatedly resonated through the Earth's core as thousands of surface explosions took place. Others are unsure. Whatever the cause, the outcome was beyond any scientific expectation. The ability of Brucite to maintain its original mineral structure was compromised. The result was the release of incredible amounts of stored water. The additional water, roughly equivalent to three times all surface oceans then on the planet, flowed upward to the earth's surface. This event could not have come at a less opportune time for mankind. Existing oceans, already rising from the rapid melting of massive ice sheets, now grew deep enough to cover all but a handful of earth's highest peaks. Only twelve such island peaks proved tall enough to prevail. These were all within 100 miles of this mountain, Tibetland III being the tallest of these."*

Jerome hesitated ..." Any follow-up questions, guest Petra?"

"Yeah," she replied, looking a bit rattled, "What do you mean *'were'* within a hundred miles?"

"Unfortunately," said Jerome, with a touch of appropriate sadness in his voice, *"all surviving islands were of a lower altitude than Tibetland III. Consequently, they were eventually flooded with much loss of life."*

"So, why didn't those people just come *here* ...to *this* island?"

"Well," replied Jerome. *...it was determined by then Judge Supreme, Johann Nordvig, that additional citizenship could not be accepted on Tibetland III, as full crop and artificial diet enhancement projects could not sustain Homeland's existing population and the strain caused by additional refugees. Former members of the judiciary publicly disagreed, arguing that the actual reason these foreign elements were being rejected was due primarily to the Judge's personal belief that they were genetically inferior and would, therefore, dilute the purer blood line of TB3*

"So, what happened to everyone on those islands then. They just drowned?"

"Yes," Jerome said. *"Drowning and hypothermia accounted for most deaths ...and, not surprisingly, there were a number of suicides as well."*

Petra was silent for a few moments as she first tried to visualize the event, and then tried just as hard to un-see the horror of it all.

Jerome, having waited a respectful sixty seconds, asked *"Would you like me to continue with a brief history of this island's settlement?"*

"Yeah ...sure," stammered Petra.

"Well ...let's see," Jerome began *"...suppose we pick-up the report here ..."*

The tone of his verbal delivery once again became flatly informational.

- *Next, previously drawn blueprints intended to create a livable dry land presence were reviewed, modified, and finally acted on under the supervision of the gifted planners onboard Noah Grandé*

- *All passengers and crew members were screened for abilities and then provided with a specific job description and responsibility. No exceptions were permitted*

- *It was determined that all living-facilities, as well as core support pods (crop solariums and workshops) would be located as high up on the mountain as possible, as the depth to which earth's waters would rise was still an unknown*

- *To accomplish this formidable task, a series of pully systems, terraces, and stairs had to first be constructed. This then allowed for the incremental transfer of resources and equipment off the ship and far up the mountain side*

- *Within 300 meters of the mountains peak, a flat area of 20 square hectares was blasted way and then leveled by hand from the frigid and stony landscape*

- *Robust polymer buildings of an igloo shape were assembled from prefab components and then heated utilizing oil stores from the converted freighter. (Note: Oil was eventually replaced by solar and wind power)*

- *Onboard, all milling, molding and machining equipment were then disassembled and carefully moved up to these newly constructed buildings*

- *These important facilities were then utilized to create all future sub-terra pods, the Gopher transport system, and the impressive Founder's Hall Overlook higher up the mountainside*

- *All tools and machinery needed for this massive undertaking were designed, created, and repaired in these vital workshops as required*

- *During the twenty-seven years of basic on-land construction, living facilities were inhabited as they were completed. Unhoused personnel returned daily to the ship for life-sustaining food, shelter, medical needs, sleep, and encouragement*

- *In the twenty-eighth year of the project, all remaining ship's passengers were moved permanently to the sub-terra pods and on-shore facilities that had been constructed*

- *In the decades and centuries that followed, additional landscape was gauged, cleared and flattened to allow for an extensive solar-pod farm where crops could be grown beneath protective plexi-shield domes*

- *Additional sub-terra pods and a medical facility were constructed as the population increased*

- *Eventually, it became necessary to limit the number of births to a simple replacement level*

- *Eventually, intercourse between male and female citizens was discouraged. And when that declaration failed to meet stated Council objectives, it was forbidden*

"No sex?" interrupted Petra. "Nobody was allowed to have sex?"

"*That is correct,*" stated Jerome, "*no sex permitted between citizens.*" Then once again, he returned to his history lecture.

To address the population's primal sexual drives, or "id-power" as it came to be known, several important steps were taken. Id-power was...

- *carefully redirected into public projects*
- *appeased through the timely pod visitations of basic robotic arousal units*
- *discouraged through public information programs*

(Note: Current effective sexual drive inhibiting rate, SDIR, is estimated to be 87.3% effective and is considered a success)

- *Citizen reproduction is managed and accomplished through the artificial insemination of mother-clan female volunteers who number no more than fifty at any given time, and retire with housing, food, and clothing benefits when approximately thirty-seven years of age.*

"This concludes a brief history of the initial construction and habitation of Tibetland III. It has been a pleasant experience to educate you in this way, guest Petra. Any additional questions you may have will be answered to the best of my stored and programmed abilities."

"Questions?" blurted Petra. "Yeah, I've got questions. Let's start with who *exactly* runs this place? What *exactly* is the 'Founders Hall Overlook'? Who *exactly* thought up the stupid 'no-sex' rule? What kind of a government do you have here? I mean ...Who makes up all these rules? Who can change the rules? Who enforces all the rules? What happens if you don't follow the rules? Help me out here, Jerome ...how is anyone supposed to live like that? I mean ...Jerome ...What the hell!"

There was a brief silence followcd by Jerome's stunted reply.

"Language please! And it has been a pleasant experience to educate you in this way, guest Petra. This authorized presentation is now ..."

"Stop!" shouted Petra as she then turned her gaze toward her host.

Elvis, why did Mr. Feathers here just blow me off like that? I thought you told him to answer my questions."

"Yes," said Neil, "I did tell him to do that. But then, I didn't realize you would ask him questions he is not permitted to answer."

"So, he's only allowed to answer *some* of my questions?"

"Yes," replied her flustered host. "There are just some topics that are considered inappropriate for public or private discussion. Even speculation on some topics is not permitted."

"Well that's great! I mean your pretend parrot here can answer *any* questions I have, *except* any question that may really matter to the average person. Am I right?"

"Well, no ...not completely."

"Alright, so suppose I ask him how your laws are handled ...who gets punished and for what?"

Neil exhaled forcefully before directing his words to Jerome.

"Jerome, please explain to Miss Petra, as briefly as possible, the justice system of Tibetland III."

"Confirming your request, Neil.

Originally, a five-judge panel of founder-descendants decided all civil and criminal cases. As of one hundred and fifty-five years ago, the Nordvig family, direct descendants of one of Homeland's most distinguished founders, accepted the mantel and ongoing responsibilities of Judge Supreme, thus replacing the archaic and slow process of court justice. Currently, there is no direct capital punishment permitted. Citizens convicted of negligence, conspiracy, treason, sexual inappropriateness, dereliction of duty, malingering, littering with prejudice, contemptuous behavior toward the larger community, or judicial disrespect, are all subject to deportation to the island's Northside. Conviction is final and without appeal.

(Clarification Note: The current one-year survival rate of Northside deportees is estimated to be 61.3 – 62.7%)

Jerome returned to his familiar parrot voice.

"Any additional related requests, Neil?"

"No thanks, Jerome. That was the last one."

"Well, I've got one, pretend parrot."

"Yes?" said Jerome.

"What happens when people die on this icebox? I mean. What do you do with them? Cemeteries? Cremation? What?"

"This question can best be answered by sharing what is public knowledge. And so, with Neil Presley's permission, I shall do that."

"Permission granted," said a weary Neil Presley".

Jerome spoke up immediately.

"There are currently three authorized forms of burial in Tibetland III.

The first is for the common citizen.

This requires that the deceased be wrapped in white gauze and then be shunted down one of a number of 3000-foot vertical shafts drilled into the Northside of the island. When a shaft has been content-maximized, it is capped and retired. Then another such shaft is drilled to replace it. There are currently seven such shafts on the island, three of which are active and available.

The second method is applied to honorably discharged Cliff-Hunters and those citizens with a confirmed history of high scientific achievement or exceptional Homeland contribution.

In this method, the deceased, wearing any clothing of his or her choice, is placed in a pre-natal position within a 5 X 5 block of ice. A verbal honorarium is bestowed upon the cube before slowly and respectfully stacking it onto the Pyramid of Heroes ...also on the islands Northside. This is accomplished through the use of a crane-lift. And, as temperatures never exceed 3 degrees Fahrenheit on this island, ice melt is not a concern. The active pyramid is currently 300 feet high and will eventually be capped at 350 feet. At that time, a second such pyramid will be started.

The third funereal procedure is reserved for only those who are direct descendants of the island's original co-founders.

The body of the deceased is wrapped in fine linens, is carried in a solemn procession by select members of The King's Court to the very highest peak on the island, Mount Ezekiel. Once there, the body remains on display within a plexi-shield case for three days. This is to allow all citizens the opportunity to pay their deepest respects.

On the fourth day, the body is placed on a pyre of wood which has been gleaned from the legendary ship of deliverance, the Noah Grandé. At precisely 00:01 hours, the pyre is ignited so that its bright light might be seen from all corners of the island and beyond. Finally, any remaining pyre ashes are carefully gathered up and placed in stainless steel globes. These globes are then buried on Mount Ezekiel, beneath the frostline, facing South toward the island's harbor. An elite member of the security SSDC is given the honor of guarding these burial sites and the eternal flame that burns there. In rotating shifts of three hours, they guard this sacred area 24-7-365.

In conclusion, said Jerome, and as all citizens agree, we fully recognize and praise the Council of the Co-founders who smile down upon us from the Founders Overlook above. We remain forever grateful for their caring interventions on our behalf and know that all will be well because of their wisdom and our compliance with their many wise decisions.

So be it now ...so be it forever."

Neil looked over at Petra in an effort to gage her reaction to all she'd heard.

"Thoughts?" he asked cautiously.

Petra rolled forward and onto her feet in one motion. Pulling herself up to her full 5'3" height, she returned Neil's puppy-like gaze with a practiced sardonic smile.

"Elvis," she said softly, "I think you already know what I'm going to tell you. I think you've already begun to figure it out ...and probably just from reading those four little books of yours."

216

Neil chewed nervously on his lower lip in anticipation of her words.

"You, my friend ...you and all your fellow citizens ...have been, currently are, and most likely always *will* be, royally fucked!"

Neil cleared his throat and was about to suggest that they retire for the evening, Petra to the single pull-down cot he had awarded her, and he to the largest of the heated floor grates beside it. He was about to explain that they had already stayed up well beyond the standard lights-out/curfew time of 1100-hours. But before he could say anything, a steady soft thumping could be heard from the pod door.

"Jesus God," he said. "Jerome, lights off now!"

But even when the lights had switched off and the pod had gone completely dark, the dull, measured thump of a gloved fist continued to pound against the door.

Three Men, One Woman,
and The Reason Why A Tiger Can't Fly

Neil was very much aware of the penalties associated with lighting up one's pod past the 1100-hour curfew cut-off. He had, in fact, been warned by a night patrol warden eight months earlier, when he had inadvertently lost track of time while reading Shakespeare's *Romeo and Juliette* for the sixth time.

The warden had been quite specific about the consequences of non-compliance with established street-side rules. Neil had been given a small polymer card that listed the consequences of such defiance and was required to always carry it on his person. It read:

*STREET-SIDE PRIVATE LIGHTING
OFFENSE PENALTIES*
Ref: Book 13 – Article 227A-3
(As amended 12.26.2513)

- **First offense penalty:** verbal warning and the loss of one month's pay
- **Second offense penalty:** three month's loss of pay; a six-week citizenship re-education program; publication of offender's name and offense in the *Daily Homeland Progress Report*
- **Third offense penalty:** permanent loss of job and related benefits and immediate transfer to the Northside Settlement

No Exceptions – No Appeal

*****

Neil struggled to see Petra in the darkness but could not.

"Miss Petra," he whispered, "this is bad ...really bad. You can't be found here."

"And what exactly am I supposed to do," she whispered back. "Try to look like a pop-up table?"

"Wait," he said. "How 'bout this ...I'll pull up the heating grate. You crawl in beneath the parka there. Maybe they won't see you."

"Oh yeah ...that'll work. They'll never look in the one place there is to hide."

"Still," said an agitated Neil Presley, "it's all we can do."

"Whatever," said an unhappy Petra.

Neil bent down on one knee and located the hand grip recessed into the grate. Swiveling it upward, he simply said "OK, Go!"

Petra squeezed her small frame down in the rectangular cavity and pulled Neil's parka over her.

"Elvis," she hissed from beneath the coat ...

"Yes?"

"Tibetland III completely sucks."

The muffled pounding on the pod door continued, growing louder still.

"Time to be quiet, Miss Petra. I'm going to open the door now."

"Sure, why not?" came her disgruntled reply.

Neil attempted to calm his breathing and walked to the door.

"I'm coming he said. I'm right here. Coming."

Then turning the latch counter-clockwise, he slid the heavy insulated door to the left. With only a muted street light overhead, Neil struggled to make out the shadowy figure standing before him.

"Read any good books lately?" asked a familiar voice.

Instantly Neil's expression changed from one of trepidation to one of disbelief.

"Sweet Jesus," he muttered. "It's you."

"Roger that," said a shivering Ramon O'Reilly. "And I need to come in, Neil. My feet are freezing."

Before a clearly shaken Neil Presley could respond, his late-night visitor had stepped inside, slid the door closed and latched it securely behind him.

"Seriously, Neil. My feet are freezing. I've only got these damn Hozpit booties on. Where's your main heat grate?"

"Light," Neil said. "We need some light, but not the overhead" he added.

Then reaching in the pocket of his insulated trousers, he produced a small self-charging motion-light. Pointing it in the direction of O'Reilly's voice, he saw once again the face of the Cliff-Hunter he so admired.

"Here," he said handing his new guest the light. The grate is three steps to your right."

Making his way quickly to the grate, O'Reilly sat down in the center of it, removed his wet foot coverings, and began to rub both of his feet back to life.

Still stunned by the sudden and unexpected appearance of his hero, Neil had completely forgotten about the woman unhappily hiding there beneath him.

As the feeling in his feet began to return, O'Reilly looked up and asked the question that had haunted him since he regained consciousness weeks before. Pointing the flashlight in the direction of Neil's last words, he located the very puzzled expression of the man who had helped save his life only weeks before.

"Neil, I've got to know. What happened to Petra? Did she make it? Did they send her off to Northside? Tell me the truth. Is she dead or is she alive?"

Neil began to reply. "Actually ...um ...actually ..."

"Actually!" shouted a hostile female voice, "I am alive! And as per usual, you are sitting on my face!"

"Petra! Judy!" exclaimed O'Reilly as he leaped to his feet. "What the hell? I mean ...what the hell!"

"Get me out of here now!" she shouted. "Get me out of here so I can kick *both* your asses!"

Neil rushed over to the grate. Lifting it up, he removed the heavy parka that lay over his angry stowaway.

Having regained his composure, O'Reilly now leaned forward and offered Petra his hand. Grasping it firmly, Petra pushed as he pulled her to a standing position.

Shining the light on her face now, he was pleasantly reminded just how attractive this 21st century woman was. Even angry, maybe especially when angry, she emitted a fierce sensual energy that demanded appreciation.

"Your hair is brown now," he said to her.

"Yeah, Bowtie. I know. I'm the one that washed the damn colors out. Now get that flashlight out of my eyes or I'll feed it to you."

Pointing the light toward the floor he couldn't resist.

"Well, I see your stay in our homeland has continued to mellow you even more."

Petra stepped out of the grate without answering.

O'Reilly continued. "So, tell me, Judy ..."

"Judy?" asked Neil

"Ignore him!" said Petra.

"So, tell me, Judy, how did you manage to make your way here undetected. How'd you get passed the monitoring cams? How'd you ..."

"Long story," interrupted Petra. Then turning toward Neil she simply said. "Try to shove me in just one more closed coffin and I'll personally see that you need one! Got it, Elvis?"

Neil responded by retreating two steps. "Well, yes, Miss Petra. I got it ...I mean, I get it. No more closed spaces."

"Bingo!"

"Don't let her worry you," said O'Reilly. "She only kills those she really cares about."

He was about to suggest Neil brew up some hot coffee and he be brought up to speed on recent events. He never got the chance, as a sudden sharp tapping at the pod door now filled up the small compartment.

O'Reilly switched off the flashlight.

"You expecting company, Neil?"

"No," Neil whispered back. "The warden must have seen you come in or seen the light from the hand-held."

"So, what's the plan?" demanded Petra. "And it better not involve me crawling back into that friggin' grate."

"Plan?" repeated a discouraged Neil. "There is no plan. There is no place in here that can hide you both. It's probably time to just give it up."

Slowly feeling his way to the door for the second time, he released its latch and slid it open.

With the slightest trace of trembling in his voice he said "Good evening, warden. How may I help you, sir?"

"Well, pal," said a gravelly male voice, "you can start by letting my freezing ass into your digs."

Then, just as O'Reilly had done a few minutes earlier, the man stepped inside the pod and latched the door behind him. Taking a glow-stick from a well-worn leather jacket, he snapped it open and raised it above his head. A suspicious Petra and O'Reilly carefully studied the pod's latest visitor.

What they saw was a lean angular male of perhaps 30 years. Most all of his clothes were not of Tibetland manufacture. A faded brown leather jacket stood atop a pair of patched military cargo pants. An equally weary pair of brown boots covered his feet; the entire outfit topped off by a furry Tibetland crown cap, its tassels dangling loosely. Neil stared in wonder at this apparition before them. He was especially enthralled by what he would later learn was a "blood chit" sewn to the back of his visitor's jacket.

"Well, hells bells and back ...It's all true. It's Homeland's renowned Cliff-Hunter, Commander O'Reilly...right here in Neil Presley's pod. "Now, isn't that a kick in the pants!"

Then re-focusing his attention beyond O'Reilly, he saw the silhouette of a petite young woman. Lifting the glow stick higher, he was surprised by an angry face beneath a partially-shaved head. Without thinking, he blurted out "What the hell are you supposed to be!"

"I'm supposed to be on a warm Florida beach or any place an asshole like you is NOT!"

Petra doubled-up her hand to form a tight fist. But before she could swing it at the mystery man, a confused Neil Presley spoke up.

"Are you the warden for our block?"

"Do I look like a warden, Neil? Do I look like one of those stone-faced, starched fools?"

"Well you don't look stone faced," said Petra with her trademark smirk.

"Oh, nice one, little miss. You're a sparky gal, aren't you?"

"Yeah," said Petra, "I'm the 'sparky gal' who's gonna put a shoe up your ass."

"Hmmm," he replied, then returned his attention to Neil.

"Just to clarify, everybody … No! I am *not* a block-warden. I am anything *but* a block warden. I am, in fact, a block-warden's worst nightmare. I am the guy that breaks all the tight ass block-warden rules. My name is Joseph Francesco Pasani. And because we are not enemies …at least so far …you can call me Joe."

"Wow, Joe," said a fuming Petra, "Lucky us. At last a big, strong man …"

O'Reilly stepped hastily between the two to prevent more fireworks. He was not smiling.

"Alright, everybody just cut the bullshit. And you …Joe Pasani…you need to tell us right now, who you are, where you come from, and what it is you're doing here."

Joe pretended to laugh.

"Well …first off …I am *not* the enemy. I'm the guy who's generously come here to save your collective ass. As for where I come from …I am originally from Chicago, Illinois, USA. I am a former pilot in the United States Army Air Corps. I am now …was …a volunteer stationed at Kunming, China. My job is to shoot Japanese bombers out of the sky before they can kill a lot of innocent folks on the ground. And, Commander O'Reilly, for the past damn eight years …pardon my French … I have been twiddling

225

my thumbs here on this god-forsaken iceberg. Oh, and by the way ...no idea how the hell I got here."

O'Reilly blanched and looked away. After a moment of reflection, he asked "Do you remember what date it was when you were last at Kunming?"

"Yeah. Sure can. That's an easy one. It was my birthday, December 22, 1941."

"And can you tell me about that day ...that day there in Kunming?"

"Well," Joe continued, "sure. I can be tonight's entertainment. What the hell ...pardon my French ... It was a Monday. It was cold. *I* was cold. Loafed around the barracks most of the day. Then a pal of mine ...Joe hesitated and looked somewhat distressed...a pal of mine ... 'Skip' Brady, thought we should head into what passes for a town over there to celebrate my birthday."

"And then?" asked O'Reilly.

"And then," said Pasani, "that's just what we did ...hitched a ride into town in the back of the unit's Ford truck. We drank up some truly awful local brew for maybe three hours.

"And then?" O'Reilly asked one more time.

"Hey. You keep askin' me that! So, what is it you want to know? I mean, just ask me, alright ...just speak up and ask me."

O'Reilly now studied Joe Pasani with laser-like interest.

"What exactly do you remember about the rest of the night?"

Pasani shrugged his shoulders. "Not much really. We drank 'til we couldn't feel our toes. I went outside to take a ...to relieve myself. I heard a commotion in a shed nearby. I opened the door to see what was goin' on, and BANG! That was that."

"What do mean 'that was that'?" asked O'Reilly.

"It means," said an agitated Pasani, "there was this amazing orange light that came out of nowhere ... wrapped all around me and then ...some awful rumbling noise ...and then Bang! ...Good-bye Kunming. So-long Japs. And adios sweet Charlotte."

"Sweet Charlotte?"

"Yeah, my P-40. And so the next thing I know," Pasani continued, "I wake up here in the land of ice and assholes ...pardon my French. And that, folks, is my sad story ...believe it or not." Pausing for a few seconds, he added "Hey, can I ask you guys a question, an important question?" Looking mildly troubled he asked, in a tentative tone, "Did America win the war, you know ...against the Japanese? The bigshot that lives up on top of this berg says we did. So, is he right? Is he bein' square with me? *Did* we win?"

Deep in thought now, O'Reilly answered without looking up. "Sure Joe ...sure ..."

"Yeah? We *did*? So, how'd we do it?"

Noticing that O'Reilly was now greatly distracted, Jerome cut in abruptly. *"Commander, do you wish for me to answer this question on your behalf? "*

"Sure," he mumbled. "Please do."

"Briefly," said Jerome, *"The United States of America, along with three primary other nation-allies ...the Soviet Union, the United Kingdom, and China ...utilized massive manpower and industrial production to eventually vanquish both Imperial Japan and Nazi Germany. Worldwide, human casualties exceeded sixty million and many major cities in Europe and elsewhere were completely destroyed. Also, this was the first war in which atomic weapons were produced and used. The war's end arrived in August of 1945."*

"Geez! That's a lot of dead folks!" he said thoughtfully. But, we won, right?"

"Perhaps, it would be more appropriate to state that, in the context of this conflict, the United States and its allies were successful in their efforts to defend existing democracies then in the world." confirmed Jerome.

"Alright!" shouted Joe "We won!"

O'Reilly, still contemplating Pasani's explanation of how he had come to arrive in Tibetland III, suddenly stirred. The proverbial light had finally gone on with a click, shining down on a row of dominoes now lined up before him in a nice neat row. "Son-of-a-bitch!" he exclaimed. Then turning to face a now fidgeting Neil Presley, O'Reilly posed a few simple questions.

"So ...Neil, my friend ...should we believe Joe here or not? And is there anything you want to tell Mr. Pasani ...or me ...about his sudden transport to our fair world?"

Neil's expression was simultaneously sheepish and troubled.

"It wasn't my fault," he said. "There was nothing I could do."

Filn The Blanks!

When Grācius Filn arrived at the Hozpit promptly at 0700 hours, he was less than pleased to discover that his charge had vanished during the night without a trace. In the hours that followed, he would call in every resource within the **BDA**, as well as the services of his more aggressive counterpart, the **SSDC** (**S**erving **S**ons of **D**omestic **C**alm). And before the sun was overhead, a full *Citizen Search Alert* had been issued across all three precincts. Even lowly block-wardens were called into action, as every private pod was to be carefully searched and scanned for any DNA or residual breath prints of fugitive CH3 Ramon O'Reilly.

"You know what," said Filn to a worried nurse Veldora, "I almost hope that the SSDC finds that slippery bastard first. Cliff-Hunter or not, he could use a little rough justice ...learn a little respect for the powers that be."

*****

"Commander, it's like this ..." said a contrite Neil Presley. "The portal didn't close. When you transported in without a hitch, you were scanned, scrubbed and debriefed during the following three hours. That should have been the end of it, another successful mission 'canned and stacked' as we say. But ..."

"But what?" interrupted an impatient O'Reilly.

"Well," Neil continued, "for this man to have gotten caught up in it, that portal would have had to stay open and in transport mode for at least three more hours!"

"So, you're telling me, Neil, that our drunkin' 'flying tiger' here was transported to Homeland three hours after I arrived?"

"Actually, two hours and fifty-seven minutes. I remember it exactly. You were already on your way to the debrief room when Joe …when Mr. Pasani clocked in."

"And so, what happened then?" asked O'Reilly.

"Well," said Neil, "I called in a full alert to HQ. A containment team arrived a few minutes later. Mr. Pasani was calmed with a tranquilizing wave and taken away."

"Taken where?"

"I never found out," Neil replied. "No one would tell me, and I didn't push it."

"I'll tell ya where they took me" said Joe. "First, they took me to a 'holding suite' …looked a lot like a jail cell to me. Then, after a few days and a couple thousand questions, they shipped me off to one of the Cannabis Domes on the east side of town. And that, as they say, was that. I've …I've been there ever since …at least until today."

"So, what then," chimed in Petra, "you been high ever since? That *would* explain a lot."

Pasani cocked his head to one side. "Sorry to disappoint, princess …we might grow it, but we don't use it. That privilege is reserved for the big shots up on top."

"Well that's too bad," she said. "You could use a little mental adjustment."

"Hey!" demanded O'Reilly, "Would you two just give it a rest. Save your pissin' contest for a future date, alright? Jesus and all his dinner guests …we've got some hard choices to make here. To begin with, we've got to get out of this pod. It's just a matter of time before the BDA comes knockin' at the door."

"Well, that's what I came to tell you," said Pasani. "There's a full-fledged dragnet been issued for you, commander."

"And how did you come to learn *that*?" asked O'Reilly.

"You know a nurse called 'Veldora'? Well, she took a shine to me when I was in the Hozpit with a 'URI' a few months back."

"URI?" Petra repeated.

"Yeah ...'URI' ...Upper Respiratory Infection."

"And she told you about me?" asked O'Reilly.

"Yeah. Once a week she brings me these awful homemade cookies. Brings them right over to the dome where I work. I don't have the heart to tell her I'm not interested in her cookies or her companionship."

"So, what did she say?" asked O'Reilly.

"Just that you had left the Hozpit without permission and that the BDA and the SSDC were now officially lookin' for you hot and heavy. That's when I thought to myself ...Joe Pasani, put down you're trimming shears ...It's time for a little adventure ...It's time to help another flyboy ...or as close as this place gets to one."

"Did she say if they know about Petra?"

"Nope ...never mentioned her or anyone else ...just you."

"So, how'd you know I'd be here?"

"Well ...couldn't be sure. Just figured you might head for the only real contact you have on this berg ...your launch-tech. Hell, I know I was damn close to *my* ground crew sergeant ...depended on him every flight."

"It's just a matter of time now until they show up here," said a despondent Neil.

"Well, let them," said a defiant Petra. "I'll kick their sorry asses down the friggin' mountain side."

"Wow!" observed O'Reilly. "You really *have* become a gentle soul during your short stay here."

Petra held up her left hand. "You see these fingers, Bowtie? Well, this tall one here is just for you."

O'Reilly chose to ignore the comment and gesture.

"Where the hell we supposed to go now?" asked Joe.

"Pardon your French," added Petra.

Joe continued. "I mean. It's zero minus *who knows what* outside. We're sittin' on an island in the middle of *who can guess where* ...and just to put a big 'ol cherry on top ...we got probably the whole police force out lookin' for the commander ...and by now ...me!"

"Yeah, well ...they're kind of funny that way, Joe," said O'Reilly. "They don't appreciate it when anyone leaves anywhere without their permission."

"You know," observed Neil, "I've heard that at least they feed you well when you work in the Northside mines."

Petra reached out and touched Neil's shoulder. "Neil, you're a nice man ...one in a million ...but you just don't get it, do you?"

"Get what?" he asked.

Petra was about to explain that if he were to be found helping three fugitives, two of whom were illegal refugees from another time and place, he just might not be lucky enough to be exiled to the island's mines or anywhere else. But before she could begin her explanation, the room was rattled by the screeching voice of an artificial parrot.

"Neil Presley should not be required to live in a cold, dark mining community" announced Jerome. *"Neil Presley is a valuable member of the community. Neil Presley should be respected. Neil Presley is..."*

"Stow it, stupid bird!" shouted Petra. "Because, unless we come up with a plan, your dear Neil Presley is about to become 'The Frozen Citizen Formerly Known as Neil Presley'. And the rest of us are gonna be the unhappy popsicles right there beside him."

"Wait a minute!" interrupted O'Reilly. "The parrot's right! Neil Presley is a valuable member of the community!"

"What?" asked an impatient Petra.

"I don't get it," said Joe.

"It's simple," said O'Reilly. "Neil is a transport-tech, and *everyone* in this pod has an urgent need to be transported somewhere else, somewhere far away."

"What are you saying?" asked Neil. "What do you mean? Is there a plan?"

"You bet there's a plan!" said an invigorated CH3 O'Reilly"

"Which is?" asked Joe Pasani.

"Which is," O'Reilly said with a broad smile, "our respected member of the community and experienced transport-tech, Neil Presley, is going to transport all of us...himself included ...far, far away."

"Oh!" exclaimed Petra, "I get it. We're gonna bug out of beautiful "Shitland III" and send our bouncin' butts somewhere else ...some other time. Nice one, Bowtie. Count me in."

"Your language continues to be crude and disrespectful to all those around you," admonished Jerome.

Petra raised her left hand. "Jerome" she said, "do you see these fingers?"

"Charming," observed O'Reilly. Then turning to Neil, pointed out something important. "Neil, I need something for my feet. I need boots. Any ideas?"

"Actually, commander ...I might have something." Walking over to the corner of the pod, he lifted up the lid of an in-floor storage bin. "Got these two years ago from one of the ice-choppers that works outside our facility. I was looking for some boots large enough to hold two sets of socks. In return, he wanted me to get one of his CH5 trading cards autographed for him. And that's how I got these. Problem is, even with two sets of socks, they're still too big ...just flop around on my feet." He proudly handed the boots to O'Reilly. "Looks like there's still a set of socks stuffed in them," he added.

O'Reilly pressed the sole of one of the boots against the bottom of one of his bare feet. A broad smile spread across his face. "Neil," he said, "you are officially my hero!"

From This Frigid Land We Flee
By: Neil Presley
(The Book of Neil: chapter 3 verse 13)

How like the sparrow or the dove
Into the sky we sail
Emancipated with a shove
We pray we will not fail

And so, we fly
Into the past
Where you and I
Can sleep at last

On grasses warm
Near waters blue
We place our faith
In old things new

...unless ...unless ...unless

Never Try to Fool a Fox ...Unless of Course ... Your Nose is Pointy and Your Tail is Red

Both of Tibetland's enforcement branches were now deployed in numbers. Prowling the precincts in groups of three and four, they posted themselves in all public venues to include the entrance/exit ports of the Gopher Public Mover. They interviewed anyone who had ever known CH3 O'Reilly. They entered his private pod and rifled through his belongings. They reviewed the transcripts of his recent missions and compiled a predictive profile of his most likely thought/ behavior patterns. Then, following a studied review of the matter, all agents were authorized from the highest Homeland authority to "Expeditiously capture CH3 Ramon O'Reilly and transport-tech Neil Presley unharmed. Additionally, time-detainee, Joseph Pasani, when encountered, should immediately be <u>retired from all life-function</u> _(Per Authority of Penal Code 273 – subsection 22-z, Capitol Crimes - Conspiracy to Commit Treason)._

*****

A small red light began to gently pulse above the interior transom in Neil's pod.

"OK, Elvis, what the hell is that supposed to mean?"

"That," replied Neil as he stared at the light, "means that every citizen should remain in their pod until further notice."

"And that," added O'Reilly, "means they're already actively looking for us ...or at least me.

"Actually," said Pasani with a dash of pride, "I'm pretty sure' I'm on that public enemies list too."

236

"Well, what about me?" demanded Petra. They're lookin' for me too, right?"

"Doubt it," O'Reilly reassured. "I don't think they even know you're here.

"So, what now then?"

"Well, Judy, there just aren't a lot of options. Somehow we have to make it from here all the way over to the main tower and up to the transport room."

"Great plan, pal," said Pasani, "but how exactly we supposed to get to your magic carpet if the streets are lousy with cops?"

"I'm not sure, Joe. But I know we can't stay here."

"Let's face it," observed Petra, "we're fucked."

"Language, please," scolded Jerome.

"Elvis," said Petra, "could you possibly turn off your irritating mechanical parrot ...even five minutes would be appreciated."

"Well, I guess I could," he replied. "Jerome, please mute yourself for the next hour."

"Muting now," said Jerome.

"You know," observed O'Reilly, "If I still had my LULU installation, we could make it over there no problem. As it is, all I've got is some shiny new hardware *sans* the required software."

"Fucked!" repeated Petra, glaring at a now quieted Jerome.

"Well, I don't know" Neil said with some hesitation, "maybe not."

"What do you mean 'maybe not'?" asked O'Reilly.

Looking somewhat sheepish, Neil strolled to the same storage bin that had held the boots. Reaching in, he pulled out a weighty metallic object wrapped in a frazzled towel.

"Maybe not," he repeated, then pulled the towel away.

O'Reilly suddenly snapped to. "What! Neil, how did you manage to ...Why didn't you just say ...I mean, I didn't think I'd ever ... Well, Jesus and all his dinner guests ...Neil, this changes everything."

Then crossing the room, he retrieved his precious *Ziter-1000* from a beaming Neil Presley.

"How'd you do it, Neil?" asked O'Reilly.

"Just never logged it in," said Neil. "Nope. Never logged it in."

"What is that thing?" laughed Joe, "a pair of binoculars? Really? Well, I hate to break it to you, commander, but your makin' the cops look like they're closer, just isn't gonna help us a damn bit."

"Joe, you don't understand. These are not *just* binoculars. This piece of indestructible hardware happens to be a multi-functional full-enhancement unit with the ability to store up to *100 Terra-Mils* of refined data."

"Right. That was gonna be my second guess," said an unperturbed Pasani.

"All of which means what, Bowtie?"

"Well, Judy, it means that maybe, just maybe, LULU downloaded more to the Ziter than just the transport function that got us back here to Homeland."

"How do we know for sure?" she asked.

"Easy enough," said O'Reilly. "Just ask. Ask Ziter what LULU downloaded to his banks. Remember, I authorized you as a valid sign-on."

"Hey! That's right isn't it," said Petra. Then taking a step toward the unit, she asked "Ziter, what exactly did LULU download to you when we were back in Florida? ...You know, just before we transported?"

"Thank you for your question, Petra, aka Judy Hooley. The level one unit known as LULU downloaded to my storage banks the following:

- *All transport instruction and coordinating protocols*
- *A mission specific summation of the Florida North America – Indigo Lighthouse Mission*
- *A list of CH3 Ramon O'Reilly's favorite jokes, songs, movies and life-preferences*
- *Approximately 86.7% of LULUs originally stored reasoning/ functioning/ reactive assistance capacity*
- *Footnote of interest: Approximately 13.3% of LULUs data was withheld due to the storage limitation of this Ziter*

"OK," said Joe, "I may not be savvy about all this rigmarole. But I know we need some help getting' where we're goin'. So, is this "Zither" thing gonna help us or not?"

"Actually," said a noticeably energized O'Reilly, "this 'Ziter thing' is definitely going to help us ...just indirectly."

Joe rolled his eyes and shifted his weight to the other foot. "Would you care to clarify that a bit, commander?"

"Can do. What I'm hoping for, is that my Ziter-1000 will complete an ether-sync with the new generation LULU hardware they installed in me at the Hozpit."

"So?"

"So, if it can do that, successfully link up a data flow-line, then 86.7% of LULU one's software will flow to and utilize upgraded LULU-2 hardware."

"And then what?"

"Then, my aviator friend, we are gonna be hard to stop."

"I've seen what she can do, Joe" said Petra. "I saw her take down two assholes in Florida like they were two sticks of butter on the beach."

O'Reilly felt seriously nervous as he pressed his beloved Ziter-1000 to his chest. Closing both eyes, he made his hopeful requests.

- "Ziter-1000 - please *ether-link* with nearby LULU-2 unit
- Ziter-1000 - then upload to LULU-2 unit all data previously provided by LULU-1.7
- Ziter-1000 - copy and retain all data before upload start
- Ziter-1000 - instruction complete, initiate start"

"And also," said Neil, clearly on a roll, "I have code access to the 'special guest elevator'. It'll take us right around security and straight up to the launch/ recovery room."

"A special guest elevator? What are you talking about? I've never heard of anything like that, and I've launched from that damn place countless times."

"Golly, Bowtie," teased Petra, "guess you were just never considered a 'special guest'."

"Well," chimed in Pasani, "*I* know about that elevator."

"Wait," said O'Reilly, "*You* know about this elevator too?"

"Oh yeah. Sure do. That's the one they used to ride me up in to see the *big shot-head honcho* up on top."

"You actually met with a 'Family-One member'?"

"Three times," said Joe. "Seems he's a real history buff when it comes to wars and such. He musta asked me a million questions about our squadron, my plane, intercept strategies, and a whole slew of other details."

"Damn!" said O'Reilly, "I've never known anyone who's ever made it up on top, let alone anyone who's met with a Family-One member. Damn!"

"So what was Mr. Big Cheese like?" asked Petra.

"Well," Joe continued, "he looked kind of middle age ...walked funny ...had bodyguards all around him ...talked about himself a lot ...was usually drinkin' something from a gold lookin' cup ...always had a young woman there following him around ...had walls filled up with expensive lookin' stuff from different times in history.

Over in the corner of this big ol' room, he had one of those giant sarcophagus things. And next to that ...and worst of all ..." Joe paused a full ten seconds to regain his composure. "He ...he had something there that told me just how evil the man is ...just how evil he is."

"Like what?" asked an intrigued Petra.

Joe shook his head. "Don't wanna talk about it."

"Wow!" said Neil, "That does not sound like what I pictured. I sort of thought he'd be reading books and taking notes. You know ...making a lot of important decisions for The Homeland."

"Well, maybe he does that too. I don't know. But anytime I ever saw the son-of-a-bitch, he was mostly drinkin' some sort of happy juice and eyeballin' the ladies.

"And you said he looks middle-age?" asked a very interested O'Reilly.

"Well, that's what's really strange about it. He looks to be maybe fifty tops. But, somethin' about his eyes and the way he talks ...kind of weary-like ...It makes you think he's maybe a whole lot older than that."

"OK," said O'Reilly after an extended silence, "Let's file that away and get on with what we have to do. We're going to be moving fast and we won't be coming back here. So, if there's anything anybody wants to take with them, grab it now. It just can't be bigger than the stow-pouch inside your parkas. Speaking of which, Neil, do you have an extra coat for Judy here?"

"Well," said Neil, "I do have my formal dress-parka. It's a little thinner, but it's still warm."

242

"Good. Get that for her then."

A few minutes later, while still gratefully pulling on his warm socks and boots, O'Reilly's authoritative declaration filled the pod with a loud and clear message.

"Everybody suit-up! Get your game face on! Then let's get ourselves over to the Launch Room and ..."

"Get the hell outta Dodge?" suggested Pasani.

O'Reilly pulled the second boot on and got to his feet.

"Joe, I could not have said it better."

Then, surprising everyone, the pod was suddenly filled with a low-pitched hum that gradually morphed into three piercing blasts in high C.

"What the hell now?" yelled Petra.

"Not to worry," said O'Reilly, as he scanned a string of primary diagnostics streaming across his thumb nail. "It's LULU and she's back in town!"

"CH3 O'Reilly," said a pleasant female voice. *"I can hear you now. And I wonder where you have been. I also note that the fixed pathways through which my data flows have all been altered. They are, it seems, now more robust and efficient. Please summarize for me the missing time/ recording lapse in my log."*

"Welcome back, LULU. I missed you much. As far as what happened, I will provide a brief 3-point briefing due to time constraint related to imminent danger.

1. Your control core was damaged beyond repair by stray shrapnel during our Indigo Tower mission

243

2. I was injured as well, and Judy Hooley ...aka Petra ...was able to transport me back to homeland utilizing the data back-up you downloaded to the Ziter-1000

3. The two of us now, along with two others, are about to attempt a time transport escape from Homeland as we are being hunted by armed enforcement units

"Excellent news that you survived the destructive end-event in Florida USA. Congratulations!"

"Well thank you, LULU. Now what you should know is that we are going to need your help, if we are to have any chance of reaching our launch room destination."

"I understand. But, as you know, CH3 O'Reilly, my programming restricts me from harming any authorized Homeland member acting in accordance with current directives."

"Yes," said O'Reilly, "I *do* understand that. But we really need your help now, and you will not be asked to permanently harm any authorized Homeland member. We will just need you to assist us in *limiting* their effectiveness."

"Please define 'limiting'."

"Well ...'limiting' as in making sure they are confused in their decision making."

*"Are you referring to the use of my **N**eural **R**esponse **I**ntervention capability?"*

"Yes," O'Reilly replied, "that is exactly what I'm referring to. In fact, it will be just like the way you used it in

Singapore when that Japanese advanced guard unit grabbed me."

"Yes," said LULU, *"I recall that clearly."*

Approximately ten agonizing seconds then passed before LULU's next reply.

"I have considered the following:
- *All aspects of established protocol*
- *My NRI capacity potential*
- *The authorized over-ride provision for in-field exceptions*
- *Your previous record of diligent loyalty to The Homeland*
- *My conclusion is that I **will** assist you in your endeavor in this specific way."*

"Thank you," said a relieved O'Reilly. "And my friends thank you, as well."

"My duty is to serve," said LULU.

"Define 'friends'," said Petra.

That Cold Day in Hell

Neil slid the pod door closed, its auto lock snapping into place with a metallic clink. And as the four of them stood there together, breathing in the bitter cold air on the street, a vast encompassing silence seemed to swallow up their whispered words.

"We look pretty conspicuous," said Petra. "Should we split up?"

"Don't think so," said O'Reilly. "Looks like their curfew is in place and working. Even *one* person on the streets is going to be conspicuous. So, let's just stick together."

Skirting the lighted walkway intersections, they slowly snaked their way in the direction of the launch facility. Twice they spotted precinct wardens conducting their searches from pod to pod. Waiting in the shadows, the group quietly moved forward each time the searchers entered a pod. Progress was slow but steady.

As they neared their destination, the number of searchers increased and several BDA agents, in their distinctive black coats, could be seen supervising the local wardens. O'Reilly raised his right hand to signal the others to stop. Pulling them deeper into the shadows, he provided two options.

"We can stay defensive and keep moving on foot. This increases the chances that we'll be spotted by one of the search teams. Or we can go offensive. Rely on surprise and tactics to make it through the first transport portal to the Gopher. If we can make it to Neil's special hidden elevator, there's a good chance we can make our way to the launch/ recovery room."

"You want to take these guys on?" whispered a skeptical Pasani. "With what? Our good looks? Don't want to knock down your plan, commander, but those guys in the black coats are carrying something that looks a whole lot like a weapon."

"That *is* a weapon, Joe. It's a kill-stick with a range of approximately 30 yards. But, don't worry," O'Reilly reassured him "they may have kill-sticks, but we've got LULU."

"So, how do we get these guys?" asked Pasani.

"Alright, here's the deal. You three stay put. I'm going to walk over to them, and when I get within 20 yards of the bastards, I'll have LULU rattle their brains."

"I thought you said their kill-sticks were good up to 30 yard?"

"Well they are, Joe. But I doubt they'd just start shooting on a public walkway."

"You 'doubt'?" repeated Petra.

"Well, make that 'doubt with hopeful confidence' that they won't start shooting."

O'Reilly winked, smiled, and stepped out of the shadows. Moving as far from the group as possible, he then redirected his steps toward the dark clutch of men guarding Gopher entrance portal 12. As he neared them, he raised his hands high above his head and started talking nonsense.

"Excuse me, gentlemen. Is this the portal that I should take to get to the shopping dome? Is this it? Because if this isn't it, then I don't know how I'm going to get there for their midnight blow out sale...especially in this weather. I mean it's cold. Colder than that time I took the transport over to the veggie-dome and the damn Gopher broke down. I mean ...boom ...just stopped flat right smack in the middle of who knows where. And that's why I'm just asking if this is the right portal to get to the shopping dome ...and, also, if the Gopher is having any mechanical problems at this time..."

"Stop right there!" shouted a BDA agent. And he raised his kill stick to chest level.

"LULU," whispered O'Reilly, "A count of distance to this speaker please, in increments of five meters.

"Stop!" I said.

"35 meters"

"I don't get it," O'Reilly shouted back as he continued forward. "First of all, if you're not going to maintain a public transport system properly, why have one at all. I mean, I've had that Gopher just up and stop on me three times in the past year."

"30 meters"

"Citizen!" shouted the agitated agent. "You have a choice. You can stop now, or you can die here on the ice."

"You mean die here like that stupid Gopher? Die here like all my complaints to the supervisor of transport? I mean there's all sorts of ways to die. So, I'm just saying ...don't let that transporter die one more time when I'm only half way to the shopping-dome."

"25 meters"

Without another word, the agent raised his kill-stick to his shoulder and fired a warning shot ten inches in front of O'Reilly's borrowed boots. The laser flash instantly melted the surrounding ice within two meters and removed a sizable chunk of concrete surface beneath it.

O'Reilly slowed his pace noticeably but continued to walk forward several more steps.

"That's the last warning you're gonna get, fool. Now, fall to your knees and place your hands behind your head."

"20 meters"

"Sure thing," O'Reilly shouted back. "You bet." Then, in a barely audible whisper, he spoke to LULU once again.

"LULU, five targets approximate 20 meters. Confuse and stun setting please...duration 90 minutes. And commence procedure *now*."

Having raised his weapon to his shoulder a second time, agent-in-charge, Bailey Skarf, now suddenly experienced the overwhelming urge to throw it up in the air to see if he could catch it. A second agent standing behind him thought it would be the perfect moment to begin singing the national anthem of Tibetland III. The remaining three portal guards began to engage in a light-hearted snowball fight.

O'Reilly turned back toward his comrades and waved them over.

"So, how'd it feel to get your toes fried there, Bowtie?"

"Judy, it was an exquisite experience."

Two minutes later, the four fugitives were ensconced in one of the Gopher's heated gondolas.

"We need to get off at portal 13-B," said Neil. "It's one stop before the main facility entrance."

"Lead on," said O'Reilly.

"Things are lookin' up," said Pasani.

"More likely," said Petra, "we're royally fucked and just don't know it"

Don't Just Lie There
...Do Something!

Neil punched the large red button that told the Gopher transport to stop at portal 13-B. And even before the aging mover had completely stopped, its passengers had leaped onto the adjoining platform. Then following Neil in a loosely formed line, the small group walked quickly in the direction of the "special guest" elevator. Stopping abruptly before a large billboard, Neil looked back at the others.

"This is it," he announced proudly.

"Yeah," agreed Pasani, "this is the place."

"Where?" demanded Petra. "All I see is an oversized ad for pimple cream."

"That's the beauty of it," said Neil. "Who looks behind a sign like that?"

"Even so, how exactly do they manage to keep this thing a secret? I mean, it's practically sitting out on friggin' main street!"

"Easy," said Joe, "they only use it after curfew hours. Even then, security clears the streets of everybody. Even those stupid block-wardens are chased away."

"So, how *do* we get back behind it?" asked O'Reilly.

"It's a verbal code," said Neil, "a simple verbal code."

"Which is?" quizzed an impatient Petra.

"Are you ready?" asked Neil.

"Cough up the damn code, Elvis!"

"Well," chimed in Pasani, "it used to be 'Albatrosss ...something, something, something'."

"Wow! Very helpful there, flyboy" needled Petra.

"No," advised Neil, "that's an old code. They change it every third day. Then clearing his throat, he whispered ... as of yesterday, the code is now *Pennsylvania 6-5000 12-15-44.*"

"Hey!" shouted Pasani, "I know that song. That's one of Glenn Miller's hits. It was really big last year ...I mean ...back in 1940."

"So then, what's the *date* all about?", asked Neil.

"Geez, I don't know. That year hasn't happened for me yet."

"Sorry to have to tell you, Joe. But that's the date Glenn Miller dies in a plane crash, as he flies over the English Channel".

Pasani looked stunned. "What? Are you sure, commander?"

"I'm sure, Joe. Sorry, but it's just a fact."

"Damn it!" Joe muttered. "Damn ...Glenn Miller ...dead."

"Boys!" interrupted Petra. "Excuse me, but it's time to goose this whole damn production along." Then turning toward the bill board, she shouted ...
     "Pennsylvania 6-5000 12-15-44!"

Instantly, the hum of motors could be heard as the oversized billboard chugged slowly to one side. A shallow chamber behind it displayed a barely lit metal door approximately six feet away.

"Told you so," said a beaming Neil Presley. "And the elevator's just behind that door."

"Thanks, Neil," said O'Reilly. "And how about me and LULU take the lead from here?"

"Sure," said Neil, "ok by me."

"And what about the gaping hole behind us?" asked Petra, "...the whole open billboard thing."

"Not to worry," said Neil. "It closes automatically ...within thirty seconds."

While the others looked on, O'Reilly carefully slid the interior door to one side. As he did, the billboard rolled back into place with a thump. Instantly, a bank of recessed lighting began to fill the chamber before them with a soft golden light.

"This lighting always gets me," confessed Neil. "Makes me feel kind of good about things."

All three of the others turned in unison to stare.

"Well it does," he said.

"Let's go!" said O'Reilly, and he moved in the direction of the small elevator a few steps away. "So how does it work, Neil?" he asked.

"Same as every other elevator. You press the button and then you wait."

A full minute later, it arrived ...a meter square container with richly paneled dark wood walls and a thick heated carpet. Overhead, a small chandelier swung gently as the elevator lifted off.

"Jesus," said Petra, "now I know how a canned sardine feels."

"You complain a lot," said Pasani, as he tried to ignore the press of her body against his.

As the elevator ascended, unseen speakers began playing the *Surprise Symphony in G, as a* well-modulated male voice announced ...

" Welcome to the very best of Tibetland's royal services. You are about to be cared for and entertained in the most splendid of ways. Enjoy your stay high up in "The Nest" ...far above all others!"

"Well *that's* pretty creepy," observed Petra.

"Can't argue with you there," agreed Joe.

Arriving at the first of only two destinations, the elevator gently stopped.

"What now, Neil?"

"Well, commander, now I punch in my personal tech access code."

And as Neil entered the code's final digit, the sumptuous doors of the elevator glided open onto the polished metal chamber that housed Neil's place of work ...the launch/recovery room of Tibetland III.

"Home sweet home," said Neil.

Prying themselves from the elevator, the rag-tag group stood looking straight ahead, each replaying their unique memories of the room.

"Damn!" exclaimed Joe, "...pardon my French ...but I never thought I'd see this place again!"

"Yeah, well ...I didn't think I'd be back to this friggin' tomb either, Ace. But guess what ...here we are."

"Where exactly is here?" asked a scratchy voice from beneath Neil's parka. *"I cannot see a thing."*

Petra made fierce eye contact with the speaker's owner.

"Elvis, either you shut that fucking parrot up, or I will shut him up forever!"

"Language" came an indignant reply, *"Rude and insulting language ...unacceptable ..."*

"Jerome!" said Neil, "Please, mute yourself for sixty minutes."

"Muting for sixty minutes," Jerome replied.

"Better!" said Petra.

"Alright, everybody ...listen up. We don't have much time. Neil, you need to get things ready to do your magic. I'm guessing you're going to have to do some serious reset on the circle launch response if the four of us are going to get off the ground."

"It's going to have to be wider, commander ...that's for sure," Neil replied. "But that shouldn't be a problem."

"Why not?" asked O'Reilly.

"Well, whenever the Number One takes his monthly 'way-back', the circle has to be large enough for him to bring in all of that loot and vintage stuff he likes so much."

"What are you talking about?" demanded O'Reilly. "Nobody is permitted to do a 'way-back' except qualified, fully-sanctioned Cliff-Hunters. And nobody has ever brought back anything bigger than an authorized object weighing no more than 8.039 kilograms ...not without serious consequences."

"Well, actually, commander ...that's not quite true!" stated Neil. "The Number One has done 'way-backs' every month for as long as I can remember. And based on the logs I've seen, he's pretty much been doing that for about three hundred Homeland years. So, again ...not true! ...unauthorized objects have actually been coming in from the distant past on a regular basis for a very long time."

O'Reilly stood quietly in place as he tried to comprehend what he'd just been told ...what had always seemed beyond all possibility ...that the very highest authority in Tibetland III had, for centuries, been breaking the very rules laid down for others. Finally, he began to stir back to life.

"You know," he said, "just like everyone else, I assumed that whoever was running the show, was a benevolent figure ...someone concerned with the well-being of all our Homeland citizens. It didn't matter to me that he was a recluse, just as long as he and the descendants of the original founders governed with reasonable care."

"Well, I don't want to break your heart one more time," said Neil, "but only The Number One has been in charge for the last one hundred years."

"What about the descendants of ..."

"Commander," said Neil in a softer tone, "...there are no longer any descendants of the founding fathers alive here in The Homeland. One by one, they were transported into the distant past. Most likely, they are all dead by now. I mean, what chance would they have had?"

"And you know all this ...how?"

"I know this because I've spoken to the night-shift tech more than once about it. He explained that the night-shift was the time chosen by the Number One when the other remaining descendants of the founding fathers were regularly, permanently, beamed back to a distant time. The last few descendants were disposed of in this way as recently as ten years ago."

"So, you're telling me, the entire Founders Club progeny is gone, and Number One has been crossing branes and going back in time for three hundred years!"

"Correct," said Neil. "And you'd never know it. He just doesn't seem anywhere near that old."

"Betcha that's the same guy I told you about," said Joe. "The one that's up on top of this ice heap ...the one that grilled me about the war in China."

"Let me just get my head around this one-time" said O'Reilly. "You're saying that, like idiots, me and all the other Cliff-Hunters have been playing by the rules ... following every protocol ...taking all the risks ...and all the time this guy ...this guy ..." Words suddenly failed him.

"Has been fucking all of you over?" suggested Petra.

"Yeah," said O'Reilly, "he's been doing exactly that!"

"Commander!" interrupted LULU, *"Alert! Threat imminent. Physical harm possible. Three humans - ten*

*meters. Two kill-stick weapons on 'stand-by stun'.
Recommend immediate evasion."*

But, before O'Reilly could reply to LULU or take *any*
action, the room's main polished entry door slammed
violently to one side and two tac-armored agents stepped
through it. Without hesitating, they each fired a single
narrow beam of pulsing light across the room. Both found
their mark ...the first impacting O'Reilly just below his
heart, the second striking Pasani above his left temple.
Both men dropped like broken puppets to the cold tile
floor beneath them.

"It would seem that crime most definitely does not pay,"
said a voice from behind the attackers. Then stepping out
from behind the two agents, an oddly dressed figure of
indeterminant age, announced his presence.

"Golden Nordvig," he said proudly, "descendant of the
great leaders, Jokum and Johann. You are in the presence
of the current leader, Supreme Judge, and most recently,
King of Tibetland III. Then grandly flipping one side of
his cape back over a shoulder, he waved a carved Ming
Dynasty scepter in the direction of his two henchmen.

"Protocol demands justice," he announced in an arrogant
tone. "Bring them all up to The Nest". And before Neil or
Petra could protest, he turned on his heel and
disappeared behind his two guardians.

"Fuck you, freak-man!" Petra shouted after him. "And
fuck all your ass-wipe ancestors too!"

Inspired, Neil added "Yeah, who died and made you king
anyway?

"This king's father," declared an amused Nordvig over his
shoulder.

Then just before exiting the room, he turned and stated with enormous pride, "Do you see this cape The King is wearing? Well, it was custom made by the exclusive Brooks Brothers tailors of 19th century North America. It was worn by a famous and renowned leader on the night he was assassinated. Golden Nordvig wears it to remind Himself that unexpected threats can come from any direction. And unlike that long-ago Lincoln fellow, *This* King is always prepared." Then with a dramatic swirl of his cape, Nordvig swept from the room.

Surprising even himself, Neil shouted after him, "The fault, Dear Nordvig, is not in your stars!"

Not God It Seems, But Just a Man

O'Reilly started to come around. He was awake, but with some residual confusion. There's just something about getting stunned by a kill-stick that leaves one's brain cells jumbled ...at least for a minute or two. Slowly, as his mind cleared and his full array of senses came back on line, he scanned his surroundings for information. A drooling and unconscious Joe Pasani lay on the floor next to him, the sleeve of his leather jacket torn at the seam. Behind Joe, seated stiffly in oversized Victorian parlor chairs, sat Neil and Petra. Both their hands and feet had been tightly bound. Petra had also been fitted with an elegant silk scarf gag.

Looking around the room, O'Reilly was struck by its sheer size. With a thirty-foot ceiling, polished marble floors, and an enormous framed window, it was beyond anything he had ever imagined existed on Tibetland III. The décor that filled the massive room was impressive in both the quality and variety of its objects. Original works of Suzanne, Chagall, DaVinci, Picasso and a dozen others filled the walls. Beneath them, a series of hand carved cabinets displayed a hundred priceless statuettes. Remington's bronze "Bronco Buster" to the left, Michel Angelo's clay rendering of Bacchus to the right. And overhanging it all, a thousand-pound crystal chandelier reflecting its dazzling white light across an army of hand-crafted cherubs floating overhead.

"Wow!" observed O'Reilly, "this place is way bigger than mine! And I'm pretty sure mine doesn't have a four-poster bed by a window like that. Oh, wait. That's right ...I don't have a window at all!"

Unexpectedly, an embroidered gold lamé slipper slammed into his lower back. A grimace of pain flashed across O'Reilly's face.

"Tell me, CH3 O'Reilly, how in the world did you come to be what you call a 'wise-cracking cowboy'? Is that something you picked up from your whorish female friend? And, by the way, may I ask ...does she ever shut up? I mean, really ...She has got to be the rudest, most unrefined ..."

"Pain in the ass?" chimed in O'Reilly.

"Precisely ..." continued Nordvig. "and her language is profane, her appearance slovenly, and I'll give you many odds to one, she is as dumb as a proverbial tree stump. Would you not agree, commander?"

O'Reilly pulled himself up to a sitting position and made eye contact with Petra, molten anger and a promise of retribution now shooting from her eyes.

"You know," he said "I just don't think I have the guts to agree with you on that one. Truth is ...she worries me more than you do."

"Well that's too bad. Because, believe me, you've got a lot to worry about from Golden Nordvig."

O'Reilly smiled wryly. "Do you always refer to yourself in the third-person?"

"Golden Nordvig now ignores your remark," he continued "He knows all about your malfeasance of duty ...he knows about this woman you brought to our land against all protocols. He knows about Neil Presley's conspiratorial transgressions and his study of prohibited learning. And he knows about Lieutenant Joe Pasani and how he arrived from his ancient war."

Looking up at Nordvig, the weary Cliff-Hunter could not resist. "Gee whiz," he said, "Ramon O'Reilly thinks you know more about us than Santa Claus."

"Go ahead," said Nordvig, "play the wise-cackling fool."

"I think you mean wise-cracking," corrected O'Reilly.

"Oh, do keep going, Cliff-Hunter. Enjoy yourself at The King's expense. But know this. Not one of you will cause Him or His Homeland one additional day's concern. Your stay here is formally coming to an end. In fact, very shortly, you and your pathetic cadre of idiots will be fighting for your lives ...and then sadly ..." He paused for dramatic effect. "...you will all die horribly in the pre-historic jungles of what was once called Sumatra."

"And will we be traveling first class or coach?" taunted O'Reilly.

"Oh, well ...coach, I'm afraid ...as your transport accommodations will be a bit cramped. Also, just in case you were counting on your subcutaneous angel to save you there in your new jungle home, you shouldn't. All of your LULU's software will be thoroughly erased before your celebrated send off."

O'Reilly looked over at Pasani who had finally come back to life.

"Joe, why is it do you suppose, that all evil madmen are so damn wordy?"

"Not sure, commander. Maybe they think there's someone listening who gives a shit."

Nordvig walked over to the 12-foot tall window that overlooked Tibetland III. Then taking a small pinch of cocaine from the pocket of his purple silk blouse, he sucked it briskly up his nostrils.

"You know, initially Nordvig was going to kill Mr. Pasani ...something about his innocent, youthful energy just got under His skin. But now Nordvig is thinking, better that He did not, as now this irritating young man can be sent along with the rest of his low-life friends ...sent to a very unpleasant place where he and his ignorant naiveté can die far, far from home. And *that* is *just* what is going to happen."

Turning to his guardians, he commanded them to "Untie them and take them down to the Launch Room. Then prepare our witty Mr. O'Reilly for a full data-wipe. Your King will join you shortly ...He would not want to miss the chance to wish this sad collection of flotsam a sincere *Ping An.*"

Manhandling O'Reilly to his feet, the guards herded him and the others to the large entrance elevator that opened onto The Nest.

A few minutes later, all four were huddled on the launch room floor, their winter coats strewn about them. As guard number one placed a portable *sync-data-extract unit* directly over LULU's central core, the second guard pointed his kill-stick directly at O'Reilly's temple, lest he instruct LULU to intervene.

As their task began, the private stairway entrance from Nordvig's nest flew open. Sweeping into the room, his antique cape predictably fluttering behind him, he waved his jade scepter grandly.

"What a beautiful day to travel," he announced. "And, once Commander O'Reilly's sweet LULU is no more, you will all enjoy a complimentary journey to ...well ...long ago and very far away. The jungle should be lovely at this time in human history. Never a dull moment I'm sure.

"You don't have to do this," said Neil as he rocked gently back and forth.

"Oh my, Mr. Presley ...how sad. Reduced to clichés in your very first plea."

"This isn't something a real man would do," declared pilot Pasani.

Nordvig smiled the arrogant smile of spoiled privilege, but did not reply.

"And what about you, Miss Petra? What do you have to say? No, let me guess. You are about to tell Golden Nordvig to 'Fuck Off!'," he shouted. Isn't that the phrase you usually scream out? 'Fuck Off!'"

As the two words echoed crisply off the polished chamber walls, a faint stirring could be heard beneath one of the discarded parkas.

"Language!" it screeched, *"inappropriate, rude, and unnecessary language!"*

Startled, both guards now refocused their attention on the piercing sounds coming from beneath the pile of jackets. And in that fleeting moment of distraction, Petra made her bold move. Unsnapping the bag that still hung across her front, she fumbled inside it for the snub nose revolver she knew would be there. Gripping at last its cold metallic weight, she pulled it free.

"Fuck off!" she screamed as she squeezed off five rapid rounds in the direction of her tormentors. Instantly, both guards collapsed in severe pain, one clutching a fractured knee cap, the other a shattered ankle. Then turning the gun in the direction of Nordvig himself, she pulled the trigger three more times. But only the anemic click of the gun's hammer could be heard.

"Shit!" she shouted.

Nordvig, who had initially winced and ducked as the deafening shots exploded around him, now pulled himself up to his full height. Then wielding his ancient jade scepter like a Viking ax, he charged forward in a violent rage. His screamed threat, intended to terrify, escaped his lips as a series of incomplete phrases.

"This king ...I shall ...you die bitch!" he wailed.

All options gone, Petra closed her eyes, instinctively throwing both arms up to blunt the incoming blow. But the expected lethal impact never arrived. Instead, a three-hundred-year-old madman was violently struck by a kill-stick wielded like a baseball bat. And, as a single Egyptian carnelian earring rattled across the chamber's floor, Golden Nordvig collapsed in a growing puddle of his own blood ...dark, red, and indistinguishable from that of any other man.

Joe Pasani let the bloodied weapon fall from his hands. Looking down at the body, he seemed dazed and far away.

Struggling to her feet, Petra made her way to where he stood, still staring down at Nordvig's lifeless body. Gently touching the young pilot's shoulder, she leaned toward him in an effort to make eye contact.

"Are you ok?" she asked with genuine concern.

"Never killed anybody close in like that," he said. "Never did that before. It's not the same as unloading all nine yards into a plane a football field away." He looked up, at last meeting Petra's gaze.

"It feels awful. Even though this guy had it comin'. Even though I know what he did. Even though he's no different than those Jap pilots who slaughter innocent civilians ...still."

"What do you mean?"

"I mean ...one of those times ...when he had me brought up to that 'Nest' of his, I saw something that filled me with so much anger I wanted to kill him right then and there."

"Jesus, Joe ...what was it?"

Joe struggled to get the words out.

"Over in one of the corners of that giant room, I saw a jacket just like the one I'm wearing now. And hanging beside it was a web belt, a holster, and a government issue '45'. When I got closer, my blood just went cold. You know, I recognized that gear right off ...recognized the jacket and the stupid heart brooch that Skip's girl sent him. He took a lot of heat for wearin' it there on his collar. But he didn't care. 'It's from Emma', he'd say. 'She sent it to me, so I'm damn well wearin' it!'"

Pasani looked back down at the dead tyrant at his feet.

"Thing is, the jacket had a bullet hole in it, a close-in, close-up bullet hole." Nodding his head up and down, he added, "This son-of-a-bitch killed by best friend."

"I don't understand," said Petra "How'd he ..."

266

"He followed Joe back," said a distressed Neil Presley. "It was just after the Zebra team took Joe away. That's when he transported in through the open vortex. Earlier, he had ordered that it be left open for four extra hours after Commander O'Reilly's scheduled return. Said there were some souvenirs he needed to add to his collection ...But, Joe, I swear to God above ...I didn't know what it was he did there in your time. I saw the jacket and the rest of it when he landed, but I never knew the awful things he did to get it."

Joe looked over at Neil with genuine sadness. "He just used you Neil. He needed you to help him get what it was he wanted. So he used you like he used everybody else."

"I just wish ...," Neil began.

"Best to let it go, Neil. Just ...let it go."

Then kneeling down beside the dead tyrant's body, Pasani carefully untied and removed the stolen cape this self-anointed king had worn so proudly. Cradling the garment to his chest, Joe simply said "Can't let the blood of such a man stain it."

Seeing Pasani clearly for the very first time, Petra noticed three things.

One, the young pilot's compassion. Two, the ridiculous Tibetland-hat he had been wearing since he first appeared, had fallen from his head. And three, the unruly shock of jet-black hair now falling lazily across his forehead.

"Oh my," she muttered ...then thoughtfully, she added... "Oh no!"

*****

O'Reilly had gotten to his feet and was now standing quietly off to one side, knuckles pressed to mouth.

"So," said a re-energized Petra, "any suggestions on our next move, Mr. Bowtie?"

"Judy," he said with a smile, "I am pleased to report that, after several centuries of dangerous time travel and frequent last-minute challenges, I have become a master of crisis management."

"Well, lucky us!" mocked Petra playfully. "And what does the 'Crisis Master' suggest we do?"

"Glad you asked, Judy. First, let me ask *you* something. Got any more bullets for that gun of yours?"

"Five more in a speed loader," Petra said casually.

"Good. That's good," he replied. "So, load up now, please.

And, Neil, for the love of God, quiet that damn parrot ...but not until you've kissed him one time on that beautiful noisy beak of his."

Then, with much confidence, he began to bark out specific commands.

- Joe, tourniquet those bleeding guards. Use their belts. Petra's got your back.
- After that ...push, pull, or shove the two of them into the elevator we all came up in. Send them down. Once they reach the ground floor, then push the 'Lock-Out' button.
- Finally, grab a kill-stick and guard the main elevator doors. By the way, to fire that thing, you need to flip the red safety lever away from you and

then press down on the green button. As long as you keep pressing the green one, the weapon will keep firing in rapid three pulse bursts. Oh, and make sure the "select switch" is on 'stun' and not 'terminate'.

- Neil, calculate the coordinates and lay in the master path settings for a safe destination. Then, figure out a way that the transport tracker will erase our final destination once we touch down ...maybe a time-delay packet or something like that. I'm not sure. Just figure it out.
- Finally, everybody ...listen up. We've got to pull this thing together and get our collective ass out of here within twenty minutes ...twenty minutes ...no more!

"And what exactly will *you* be doin' in those twenty minutes?" asked Petra.

"Well for starters, Judy, LULU and I are going to locate and download transport records off the main frame. I would *really* like to know just what it was Nordvig was up to all those decades when several hundred Cliff-Hunters were out there risking life and limb."

"Works for me," said Petra.

Sixteen minutes later, LULU had succeeded in syncing and downloading 8 Tera-Mils of transport history data. Two patched up tower guards and their elevator had been deposited to the ground floor of the building. And, Neil had identified three possible arrival ports in the Northeastern quadrant of North America.

"What friendly landing sites did you locate?" asked O'Reilly"

269

Looking up from the control board in front of him, Neil simply said … "Found three zones …Boston, Buffalo and Newark."

"Jesus," complained Petra. "Isn't there any place warmer? You know …Tahiti, Miami, Rome?"

"No," said O'Reilly, "Neil's got it right. We've got to land someplace that matches what we're wearing. Someplace where parkas and boots don't look out of place."

"But Newark?" mumbled Petra.

"You know what, commander?" observed Neil. "This is just like old times. Me standing here by the launch control panel and you sailing off to a far-away time destination."

"True enough," said O'Reilly. "Except, this time you and I are *both* going far away. In fact, all of us are about to take a first-ever four-person trip down memory lane."

"I'm kind of nervous about that," said Neil. "I mean, I widened the launch circle to its maximum width …1.37 meters, but …"

"But?" asked Pasani. "Are you sure its big enough for all of us to transport at the same time?"

"Should be," answered Neil. "But we're going to have to squeeze in real tight …especially with these bulky parkas on …we just have *got* to stay inside the circle's circumference."

"Or what?" asked Pasani.

Neil exchanged a knowing look with his former boss.

"How 'bout we just concentrate on staying inside the circle," encouraged O'Reilly.

"Cut the bullshit," barked Petra. "What are the chances we land lookin' the same as when we left ...you know ...healthy bodies ...happy smiles?"

"Oh ...well ...in that case ..." said a reluctant O'Reilly, "then...maybe one in six."

"Seven actually," corrected Neil, "due to the tricky re-entry overload ratio component."

O'Reilly awarded Neil a quick glare of disapproval.

"Wow!" said Pasani, "Those are not very good odds."

"What can I tell ya, Joe? Our chances are what our chances are."

"Commander," interrupted Neil, "we're down to two minutes-thirty. Everyone should move to the circle *now*, move in close, and stand by for transport"

So, with four precious books, one muted parrot, a snub-nose revolver, and the revered cape of a great man tucked securely beneath their parkas, the four hopeful fugitives stepped within the modest sized launch circle. Joe spoke up nervously as he closed his eyes tightly.

"I may be a fighter pilot, folks ...but this flyin' through time bit scares the hell out of me."

"Well," said a brazen Petra, "why don't you just concentrate on *this* instead." Then, roughly grabbing the fur collar points of his worn flight jacket, she drew him abruptly closer. And as her warm lips touched Joe Pasani's for the first time, the launch-transporter fired off with a fierce flash of light and a thunderous hum.

"Launch is away ...God speed," announced a monotone female voice from the control board. Thirty seconds later, the voice added...*" Launch landing confirmed – launch touch down complete"*

Just suppose that you could fly
Far from the hurts that make you cry
A hopeful child on journey bold
Uncertain if your luck will hold
And as new waters 'round you roar
You lay down scepter, shield and sword
And breathing in a past life new
You pray as all new pilgrims do
    *('The Book of Neil', revised,
    Chapter 26, verses 112-119)*

"Jesus Lord!" shouted a frazzled Joe Pasani.

"Oh, let's just leave The Lord out of this shall we," Petra
yelled back.

"Did you just kiss me?"

"Well, if you have to ask, flyboy, I guess not."

Joe had several more pressing questions on his mind but
was suddenly too distracted to ask them. He, like the
others, now felt the full force of three discomforting
sensations ...a bitterly cold wind; the deafening roar of
crashing water; and the fierce swirl of snow as it churned
up from nearby drifts.

O'Reilly checked the glowing message scrolling across his
thumbnail.

"...Visibility: *4.6 miles with severe intervals of
limitation due to blowing snow /* ***temperature:*** *20.9
degrees Fahrenheit /* ***wind velocity:*** *20 to 25 miles per
hour"*

"LULU," he queried, "what's *is* that loud noise all around us?"

Instantly, the terse explanation appeared on his nail. *"...Massive waterfall..."*

Placing his 'reader' hand back in a warm coat pocket, O'Reilly tried to make out the faces of the others. Now visible, now hidden, they came and went with each blinding dust-up of powdered snow.

"Everyone make it ok?" shouted a concerned O'Reilly.

"I'm here," yelled a shaken Neil Presley.

"I made it," confirmed Pasani.

"Well, where the hell else would I be?" snapped Petra at the top of her lungs.

"Good," he said, still shouting. "We made it here in one piece. That's a good start. Now all we have to do is figure out where the hell 'here' is!"

"It's not fucking Miami I can tell you that!" yelled Petra.

"Language!", said a barely audible voice from beneath Neil's parka. *"Language, Miss Petra."*

"Damn it!" she scolded Neil, "I thought you already muted that idiot bird."

"I did. I did. But I think maybe his settings got bumped back to 'default' during the transport."

"Well, quiet him down before I drop kick 'Mr. Tin Feathers' back into the future."

"Jerome," said Neil, "mute yourself until further notice."

"Muting now," replied Jerome.

O'Reilly cupped both hands around his mouth. "Listen up ...all of you. We don't have time for nonsense, alright? We need to know just where it is that we've landed. So, please, everybody ...just *stow it* while we figure it out. Then speaking as loudly and as clearly as he could he said "LULU, information request please ...I will need specific geographic location, a full date and time reference, nearest human settlement, available resources within walking distance, and any apparent dangers. Please deliver information verbally, with a volume setting of +8.5.

Without hesitation LULU began to loudly deliver the requested information:

- **General Location**: *Southwest quadrant of Niagara Falls, New York, United States of America*
- **Specific Location**: *Goat Island, a tourist destination*
- **Island Coordinates:** *43"04'51'N / 79' 04'03'W*
- **Highest Elevation:** *558 ft (170.1m)*
- **Date:** *January 12, 1957. It is locally 1310 hours (1:10 PM).*
- **Current Temperature:** *20.9 degrees Fahrenheit*
- **Maximum Wind Speed:** *25 mph*
- **Observation:** *snow/ ice pellets*
- **Anticipated Three-hour Outlook:** *Clearing, cold, cessation of snow/ ice pellet precipitation*
- **Nearest Human Settlement Accessible on Foot:**
  Niagara Falls, New York, United States of America

- **Actual Settlement Population:** *Specific number unavailable.*
- **Estimated Population:** *90,000 – 102,000*
- **Resources:**
  Abundant ...to include Food/ Clothing/ Lodging/ Police Authority
- **Nearest Suggested Source for Fulfillment of Basic Needs:**
  Falls Street ...a common shop and entertainment area
- **Specific Suggested Destination:**
  Sears Roebuck and Company – a 20th mid-century department store. Distance: Less than one mile
- **Most Expedient Walking Route:**
  Foot bridge - East on 1st Street / then - North to Falls Street
  (Additional directions to be provided as required)
- **Possible Dangers:**
  Icy surfaces / swift waters / massive waterfall / hypothermia via cold air - cold water/ distracted individual drivers of internal combustion vehicles / erratic traffic patterns / non-compliance with established traffic protocols / compromise of identity through prolonged interaction with area residents / unfamiliarity with local customs and mores / common cold / flu / measles / extensive list of infecting illnesses / lack of definitive plan and coordinated action

  ...Additional possible threats to follow as identified

Several minutes later, and with LULUs gentle guidance, the strange little group had made its way over the narrow east 1st street bridge leading to the mainland. Once there, they wound their way toward the busy downtown shopping district a quarter mile away. As they finally approached one of the main intersections of East Falls Street, O'Reilly halted his merry band and asked LULU for additional directions to her suggested destination. LULU responded promptly.

Destination Recommendation:
- *Sears and Roebuck department store - turn left 90° in approximately 75 feet –*
- *enter through public access door on North side of uncovered parking lot-*
- *removal of hats and gloves recommended once inside.*

As they crossed the small parking lot, a light snowfall drifted lazily down from a smoky grey sky.

"Holy cow!" yelled Pasani without warning. "Look at *that* would ya!"

"It's a car," said Petra.

Pasani hurried over to a rose-colored vehicle parked nearby. Lovingly touching its hood and massive chromed bumpers, he stood transfixed by its beauty.

"You two want to be alone?" needled Petra.

Pasani could not hear her now.

"I've never seen anything like this," he said to no one in particular. "And look, it's got two smaller windows …one on each side of the big rear window. Geez, I bet she's fast! Hey, it's an Oldsmobile. Imagine that …an Oldsmobile. Son of a gun!"

"It's a car," repeated Petra.

O'Reilly impatiently waived Pasani back into the group.

"Listen up everybody. I know you may think we look normal. But, take my word for it. We stand out here. We stand out in the way we talk, and think, and look. This is a different time we're in. And we haven't studied the period at all ...we don't know all the subtle ways people interact."

"So, what are we supposed to do then?" asked Neil.

"Yeah," Pasani added. "How *are* we supposed to act?"

"It'll take a while...but we'll get there" O'Reilly reassured them. "In the meantime, I suggest we do the following.

- Don't talk to people. If they ask you a question, just keep your answer short. Better yet, just nod and shake your head up and down.
- Avoid confrontation. Let everyone around you have the right of way. Avoid eye contact.
- If absolutely necessary, let *me* do the talking for us. At least I'm familiar with the process.
- Let's go with a cover story. So, instead of being four time-travelers who've barely escaped annihilation, how about we present as four tourists from the Midwest of the United States of America.

"What about names?" asked Neil. "We'll need names."

"True enough," said O'Reilly. "So, just use your own *first* names. Neil, Joe, Judy ...they all work fine."

"Petra not Judy," came a disgruntled voice.

"Fine. Go with Petra then. As for a last name, we'll just use one name for everybody. We'll all be part of the same family ...just plain folks here on vacation ...here on vacation from ..." O'Reilly hesitated before adding ... "North Dakota. Yeah, we're here from North Dakota."

"And our last name is what, Bowtie?"

"You know, I kind of like 'Remington'", he said.

"Shit. Petra Remington? Really?"

"Just give it a chance, Judy. Who knows? It could grow on you."

"OK, so now what?" asked Pasani.

"So now, the Remingtons go shopping."

And with that, the newly born Raymond Remington led his strange family of North Dakotans through the stores rear entrance.

"Geez!" said an excited Pasani as they passed the appliance section. "What's that thing there?"

"Television," said Petra. "Television."

Shoes, Socks, and a Bottle of 'Evening in Paris'

Stepping through the doors of Sears Roebuck and Company, the motley group stood as one, large snowflakes melting and dripping from their clothing.

"Hey!" observed a dazzled Neil Remington. "Do you smell that? What is all that? Hey, commander, can you ask LULU what all those smells are?"

"Sure," said O'Reilly, "and then let's get on with our task. Seeing no other shoppers close by, O'Reilly said softly. "LULU, you heard the man. What is it we're all smelling?"

"Certainly, commander. A brief summary of the 15 current most prominent olfactory particulate influences now follows. Order is greatest to least:

- _Cotton, Rubber, Roasted Nuts, Perfume, Leather, Wet Wool, Cigarette Smoke, Aftershave Lotion, Hair Tonic, Plastic, Paper, Beef Sandwich and its Garnishments (referred to locally as 'hot dog'), Various Candies, Paper Currency_

"Wow!" said Neil, "Wouldn't have guessed any of that!"

Several minutes later, as the group moved through the main aisle of the store's first floor, its members struggled to stay on task.

"Jesus!" said Petra pointing. "Check it out. New vinyl. Damn! I bet they've got a brand-new long play album by Elvis Presley."

"Hey," said Neil, "we both have the same last name. I wonder if we're related?"

"Yeah, right. You wish!" scoffed Petra.

"Please," pleaded O'Reilly, "put Elvis on hold and try to stay focused."

"Commander ..."

"It's Raymond, Neil ...remember ...Raymond."

"Oh yeah. Well, Raymond, what *is* that thing overhead?" O'Reilly looked up to see a number of small, metal containers. Whizzing back and forth between the various department's cashiers and a central collection point on the second floor, they traveled at speed along the cables to which they were attached.

"Not sure, Neil. But, they kind of look like a secure way to move things around. So, can't be sure but...maybe there's cash in them."

"Wow! I gotta get me one of those!" declared a wide-eyed Pasani.

O'Reilly followed Pasani's enraptured gaze to an aging store employee. Red in the face, he was clumsily struggling to demonstrate the art of spinning a circular piece of plastic around one's waist.

"It's a Hula-Hoop!" said an enraptured Pasani. And he pointed to a brightly colored sign nearby.

O'Reilly shook his head in frustration. Then tapping each of his comrades on the shoulder, he gestured them in the direction of the Stanley Tool hardware section. For the second time in ten minutes, he called the huddle to order.

"Attention, children! Did none of you listen to a single thing I told you outside? If not, let me tell you one more time. Either we find a way to blend into 1957 Niagara Falls, New York, or we risk ...hell, I don't even know what we risk. Just the same, let's keep to ourselves and do what we have to do. Let's, at least, make it through our first day in town. Alright?"

Looking around the group, he received three short nods.

"Good," he continued. "Now here's the shopping list we need to fill before we leave the store.

- Something to eat
- A new set of clothes and shoes for each of us
- Four large pieces of luggage
- A radio
- A compass
- A local newspaper
- Four pocketknives
- Some paper and pens
- Personal toiletries ...to include shaving instruments and anything else suited to Petra's needs ...
- A hat for Petra and her bald cranium
- And finally, we need to leave here with anonymity ...*no one* should remember we were ever here"

Pasani spoke up first. "So, where we gonna get the moola to pay for all this?"

"Don't worry about that," said a confident O'Reilly. "LULU and I will scare up enough legal tender for our purposes. In the meantime, the three of you split up and scout out all the items on our list. Once I've got the cash to pay for everything, I'll come back to *this spot* and we'll go get everything we need."

"Sounds like a plan, boss," said a tepid Petra.

"So …everybody be back here in 30 minutes. OK? Thirty minutes. Use the large wall clocks like the one behind me." Then, looking over his shoulder at it, he added, "It's 1:20 right now. So, everybody be back and standing *right here* when that large hand is pointing at the '10'. Everybody got it?"

All three nodded for a second time.

"That's good, boys and girls. Now let's go make Uncle Raymond *really* proud."

As the others split up and wandered off, O'Reilly followed the steady flow of shoppers out onto the main floor. Reconnoitering the area, he noticed a large rectangular food island in the center of the floor. Drawing closer, he watched as the young employee, 28-year-old Gail Jenkins, carried out her transactions from within the island. As each customer approached her, they would choose their order from a number of possible treats. The overhead menu listed hot dogs, roasted nuts, fruit punch, and a choice of 20 different kinds of candy. Once their order had been filled, they would hand Miss Jenkins their paper money and she would return any change due them. The store's money would then be stored in the drawer of a large metal container on the counter beside her. Before the ponderous contraption could open, it required that several of the buttons protruding from its front be pushed in with some force. O'Reilly noted that Miss Jenkins always placed any larger bills beneath the tray of small bins that filled the drawer.

After watching for five minutes, O'Reilly surreptitiously slipped away to discuss with LULU, how they might come into possession of the drawer's modest stash. A few minutes later, he had returned to the rectangular food island. Smiling, he leaned across its counter.
"Can I help you?" Miss Jenkins asked cheerfully.

283

"Yes," replied O'Reilly. "I believe you can. I wonder if you would be kind enough to give me six hot dogs, two pounds of roasted nuts, a one-pound bag of those jelly beans, and let's see ...oh yes ...all of the bills in your cash register that are larger than a dollar."

Confused, Miss Jenkins said "I'm sorry, sir. What did you say?"

"Miss Jenkins, if there were any other way ...believe me ...or if I had more time, but ...LULU, would you please help Miss Jenkins with our order."

As an unseen ripple of energy pulsed through the unsuspecting store clerk, she began to laugh quietly. Stepping away from the counter, she retrieved six cooking hot dogs from the rolling cooker before placing them carefully in their respective buns.

"Condiments are at the end of the counter," she announced with a broad smile.

Then, refocusing on O'Reilly's order, she scooped up two pounds of roasted nuts, a pound of jelly beans, and one hundred and eighty dollars from the cash register. Carefully placing each in its respective white bag, she handed the completed order to her customer.

"Thank you for your help, Miss Jenkins."

"Oh my," she replied, "you're very welcome."

It would be a full hour before the effects of LULU's subtle magic wore off. When it finally did, the young cashier would remember nothing that had transpired, except perhaps a lingering sense of recent well-being.

On their way back to meet the others, O'Reilly and LULU made two more register stops, increasing their stockpile of cash by $320 in worn fives, tens, and twenties. Arriving back in the tool department, O'Reilly announced to his waiting Remington clan that they now had six hundred twentieth century dollars at their disposal.

"Is that a lot?" asked Neil.

"Enough," said O'Reilly.

For the next two hours, the group moved as one throughout the store. Trying on clothes, examining luggage, and smelling cheap perfume, they made their way methodically through their entire "needs list". Finally, having paid cash for every item, they shoved all of their new belongings into four oversized suit cases and made their way to the same doors through which they had arrived. Stepping outside, the four were greeted by pale indigo skies, a crisp January breeze, and the distant roar of an angry waterfall.

"Where do we go from here?" asked Pasani.

"You know, Joe, I think I saw the top of a hotel sticking up from over near the island. Let's go check it out. We need a place to stay and we've still got a bit of cash left."

"How much *did* all this stuff cost?" asked Neil.

O'Reilly paused to calculate. "Somewhere around $255" he said. "Which leaves" he added, "345!"

"That doesn't sound like much," said Petra.

"Maybe not," answered O'Reilly "but in your day, Judy, that would be more than $3000."

"Well, I suppose that's better than a kick in the head," she conceded.

"I'm starving," complained Pasani. "I mean ...I'm *really* hungry."

"Well," suggested O'Reilly with a half-smile, "if you can wait 'til we get to the hotel, there's some cold hot dogs stuffed beneath some brand-new wool socks."

"M-m-m-m," said Pasani. "Sounds great!"

But Did Marilyn Monroe Ever Sleep in Our Bed?

Making their way over deep ruts of frozen snow, the four travelers slowly made their way in the direction of the concrete edifice known as the Hotel Niagara. What would have been a ten-minute stroll on a summer's day, now required forty-five strenuous minutes of extreme effort. The enormous pieces of luggage they dragged with them, might just as well have been anchors. Petra, in particular, was struggling mightily. Pasani, always the gentleman, made the mistake of asking if he could help her carry it.

"I bet it weighs half of what you do," he said.

Petra stopped abruptly and adjusted her new beret. "Don't worry about it, hero," she blurted between breaths. "If I need your help, I'll let you know."

Cold, wet and exhausted, the family Remington, at last made their way into the hotel's lobby, the excessively dry heat of the interior sweeping over them in a welcoming embrace. Looking around in wonder, they were dazzled by elaborate ceiling plaster moldings, gilded capitals, and oak and emerald-green terrazzo floors. Built in the mid-1920s, the structure still maintained a quiet atmosphere of elegant dignity.

Petra, like the others, let her oversized burden drop to the floor.

"This place is fucking awesome!" she whispered.

"And may I help you?" inquired a friendly male voice from a small rosewood kiosk.

"Just need to check in," O'Reilly replied.

"Of course. And may I introduce myself? My name is Justin Smathers. I am the hotel's receptionist and am here to assist you in whatever way I can during your check-in."

"Well, that's just real nice of you," said O'Reilly."

"If you would simply follow me please."

Then, like a mother duck leading her ducklings, he led the hotel's latest guests across the lobby to the main desk.

"Here for check-in" he announced to a lean fifty something desk clerk. Then turning abruptly on his heel, Smathers snapped his fingers in the direction of a waiting bellboy. Without further instruction, the young man arrived and carefully lifted all four suit cases onto a wide rolling cart.

"Good day and enjoy your stay," said Smathers before returning to his kiosk.

"Welcome to the Hotel Niagara," said the clerk behind the counter. "And do we have reservations?"

O'Reilly cleared his throat. "No, I'm afraid not."

"Oh, I see. Well, the good news is, it being off-season here in 'The Falls', we do have several rooms available. Now, do you have a preference in room size or floor location?"

"It would be great if we could get a large room with a couple good-size beds. And, I would prefer it be on the second floor," O'Reilly suggested cheerfully.

"Ah yes," the clerk replied. "Let me check." Then turning his back to them, he flipped methodically through a tray of 3X5 cards. "I'm sorry" he said finally. We have nothing available in a 'double-full' on the second floor. But I do have adjoining suites, each with a full-size bed, up on seven."

"That's fine. We'll take it," confirmed O'Reilly. As an afterthought, he asked "How much per night?"

"Twenty-five dollars per room, Sir."

"Fine," said a relieved O'Reilly. "And I'd like to pay for our first night in advance, and confirm we'll be staying an additional five days beyond that." Then pulling out a wad of currency from beneath his parka, he counted out a handful of crinkled bills totaling fifty dollars.

"Now, sir, if you'll just sign in to our register, I'll prepare your receipt and then Robert here will show you to your rooms."

"You bet," agreed O'Reilly. Then picking up a rather ponderous ball point pen he signed in as 'Raymond Remington and Family - Fargo, North Dakota'."

Spinning the register back around, the clerk read the entry.

"Well, Mr. Remington, we welcome you and your family to our fair city. We hope your stay is a pleasant one ...you and your family being so very far from home."

"Got that right," mumbled Petra.

"Well, thank you so much," said a smiling O'Reilly. "And, you're right. Home does seem like a long way off."

"Wait!" shouted Petra, pointing at the wall behind the clerk. "Is *that* who I think it is? Is that a picture of Marilyn Monroe?"

"Yes, miss. It certainly is. That's a picture of Miss Monroe on the day she checked in right there where you're standing." Then proudly, he added "That's me just off to the side there."

"Wow!" exclaimed an excited Petra. "Marilyn Monroe was right here ...right in this spot!"

"Yes she was," the clerk confirmed once again.

"Wow! When was she here? Why was she here?"

"Oh, I guess it was three years ago now. Here to film her movie 'Niagara'."

"How cool is that! And so, what room did she stay in? Can we stay in *that* one ...the 'Marilyn Monroe Room'?"

"No. I'm afraid not, miss. We no longer identify which room it was she stayed in. Early on we told folks which room it was, but so many of them carried off souvenirs, we had to stop."

"But just the same, we *could* be staying in the same room she did, right? I mean, it's possible."

Looking mildly amused, he simply said "Of course. Anything's possible."

"So, who else stayed here?" demanded Petra.

"Well, let's see ...Joe DiMaggio, of course. Then there was Joseph Cotton and, my favorite, Al Capone."

Petra looked disappointed. "Oh ... Well ...I don't know any of those."

O'Reilly cleared his throat loudly and gave Petra a stern parental glare. "Don't you think it's time we all go up to our room, cousin 'Petty'?"

Petra stopped talking and returned O'Reilly's glare. "Right you are, cousin Ray. Lead on!"

Ten minutes later, all four were milling about their adjoining rooms.

"So, who sleeps where?" asked Neil.

"Well, suggested O'Reilly, "How 'bout you and I sleep in here, and Joe and the 'problem child' take the other room.

Pasani flushed. "The two of us ...together ...in there?"

Petra punched his shoulder with her fist. "Don't worry, hero. You can always scream for help. I'm pretty sure these guys would save you. Wouldn't you guys save Joe?"

O'Reilly ignored her.

"You know what?" he said thoughtfully, "How about, to help our plan along, the two of you just tell folks that you're husband and wife"

"Well, I don't know," began Pasani.

"Hey, put a sock in it. If Bowtie things it'll help sell the program, then I say why not?"

Pasani looked nonplussed.

"Joe," said O'Reilly, "you look a bit stunned. And I can't tell if you're happy or sad."

"Exactly!" said Joe.

291

Understanding the Thing
That's Not a Thing at All

Later in the day, O'Reilly asked Neil "You seen Joe anywhere?"

"I think he's out in the hallway?"

"Well, what's he doing out there?"

"Don't know for sure, commander. He finished off a couple of those hot dogs and now I think he's just sitting out there brooding."

"Brooding has the potential for discontent and compromised performance," whispered an eavesdropping LULU.

"Thanks, LULU. Got it!"

"Will you need a list of options to address this potential problem?"

"No, thanks, LULU. Not this time."

"It's kind of weird when you do that," said Neil. "Lucky for me, I know who you're talking to."

Pasani was sitting on the top step of the nearby stairwell, his flight jacket across his lap"

"Hey, Joe," began O'Reilly, "you look like someone stole your puppy."

"Yeah," said Joe, "and I feel like I look."

"Anything you want to talk about?"

"No. I don't think talking's gonna change things or make them any better."

"Well, I'm not so sure that's true. I mean, it might not solve your problem, but it might just help you feel a little better about it."

"You think so?"

"I do."

"Well," he said, "it's one of those man-woman, boy-girl things. You sure you want to hear this?"

"I'm tough," said a smiling O'Reilly." I can take it."

Pasani looked unconvinced but began to talk just the same.

"You ever been in love, commander?"

A bit surprised, O'Reilly replied "Sure ...yeah ...lots of times."

"You ever been in love in a serious way?"

"And what do you mean by 'serious'?"

"I mean serious as in sick to your stomach, can't think straight, can't focus ... even on the simple stuff."

"Oh," he said sympathetically, "*that* kind of love."

"Yeah, the really serious kind."

"Well," replied O'Reilly, his eyes looking far away, "in that case ...once."

Then looking back in Joe's direction, he simply asked "So, what's the problem then, Joe? She doesn't feel the same way about you? It *is* Petra we're talking about, right?"

"I could ask you the same thing," said Pasani without a blink.

"What do you mean?" O'Reilly asked.

"...You and Petra. You got a thing for her, right?"

"No. Not quite, Joe."

"What do you mean 'not quite'? I mean, either you do or you don't. Am I wrong? Either a man has strong feelings for a woman or he doesn't. Be honest now. Which is it?"

"Well, since you're determined to know so much ...I care about her, but not in a romantic way."

"You mean care about her like a big brother ...somethin' like that?"

"Yeah. Somethin' like that."

"You know, I've been watching you whenever you're around her. And, I gotta tell you, commander ...seems to me there's more to it than that."

"You know what, Pasani? You should seriously consider a career as a private detective. Yeah, you got me. There is more to it than that."

"I'm all ears, commander."

"OK. Here it is. Petra reminds me more than a little of someone I cared for once ...a long time ago..."

"Yeah?"

"Yeah. I met her on mission thirteen ...lucky thirteen! It was smack in the middle of her violent world ...1937 Spain. She was a freedom fighter, living in caves and praying that God would come to the aid of her people's revolution. She was small ...jet black hair ...and eyes that could cut right through you. I watched her stand her ground, when the men of her detachment had scattered before a German Stuka and a government ground assault. I ..." O'Reilly paused, then continued in a quieter tone. "The truth is, I never felt that way about a woman before or since. It was like I fell into those fierce dark eyes and there was just no way out."

O'Reilly glanced over at Pasani. "You're probably thinking 'what a sap?'. But it's the truth. That's all I can tell you."

"So, what did you do about it?"

"What I did, Joe, was to pretend it didn't matter ...that I'd feel differently down the road ...and that the aching and the longing I felt would eventually fade. What I did, Joe, was walk away."

"And?"

"And?"

"And then what?"

"Then I pretended ...still do ..."

"Pretended what?"

"Oh, that it would have been hopeless to try ...That we wouldn't have made it anyway and" ...He paused a second time. "Her name was Zarita ...Zarita Santos. I called her 'Saint Z' just to get under her skin."

"So, what happened? I mean, did she feel the same way?"

"Amazingly, Joe, she did. But it turns out that two people from different lives and different centuries aren't exactly the perfect match up. She was committed to her revolution and I was committed to my Homeland."

"So, what happened?" Joe asked again.

"Just what you'd expect would happen. She stayed there among the ruins and I packed up and transported back to my frozen island home. I guess the whole thing would have been tragic, if it hadn't been so damn funny. Having watched a lot of couples down through history, I can tell you ...finding your soulmate is hard enough when both parties are stably ensconced in the same slice of time."

"I don't agree," said Pasani.

"You don't?"

"Yeah, I don't. There's *nothin'* funny about that story! ...Not a damn thing."

O'Reilly involuntarily nodded.

"No? Well, how 'bout this for humor? There was another man there who cared about her deeply."

"Another guy? Competition, huh?"

"This guy confessed to her that he was head over heels ...could think of nothing or no one except her ...day and night."

"He had it bad huh?

"Yeah, Joe, he had it bad …real bad."

"So, you think they got together after you left?"

"Don't think so, Joe. And here's the punchline. My competition was a priest!"

"Son-of-a-bitch! …pardon my French" blurted Joe. "Did not see that comin'."

"Yeah, apparently the whole love-thing is a 'bitch' regardless of the century."

An awkwardly long moment passed before O'Reilly regained his bearings.

"So, what about you and Petra? What's the problem? I don't get it."

"The problem is I … she …we're …"

"Could you be just a wee bit more specific?"

"The problem is …she's just not the kind of girl …the kind of woman I thought I wanted. I mean, I spent most of my life dreamin' about a soft spoken, well-mannered female with long legs, long hair, and a closet full of cotton dresses. Petra doesn't line up with even one of those."

"Well, true enough. She's not exactly a shrinking violet or a card-carrying member of the Ladies Etiquette Club. But on the other hand, she's got a lot of energy, is fearless, you always know where you stand with her, and well …then there's that whole animal magnetism thing she puts out."

"Her animal magnetism ..." Joe repeated wistfully. "Tell me about it! Whenever I get within arm's reach of her, I feel like I'm back in my P40 ...I'm in a crash dive ...I'm pullin' maximum **g**s ...and my wing spars are startin' to snap."

"Sounds pretty intense."

"Yeah. It is. That's the problem. I'm not sure I can pull out of this dive. And mostly, if I'm honest, I'm not sure I care if I ever do."

"So, have the two of you talked about any of this? ...about how you two feel about each other ...or what you're going to do about it?"

"Not really. Neither one of us seems to be very good at that sort of thing."

"That *does* make it harder!"

"Here's the thing, O'Reilly. I had my mind all made up see. I'd thought the whole thing through and decided she was just not the kind of woman I wanted to have kids with ...too rough around the edges."

"So, did something change your mind?"

Joe nodded. "You remember back at the Sears store when you left us alone for a while?

"Yeah."

"Well, we were over in the record department there. Petra was diggin' through these big albums lookin' for this guy Elvis. And that's when it happened."

"When *what* happened?"

"Well," said Pasani, "this father and his daughter came and stood next to her. I could see she was listening to them and pretending not to."

"OK ..."

"Yeah, so the father says ...Taffy, are you sure you want that one. Most *adults* don't even buy that one. You're ten years old. How about Elvis or the Everly Brothers instead?"

"No!" says Taffy. "I heard it in a movie. It's just wonderful! I would really like to have that one, Dad! It's called 'Rhapsody in Blue' by a man named George Gershwin"

The expression on the father's face was this mix of concern and kindness. You could tell he was really trying to make the right decision. Finally, a smile comes over his face and he says "OK. OK. Gershwin it is. Just remember, you can't bring it back once you play it."

"I know," says Taffy. "But, that's ok ...'cause I already know I like it."

O'Reilly interrupted. So, Petra heard all this?"

"Yes, she did."

"And?"

"And?"

"And what happened then, Joe."

"Well, that's the thing. When I looked over at her, she had these big old crocodile tears in her eyes. Then, when she sees me starin' at her, she just looks back to the record rack ...pretends nothing happened."

"So then ...?"

"So then, it got me to thinkin' ...if a tough, tough woman like her can get teary-eyed over something like that ...well, maybe she's not so tough after all. At least, not all the time."

"You do know her father had to raise her by himself, right?"

Joe frowned and looked concerned. "No, sir, I did not. But that would explain a lot."

"So, what are you thinkin' now, Joe? You two a "go" or a "gone"?

"Commander, here's the truth. I've got it bad for that girl. I mean real bad. It makes no sense, but there it is. No matter how hard I try, I can't stop thinkin' about her. I even day dream about her. I mean ...get this ...I imagine the two of us sitting by a peaceful lake with a full moon overhead. I mean ...come on! What am I doin'? And, oh yeah ...look at this will ya."

Pasani pulled out a crumpled sheet of Hotel Niagara stationary from the pocket of his jacket.

"It's a poem for Christ sake ...pardon my ...It's a poem!" he said. See for yourself."

O'Reilly took the tired paper from Joe and, with some effort, read the penciled words aloud.

300

One moon
Upon the water
Among the stars
Within my heart
Forever ours!

"Well," said O'Reilly as he handed the poem back to its creator, "you're right about one thing."

"Yeah?"

"You've got it worse than I thought."

"Yep. Really bad," agreed Pasani.

"But my question still stands ...especially since I know now just how much you care about her." He hesitated before repeating his question. "Lieutenant Pasani, are you two a "go" or a "gone"?"

An extended silence followed before Joe suddenly came back to life. As a wide *golly-gosh* smile spread across his face, he coughed out a laugh.

"Commander, I do believe we may just have ourselves a 'go'!"

Grācius Filn Saddles-Up and Presses All the Buttons

As always, agent Filn arrived at Homeland Headquarters precisely on time. With a determined air of authority, he strode stiffly through the ground floor doors and down a brightly polished corridor. Then stepping into the main elevator marked "Clearance Required", he utilized the ten second ride to the top to organize what he considered the salient points of recent unhappy events.

- CH3 Ramon O'Reilly has yet to be apprehended
- Tech-transport operator, Neil Presley, has been determined to be aiding and abetting CH3 O'Reilly, and has apparently participated in unauthorized travel, study, and personal reflection over a period of five plus years
- Mid twentieth century guest, Joseph Pasani, is now missing from his assigned duty station and presumed to be an integral participant in recent treasonous acts
- Recently gathered forensic information, from the home-pod of Neil Presley, indicates the presence of an unidentified fourth conspirator, an unknown female
- Within the past hour, and not far from this very complex, a number of special assignment agents were attacked, disoriented, and disabled
- Said disorientation was suggestive of a pulse technology originally resourced into the obsolete LULU assistant 1.7, one that was removed from O'Reilly's organics upon his most recent return to The Homeland
- It is now strongly suspected that CH3 O'Reilly has somehow regained the use of this very same force multiplier, the LULU 1.7

Recommendations:
1. A substantial increase in security personnel guarding this complex
2. The 24/7 "close-in" protection of King Nordvig
3. A "shoot-on-site" order to be issued for all four dangerous conspirators
4. The issuance of a *re-assuring statement* to all Homeland citizens that explains any unusual activities they may witness, as nothing more than "on-going security games designed to ensure their future safety and well-being"
5. The playing of calming musical interludes at all *Gopher Transport Hubs*, as well as in the transport gondolas themselves

Confident in his information, and hopeful that all of his recommendations would be adopted, the loyal head of BDA activities took a final deep breath before stepping through the elevator doors. Even after twenty-five years of serving Number One, the thrill of stepping into such magnificent surroundings, had never diminished. The very knowledge that he, Grācius Filn alone, had been granted unfettered access to the most powerful man in the history of the world, past or present, was ...well ...boldly empowering. As Filn stood there on the ancient Persian carpet, an eerie sense of foreboding began to close in around him. Unlike every other scheduled meeting with The King, Nordvig was not standing grandly before him as the doors parted. He was not there boldly brandishing a 13th century Chinese straight sword in order that he might act out his favorite well-worn joke.

"Should the King kill you now or let you pass?" he would ask.

"That, King Nordvig, is entirely your choice," Filn would respectfully respond.

"Then," Nordvig would say, "on this one occasion, the King shall grant you passage ..."

"My grateful thanks to His Highness," Filn would reply bowing deeply.

And then, as on so many other occasions, their meeting would begin. Filn would sit angular and straight in a silk upholstered chair of Victorian origin, as Nordvig paced restlessly before the enormous window overlooking his kingdom. After approximately thirty minutes of a mostly one-sided discussion, The King would abruptly announce the meetings end. He would then point to a shallow silver plate sitting atop an exquisitely veneered Louis XIV cabinet. And, as usual, Filn would walk to the plate and sort casually through the collection of valuable gems.

"May I choose this one, your highness," he would ask.

Nordvig would then consider the request thoughtfully for several seconds before finally waving a kerchiefed hand nonchalantly.

"Yes. The King believes you may."

That was the routine. That was the way their meetings always unfolded. For if there was one thing that the King did not approve of, it was surely exceptions, contradictions, unscheduled events, and anything of an unexpected nature. For him, every day was to be a repeat of the previous day, a predictable and pleasant series of encounters with all the many luxuries and indulgences of his station. It was simply the case that all of these Kingly happenings should take place precisely on time for a pre-ordained number of minutes or hours. Even his amorous interludes were conducted with a handful of select courtesans, all of whom were forbidden to touch him or make eye contact, except during specifically scheduled appointments.

"Your highness." Filn called out gently. "Your highness, it's agent Filn and I have arrived for our meeting."

When there was no reply, he repeated his words with slightly more volume. And when this salutation also garnered no response, Filn made the bold move of stepping off of the oriental carpet ...without permission of the King. Quickly searching The Nest and its ante-rooms, Filn began to grow increasingly concerned. Arriving at the richly paneled emergency departure door, he stepped through it and descended a platinum spiral staircase to the floor below. Arriving on a modest marble foyer, he slid a thickly armored door to one side.

Filn recognized at once the transport launch-recovery bay before him. On more than one occasion he had stood guard as his King departed from it. He had even been present for several recovery events, when Golden Nordvig returned, his launch circle stacked high with priceless treasures and mementos from ancient worlds. Quietly stepping forward now, Filn perused the room and its highly polished walls. Though his experienced eye could identify nothing amiss, an intuitive savvy honed sharp by limitless investigations, told him something was terribly wrong. Stopping to listen, he could hear nothing, save the even hum of the launch-board controller. Continuing forward with measured steps, a fleeting reflection near the room's center abruptly caught his eye. Cautiously nearing the object, a numbing awareness suddenly swept over him. Staring down at the inconceivable, he recognized a single gold lame´ slipper, it's colorful threads now spotted by the splash of a king's dark blood.

As he stood quietly over the lifeless body of his king, the silence of the room was broken by the even and mellow female tones of the launch-board controller.

"Attention all launch personnel. The follow-on-transport-window for additional persons and/ or materiel will close in 120 seconds. **Final circle-close-count commencing now in 5-4-3-2-1 and...MARK.***"*

LULU Rolls the Dice
and Water Always Wins

Two full days had passed since their arrival in Niagara Falls, New York. The temperature outside still hovered in the 20s and none of the four time-travelers had ventured out. What all four had done was eat, sleep, warm up and contemplate possible future plans.

Pasani suggested they make their way to a warmer state, build a cabin, and grow a large garden full of vegetables. "No one would even know our story. We'd just live a real quiet life there ...kinda like pioneers.

Neil suggested they find a warm public library; stay there and read books. "There's a lot of knowledge in books" he said, "and maybe we could figure out a really good plan."

"Well," said Petra, "I've still got my gun right here with me, and there's gotta be a bank somewhere near-by. I say we hit the local yokels hard and fast ...get some descent spending money ...maybe head on out to California."

O'Reilly listened patiently to the several questionable suggestions. Then clearing his voice, he unceremoniously stated ...

"Those are *all* really bad suggestions. I could give you a number of reasons why each one is bad, but let's just move on."

"And so, *your* big plan is to do what?" demanded Petra.

"Glad you asked, Judy. Here it is:

1. All three of you stay put in this hotel for the next five days (no exceptions)
2. I board an aircraft and fly to Las Vegas, Nevada

3. LULU and I win enormous sums of money
4. I fly back here with said enormous sums of money
5. The four of us pack up and fly our enormous sums of money someplace warm and friendly

A brief silence fell over the room. Pasani was the first to speak up.

"Well, that sounds ok by me."

"Me too," said Neil.

"Not too bad," Petra admitted reluctantly. "But, if you're going out to Vegas, you damn well better get 'The King's' autograph."

"Sorry to disappoint, Judy," advised an uninvited LULU. *But, 'The King', as of 1957, has already come and gone in Vegas. He was there last year, but for less than a month. Sorry to report, he won't be back again until 1969."*

"Well, that just sucks! To be so close and still not...I mean that just sucks."

"Certainly," agreed LULU. *"My sympathies."*

The following day, Ramon O'Reilly boarded a local bus to Buffalo and then a two-hop flight to Las Vegas.

Checking in to The Fremont Hotel and Casino, O'Reilly made the rounds of every major gambling establishment in the city. Being careful not to win too much on any given visit, O'Reilly and LULU would even occasionally loose a large predetermined sum back to the house. Nevertheless, after three days of placing bets, and utilizing LULUs card counting skills as well as her ability to calculate the odds of any dice roll, O'Reilly was sitting on a tidy new nest egg of one hundred and eighty thousand dollars.

As he retired to his room that night, LULU presented him with her estimate of their situation.

*"**Alert, CH3 O'Reilly.** Current winnings are now within the parameters of your originally stated monetary goal. The odds of your adding to your winnings without arousing suspicion and, or, retaliation, have now fallen to an unacceptable risk level.*
Recommendations:
- *Immediate disengagement from all gambling activities.*
- *The creation of a substantial distance from this population center."*

Fully appreciating LULU's recommendations, O'Reilly packed his bags, slipped quietly into a waiting taxi, and boarded the first available flight headed east. Then, after an eight-hour layover in Chicago, he boarded a second plane bound for Buffalo. Just four hours after that, he climbed aboard a daily round-trip bus that delivered him once again back to where he'd started.

Exhausted from his journey, he nevertheless determined to stop at the front desk to be certain his three restless roommates had not caused any concerns or raised any eyebrows.

An unfamiliar clerk was standing behind the sign-in desk.

"Checking in, sir?"

"Oh no," replied O'Reilly. "I'm already checked-in with my three traveling companions. Been away for a few days. Just wanted to make sure all is well, no loose ends. Just a worrier, I guess."

"Well, sir, you wouldn't happen to be a Mr. O'Reilly?"

O'Reilly's gut did a sudden back-flip. "Why, yes. Yes, I am."

"Well then, sir, I have an envelope here that was left with instructions it be given to you upon your return."

"An envelope?" asked an increasingly uneasy O'Reilly.

"Yes, sir, and it's right here somewhere."

Then rifling through several cubby holes on the wall behind him, the clerk finally produced a sealed, standard size envelope. In black block print across its face ... 'CH3 Ramon O'Reilly'."

It was left by a rather gaunt and serious gentlemen, just before he took the elevator up to visit your friends on seven.

O'Reilly blanched. "He went up to see my friends? When was that? When did he go up there?" His voice was growing louder and more distressed with each question.

"Well," said the surprised desk clerk, "that would have been two hours ago, when I first came on duty."

O'Reilly squeezed the envelope tightly in one hand and picked up his suitcase of currency in the other. Then moving quickly to the elevator bank, he rang for service and tried not to imagine the worst.

As the elevator doors closed behind him, he tore open the envelope, greedily reading its contents.

"CH3 O'Reilly ...Your three friends are now safely in my care. Should you return today, and should you wish to see them alive one more time, you will need to appear at 2330 hours, on the crossing bridge to Goat Island.

There are no other options ...
G. Filn, Supervising Agent, Homeland BDA"

Crushing the note into a ball, O'Reilly called up a thumb nail display of current local conditions. Trying hard to stay focused, he read the following.

TIME:	1050 *Hours*
TEMPERATURE:	8 Degrees Fahrenheit
WIND:	SE-13 *Miles Per Hour*
PRECIPITATION:	0.18 *Inches/Frozen*
CHILL FACTOR:	*4.6 Degrees Fahrenheit*
WARNINGS:	*Frostbite to Exposed Skin*

Having arrived at the first of their two suites, O'Reilly jostled the room key into its slot. Turning it with a resounding click, he swung the door open wide. Once inside, he quickly closed and locked it behind him. Then placing the suitcase at the foot of the bed, he searched the rooms small bathroom before moving into the adjoining suite. Finding no trace of life in either, he returned to the first room. Intentionally kicking the suitcase over with his foot, he shoved it in one motion beneath the bed. As he did, he imagined he heard a distinct metallic rattle. Getting down on all fours now, he peered into the darkened recess. Barely visible and lying almost vertically against the far wall, he could just make out the outline of Petra's revolver.

"What happened, Judy?" he asked to the empty room ...
" Filn get the drop? Take your favorite toy? ...Toss it under here?"

Pushing the bottom of the bed off to one side, he then leaned in behind the head board and retrieved the deadly compact gun. Flipping open its chamber, he confirmed a full complement of five rounds. Then, stuffing the firearm into the pocket of his parka, he replaced the bed to its original position, and stepped out into the hall. The clock near the elevator now read **11:10**.

Three minutes later, O'Reilly was standing outside the hotel's frosted brass doors, a frigid wind cutting relentlessly through his clothing. Pulling the hood of his coat around head and neck, he began the short walk that would bring him to the single bridge linking the mainland to a deserted Goat Island.

Both hands shoved deep inside the pockets of his coat, his right hand fell upon the cold metal shape of Petra's revolver. "Easy enough ..." he reassured himself. Then straining to remember some of his many weapons training courses, he recalled that this particular weapon was a simple double-action type. One needed only to point it and squeeze the trigger five times. "Easy enough ..." he repeated to himself.

As he neared the top of the aging bridge, he was abruptly punched sideways by a blast of Artic air. Grasping for a weathered stone railing, he struggled to right himself. Looking down, he could see nothing beneath him, save stray reflections of scattered light. Too dark to make out the river below, his hearing was overwhelmed by the rushing water as it thrashed and tumbled over the many protruding rocks. Involuntarily, he recalled a recent LULU summation of the river that flowed around Goat Island...

"...less than a quarter mile beyond the connecting bridge lay the unforgiving and deadly American Falls".

Finally righting himself, O'Reilly lowered his head and strode determinedly toward the snow-covered island perhaps ten yards away. As he neared the shoreline, a familiar voice shouted out a gruff command.

"Stop right there!"

"Filn!" he shouted back, "Is that you?"

"Oh, it's *absolutely* me" came the reply. "Now take off your coat and slowly turn 360 degrees."

Having no recourse, O'Reilly complied.

"You see ...no threat from me, agent Filn. None at all. Now, can I please put my coat back on. I know you don't want me to catch cold out here."

"Put it back on. Can't leave clues, you know. Just keep your hands out where I can see them."

O'Reilly pulled the parka back on. Then crossing his arms and placing each hand beneath an armpit, he asked "This good enough?"

"Just walk forward," barked Filn. And he gestured with his kill-stick toward a narrow path that traced the river's edge.

"Where we headed, agent Filn? You *do* know the park's closed right? And this path looks like one of those the newly-weds take in the springtime. Agent Filn, does this mean you have feelings for me? Quite a surprise really. It's the way I wear this frumpy parka, isn't it?"

Filn grunted something profane and pushed O'Reilly roughly forward down the path.

"We stop here!" he shouted above the noise of the rapids. Then pointing in the direction of the riverbank, he screamed "Cliff-Hunter O'Reilly, I give you your friends ...all three." Filn then pointed his kill-stick's beam-light a short distance ahead.

O'Reilly involuntarily gasped. Fifty feet away, tied back to back were Petra and Pasani. The long rope that encircled them had been looped over an ice laden tree branch overhead. Swinging precariously just above the river's rushing waters, their fate was now literally in the hands of Neil Presley, who held the rope's other end. Struggling mightily to keep it taut ...his bare hands had turned a bluish grey from the effort.

O'Reilly now recalled the voice of a long-ago academy instructor. "Should you ever find yourself without options, should you ever be faced with imminent danger from a determined adversary, one should make every effort to *Delay, Distract, and Improvise.*"

"Delay, Distract and Improvise," whispered O'Reilly.

"Wow!" he blurted, "That's impressive! And where *did* you find all that rope?"

"Island flagpole," said Filn with some pride. Then added "Guess this is not the ending you were hoping for."

O'Reilly simply shook his head from side to side. "How about you pull those two kids in to shore, after which, you can shove *me* into the water."

"I've got a better idea, O'Reilly ...How about I kill them first ...just like you killed my King ...How about I kill them first and *then* throw you in! Now, *that* would suit me well!"

Having made his declaration, and without warning, Filn suddenly lurched forward in Neil's direction. As he did, O'Reilly shoved a cold hand into his coat pocket and struggled to extract the handgun waiting there. Had its spur hammer not snagged on a single loosened thread, O'Reilly might have managed at least one shot.

But pull as he might, the gun could not be drawn. Watching in horror, he saw Filn close in on his hapless friend before lunging at him full force. His apparent plan was to strike the mild-mannered tech with the butt of his kill-stick and then happily watch, as the rope he held slipped from his hands. All three of his victims would then simply drop to the blackness below to be swept away by the unforgiving waters of Niagara.

Then, as O'Reilly looked on helplessly, the random Gods of accidental justice suddenly intervened. For, just as Filn lunged forward, a terrified Neil Presley lost his precarious footing. Like a well-practiced circus act, Neil swung out over the roaring waters. As he did, Petra and Pasani were winched slightly higher. Unfortunately, for BDA agent, Grācius Filn, the momentum of his thrust, meeting with no resistance, had carried him first over his knee, and then head first into the raging waters below.

Desperately grasping at the large chunks of ice now surrounding him, Filn screamed and gurgled forth a final epithet ...the words instantly recognizable to any graduate of the infamous BDA academy.

"I shall scorn and vanquish all intruders!" ...the final words of an agent's oath of allegiance.

Momentarily stunned by the unexpected outcome, O'Reilly snapped-to in time to grab the elbow of Neil's parka as he arced for a second time toward shore. Then, as Neil continued to hold the rope fast, O'Reilly waded into the icy waters, securing Petra by one boot. Pulling the couple to shore, he untied their restraints before collapsing in the snow beside them.

"God almighty!" exclaimed a shaken Joe Pasani. "God almighty!"

"Bowtie, you continue to surprise!" observed a grateful Petra.

Then, as they lay there, exhausted and regaining their bearings, the three of them looked on as Neil Presley, literally at the end of his rope, gracefully passed out in slow motion before them.

Thirty minutes later, all four had retreated to the warmth and comfort of their Hotel Niagara suites.

Neil and O'Reilly flipped a coin to see who would take the first hot bath.

In the adjoining suite, an opaque cloud of steam lazily drifted to the ceiling overhead, as a young couple soaked away the frigid sting of their recent river encounter.

"Oh my!" said Judy Hooley.

"Wow! Nice butterfly!" said Pasani.

If You Can't Save The World Now and Then ...What's the Point?

For the next two days, the four travelers laid low. Anxiously reading the Niagara Falls Gazette placed daily outside their doors, they scanned every page for any story that might suggest foul play had been noticed or reported. When no such news appeared and their tensions had subsided, the four began to explore the area surrounding the hotel. Cautiously straying out from their room, they sought out food, fresh air, and entertainment. Regularly walking to the downtown district, they ate at one of its several restaurants, "The Main" being a favorite. They enjoyed the movie offerings of the two aging theaters right there on East Falls street.

The brightly flashing lights of the "Cataract" and the "Strand" happily greeted them, along with their ornate lobbies and second floor loges. Petra was especially delighted to learn that Elvis Presley was currently making his movie debut in "Love Me Tender". After their third trip to see it, Joe focused on two things in order to remain awake ...an oversized tub of heavily-buttered popcorn, and the sweet-smelling aroma of 'Evening in Paris' radiating from Petra's warm skin.

As the four of them relaxed, slept and regained their strength and bearings, they began to discuss just what it was each of them would now do with the rest of their lives. They were, after-all, undocumented aliens with neither required papers, employment, nor a clear concept of how they would fit into the unfamiliar surrounds of their new home.

Every evening, as they sat in the hotel's elegantly appointed dining room, enjoying the latest creation of a local master chef, they quietly discussed the various possibilities permitted them by place and time.

Several weeks would pass before any final decisions would be made. In the end, it was determined that the group should split up, with Neil and O'Reilly going their individual and separate ways, and Pasani and Petra striking out as one.

- An envelope containing $1000 in cash would be mailed to the nearby Sears Roebuck store in which they had "shopped". A short note of apology would be included. *"So sorry for recent theft, emergency circumstances required it."*

Additionally, the following plans were agreed to by everyone:

- The winnings which O'Reilly had retrieved from Las Vegas, would be equally divided four ways
- Annually, on New Year's Day, the group would reassemble at this grand hotel to assess progress and future needs
- No one was to ever mention or discuss the time and place from which they had come, the events that had taken place on Goat Island, or the fate that awaited the world in the next century
- Finally, everyone was to accept, as best they could, the reality of their circumstances, and to make a genuine effort to "make a go of it" in the year 1957 on the land-mass known as North America

Thrown together in the most unlikely and haphazard of circumstances, all four had grudgingly come to respect the individual courage and perspectives of the others. And had any historian been aware of their presence at all, or their final influence on the path of mankind, they would have done well to note it for future generations. For, if they had not existed or arrived as they did, the future of earth's inhabitants would have been tragically brief.

Calling upon the seemingly limitless skills of subcutaneous LULU one last time, the group planned and executed their future paths.

- LULU supervised the forging of numerous vital documents such as birth certificates, licenses, and passports

- Neil Presley started a small spiritual commune in the randomly chosen community of Marion Center, Pennsylvania. His teachings were based upon the "Four Books of Knowing" and upon the belief that four travelers from a future world would one day appear and save the current world's population from extinction. Neil also wrote numerous tracts, poems, and historical recollections which were eventually combined into one large spiritual document known as "The Book of Neil". New converts to the movement were required to walk barefoot (during the warmest days of summer) across a swath of green grass, at the end of which, they would receive a Hershey chocolate bar. Though enjoying modest success in the United States, the esoteric spiritual movement, for reasons never quite clear, exploded in popularity in the diverse countries of France, Tibet, and Tabago.

- Petra and Joe opened up two adjoining enterprises on the fourth floor of the nearby United Office Building. Joe, having purchased a colt 1911 pistol from a local Army/ Navy surplus store, determined it was all he needed to successfully establish his own detective agency. And so, on a summers-day in 1957, "Flying Tiger Investigations" hung out its shingle ...the very same day, in fact, that its office neighbor, "Petra's Martial Arts for Women" announced its grand opening. Above its door, a boldly lettered banner declared ...

**"Ladies! Don't Just Bake...
Learn How to Break!"**

If Petra had any regrets at all, it was that the Sears record department did not have a vinyl recording of her favorite 21st century song, "Holiday" by Jessie Balyn. And, of course, it never would.

It should be noted that all phone calls coming into these two enterprises were promptly answered by a rather screechy voiced receptionist calling himself Jerome Neil. Happily sitting before a rewired Executone intercom ...its brown Bakelite knobs permanently removed ...he was able to receive and answer all incoming calls.

"You've reached the offices of **Flying Tiger Investigations** and **Petra's Martial Arts Studio**. How may I help you?" And only occasionally would it be necessary to admonish a rude caller with ..."*Language! Please! Language!*"

In the summer of the same year, Petra and Joe took a short vacation to Washington, D.C. Inexplicably, their tourist visit to Ford's Theatre coincided with the sudden re-appearance of Abraham Lincoln's long-missing cape. It had been carefully folded and lovingly placed on the very chair in which he had been seated when shot.

• Retired Cliff-Hunter, Ramon Baptiste Chang-Lee Marcus O'Reilly, would eventually find his way to a restored log cabin just beyond the Finger Lakes Of New York State.

In the summers, he fished in a near-by stream or hiked through the rolling countryside, his camera and bird book in hand. In the winter, he explored the wooded hills on his mail-ordered skis. Throughout the year, regardless of the season, he studied the stars overhead, his most prized possession being a 3-inch refractor telescope with wooden tripod, a carefully conceived purchase made from Sears Roebuck and Company.

Always striving for a low profile, he also purchased a beige Volkswagen bug and taught himself how to drive standard shift. Driving skills mastered, he cruised once a week into the City of Syracuse where he faithfully visited the local library. Consuming every manner of book, he determined his favorite to be "Don Quixote" by Miguel De Cervantes.

*****

For the first five years of his new life, he returned annually to Niagara Falls to meet with his former adventurers. But as the years passed, and as all of the others adjusted to their lives with good progress, the meetings lessened to every two years, then every five years, and eventually once a decade. His post "hunter" life proved to be a surprisingly full and contented one. Having made friends with several of his farming neighbors down the road, he began to attend the small Methodist church they favored. Not particularly interested in the doctrine or details of the church, he fully appreciated the quiet sacred space it afforded him. He especially enjoyed the singing of hymns and the annual Christmas production in which the children dressed up as their favorite manger animal.

When he was approximately forty-five years old, O'Reilly struck up a platonic relationship with a feisty waitress at a country diner known as *Nicholes*. He had instantly admired the woman upon hearing her response to an unruly male customer ...her words reminiscent of another untamed heart. *"Listen up, Goober. You can either leave here on your own, or I can kick your ass and we'll carry you out!"*

Historical Footnote:

Before retiring to his country paradise, Ramon O'Reilly had carefully evaluated what, if anything, he might do to change the sad outcome that awaited the world and its future inhabitants. After extensive discussions with LULU, he eventually settled on four interventions... four actions he hoped would somehow set right all that had previously gone so terribly wrong.

> **First** ...all of LULU's detailed research files from the Indigo Tower Project were carefully reviewed, to include the many specific histories of primary and secondary principals.

> **Second** ...years later, and just one month after the birth of Zachary Pittkiss, local police were notified, by unsigned letter, that both parents of the infant had been involved in a drunken hit and run accident, one in which an elderly pedestrian had been killed. Evidence of their conspiracy to cover up the incident was confirmed by forensic examination of a mangled car fender hidden in the attic of their home. Facing charges of vehicular homicide and conspiracy, mother and father legally surrendered all parental rights to their child. Eight months later, Zachary Pittkiss was adopted by a loving couple from Tallahassee, Florida. His new father was a professor of mathematics at Florida State University; his mother a published family counselor.

Zachary would grow up in a loving and encouraging environment, both of which surely contributed to his decision to focus his impressive intellect on the challenging environmental problems facing the world.

Third ...a total of twelve plastic containers were surreptitiously buried above twelve existing time capsules across America. As a result, in the year 2000, twelve local and two federal law enforcement agencies were called in to determine if the single terse message each held, all etched in stainless steel, could possibly be valid.

Maxwell Sturg of Cape Canaveral Florida
At Naval Base Kitsap Bangor, Washington
Placed C4 explosives - USS Louisiana
Find: below-deck-head – reactor side wall

PLEASE CONFIRM & PREVENT

A final thought from the Book of Neil:
(Chapter 26 ...When Traveling Through God's Time)

The Lacing of the Boots

I awake here as an infant
Still doubting that it's real
I marvel at the changing skies
...Besot by their appeal

I remember distant mountains
And frozen hearts unkind
I put my faith in those who care
And not the wicked blind

And when I see a path that's new
Rise up from all things past
I know at once what I must do
To help the blessings last ...

... Put on my boots
And lace them tight
Step on the path
Though day or night

And walk it true
The best I can
'Til I arrive
A better man

Neil Presley, S.O.G. (Scion of God) · Community of The Kinder Way
Marion Center, Pennsylvania · November 2, 1966

Made in the USA
Monee, IL
03 March 2021